Going
Somewhere

Going Somewhere

A Dan and Bea Adventure

GEORGE GRANT

CUMBERLAND HOUSE

NASHVILLE, TENNESSEE

Published by Cumberland House Publishing, Inc., 431 Harding Industrial Drive, Nashville, Tennessee 37211.

Cover design by Karen Philips, Nashville, Tennessee.

Library of Congress Cataloging-in-Publication Data

 Grant, George, 1954–.
  Going somewhere / George Grant.
   p. cm.
  "A Dan and Bea adventure"
  ISBN 1-58182-030-5 (pbk : alk. paper)
  I. Title.
 PS3557.R2655 G65 1999
 813'.54—dc21   99-047986

Printed in the United States of America.

1 2 3 4 5 6 7 8—03 02 01 00 99

To my Bannockburn friends
on the road again
with yet another myth in tow

CONTENTS

ACKNOWLEDGMENTS

The road to paradise is always under construction.
It thus makes for a most disconcerting journey home.

Dorothy Sayers

According to the erudite Dutch novelist and semioticist Alf Kremmer, "All works of fiction ought to aspire to experimentally capture the ultimate concerns and interests of the author, evident to all, but in a mysterious way invisible to him." As a result, he asserts, "A novel should be a recapitulation of everything past, yet entirely new; it must never be a true memoir, yet it will be inescapably autobiographical; it should be altogether unrecognizable, while it nevertheless attains an eerie familiarity." Indeed, he says, "It should be instantly ascertained on its multiple levels of paradox by the author's friends, family members, and colleagues, while remaining a genuine enigma to him. Thus, the work ought to be as much evidence of a community as it is anything else."

If ever that were true of a book, this novel is a clear and present example.

I am grateful for the community that has called forth these odd vagaries and varied musings. Gene and Susan Hunt, Stephen and Tricia Mansfield, Tom and Jody Clark, Jim and Gwen Smith, Hugh and Lisa Harris, Tom and Lucie Moucka, Steve and Nancy Dragoo, David and Carol Ann Trent, Terry and Gayle Cost, Mike and Dianne Tant, Robert and Kim Fulcher, Greg and Sophia Wilbur, Terry and Patty Gensemer, and Anthony and Sharon Gordon have encouraged me along many a highway. And my students at Bannockburn College, Gileskirk School, and Franklin Classical School stood by me in many a difficult hour, encouraged me to write, and fed me with their exotica—both temporal and eternal. We've traveled a lot of roads and many miles together.

My good friends and yokefellows at Cumberland House, Ron and Julia Pitkin, have provided me with that rarest of all creative inducements and productive provocations: a happy, healthy, and honest publishing relationship.

My editor, Heather Armstrong, had the temerity to actually edit. For that reason I had to work a lot harder than I thought I would. And for that reason the book is far better than it might have been otherwise.

To all these, I offer my sincerest thanks. I never would have gotten anywhere without them.

The soundtrack for this project—in other words, the music I was listening to as I wrote—was provided by the appropriately disparate music of the Baltimore Consort, David Arkenstone, William Coulter, and the Ensemble de Medici. Likewise, the midnight musings—in other words, the books I was reading as I wrote—were provided by the equally diverse prose of Miss Read, Colin Thubron, Jan Karon, G. K. Chesterton, and Thomas Chalmers. Their influence, I hope, is all too obvious in both content and form.

As always though, it was my wife, Karen, and my beloved children, Joel, Joanna, and Jesse, who most enabled me to write this altogether new recapitulation of everything past, this entirely unrecognizable, yet eerily familiar exploration of life, the universe, and everything edible. They have taught me what a home is—and where it is. All this remains a mystery to me.

Lententide 1999
King's Meadow

Going Somewhere

There is in all literature a sort of purpose;
Quite different from the mere moralizing
That is generally meant by a novel with a
        purpose.

There is something in the plan of the idea
That is straight like a backbone
And pointing like an arrow.

It is meant to go somewhere,
Or at least to point somewhere; to its end,
Not only in the modern sense of ending,

But in the medieval sense of fruition.

                              G. K. Chesterton

BOOK 1

LIMBO

Midway this way of life we're bound upon,
I woke to find myself in a dark wood,
Where the right road was wholly lost and gone.

Ay me! How hard to speak of it—that rude
And rough and stubborn forest! The mere breath
Of memory stirs the old fear in the blood;

It is so bitter, it goes nigh to death;
Yet there I gained such good, that, to convey
The tale, I'll write what else I found therewith.

How I got into it I cannot say,
Because I was so heavy and full of sleep
When first I stumbled from the narrow way.

Dante Alighieri

There arose in me a multitude of thoughts
Through which at last came floating a vision
Of the woods of home and of another place;
The lake where the Arun rises.
And I said to myself, inside my own mind:
What are you doing?
You are on some business that takes you far,
Not even for ambition or for adventure,
But only to earn.
And you will cross the sea and earn your money,
And you will come back and spend more than you
     have earned.
But all the while your life runs past you like a river,
And the things that are of moment to men
You do not heed at all.

                                        Hilaire Belloc

DENVER
POPULATION 467,610

HE WASN'T GOING ANYWHERE. At least, not tonight.

He knew it the moment he heard that annoying little click and buzz of the intercom followed by the disembodied voice of the pilot uttering low, muffled, staticky syllables—something to the effect of: "Well, ladies and gentlemen, good evening from the flight deck—this is your captain speaking. We've just been informed by the tower that a turbulent weather system blowing in from the Rockies has resulted in a slight delay for all departures and arrivals here in Denver. And as if that were not enough, a separate winter storm in the Midwest has socked in Chicago—they are reporting nearly a foot of snow there this evening. Right now air traffic control has us on a thirty-minute hold—but that could change at any moment depending on how these high-level precipitation packages develop. We'll need to remain on the tarmac to ensure our place in line for takeoff, so we won't be able to head back to the gate. We apologize for any inconvenience this may cause. Of course, when the situation changes, you'll be the first to know. In the meantime, sit back and relax—our flight attendants will attempt to make our time on the ground here as comfortable as possible for you."

Dan Gylberd was a seasoned traveler. He knew only too well that what the pilot really meant was the plane was stuck on the runway and there was little likelihood that they were going to make it out to Chicago this late in the evening—but FAA regulations required the airline to keep passengers guessing for as long as possible. He heaved a sigh of resignation and tried to lean back on the headrest, which hit him uncomfortably just below the nape of his neck. Through the window across the aisle he could see the dense snowfall beginning to swirl against the terminal in deep, roiling drifts.

Just my luck! he thought. It had already been a rather unpleasant trip for him. And this was just icing on the cake.

Business travel is merely one of a whole host of grave indignities that corporate life seems to have thrust upon the average American worker—but Dan was convinced that it was far and away the most insidious. Over the past several years— since he had begun crisscrossing the nation, racking up frequent-flier miles, and earning his stripes as a veteran road warrior—he could not help but notice that the quality, comfort, and desirability of air travel had deteriorated dramatically. He was certain that the Byzantine vagaries of airline deregulation had somehow managed to increase the capacity of each aircraft while simultaneously reducing its actual size. Coach seating was now apparently designed for Munchkins. Overhead compartments were about as spacious as his Honda Civic's glove box. Carriers seemed to have a knack for eliminating direct routes to whichever cities were on his current itinerary—if he wanted to go to Dallas, he had to fly through Salt Lake; if he wanted to go to Salt Lake, he had to fly through Cincinnati; and if he wanted to go anywhere else, he had to fly through Atlanta. It was now necessary to stand in more lines, endure more delays, and observe more policies, procedures, and protocols than a babushka might have to in Voroshilov-grad. Every airport in the country either was currently under construction and therefore unnavigable or was a high-tech architectural horror where travelers were herded about like Orwellian thralls. The only thing that had improved somewhat was airline food—a bag of peanuts and a watered-down Dr Pepper beats sticky, cold, reconstituted lasagna paste or gray, rubbery, unidentifiable chicken parts any day of the week.

It never ceased to amaze him that even though he hardly ever saw anything more than the inside of airports, shuttle buses, and chain hotels, his neighbors and acquaintances actually thought his job was glamorous. And truth be told, he had once aspired to his present career—for just that reason. He thought it might enable him to expand his horizons. See the world. Visit exotic locales. Meet fascinating people. Drink deeply from the draught of life.

Ha! It hadn't taken long for him to be disabused of that grand illusion. Business travel was actually little more than a mind-numbing and body-drubbing test of patience and endurance.

On this particular trip he had breezed in and out of Los Angeles, hurrying through a half dozen meetings over the course of a day and a half at a nondescript hotel near LAX—a sprawling hodgepodge of an airport that seemed to cannily mimic the anarchic expanse of the city it served. Simultaneously gaudy and tawdry, everything about the place was fast, furious, and frenetic. It always left Dan feeling exhausted, debilitated, and entirely out of control.

He had tried to get out of going on this trip in every way he could possibly think of—he told his boss that the authors he was supposed to meet with would probably rather come to Chicago and see the offices, meet the editorial staff, tour the art department, and sit down with the publicists; he complained that the slush pile on his desk was threatening to engulf half the office; he argued that he wasn't necessarily the best person to represent the publisher to new acquisitions; he tried to appeal to the inordinate cost of this last-minute shuttle mission in light of expected returns on the contracts; he even tried whining. But all to no avail.

"Look, Dan," his boss explained for the umpteenth time, "these guys don't want to see anybody but you. And it is far more cost effective for me to send you out to the West Coast for a couple of days than it is for me to bring in four high-over-head, high-maintenance authors, wine and dine them, and gobble up who knows how much time of half the staff here at the office. No, you really need to do this. Look, it's just for a couple of days. Kick back. Enjoy the ride. Drink in a little California sunshine. See the sights."

"Yeah, right. That's just what I need. A good dose of the land of fruits and nuts. That's sure to help my disposition."

"Dan, you're an incurable crank."

"Yeah, I know. Thanks."

Dan's wife, Bea, normally hated it when he traveled—practically as much as he did—especially now that the kids were all out of the nest. But this time, even she could offer him little consolation. She had been called up for jury duty and it looked like she would be out of pocket for the entire week anyway.

"Go ahead and just get this over with," she told him. "Then we can both take next week off and enjoy ourselves."

"You're no help at all. Aren't you supposed to be on my side?"

"Sorry, Charlie," she chuckled. "But this time it's just a little difficult to sympathize with you—while you're off enjoying the warm Pacific breezes, kibitzing with a gaggle of hoity-toity authors, and playing the part of a publishing bigwig, I'll be slogging through the snow in downtown Chicago and fulfilling my civic duties with the Cook County jury pool."

He realized that there really wasn't much he could say in response to that. So off he went.

Chicago's O'Hare was normally a zoo. The busiest airport in the world was always abuzz with activity, crowded with visitors from across the globe, and absurdly difficult to get into and out of with any measure of grace. During holidays, it was practically a federal disaster area—often looking more like a refugee shelter than a world-class transportation hub. Weary travelers lugging half their worldly possessions in backpacks, duffle bags, and gargantuan wheeled trunks were inevitably sprawled across lounge seats, scattered along corridors, and camped out in waiting areas.

Since this was the week after the New Year's weekend, students on their way back to school following the midterm break, soldiers returning from holiday leave, and families coming home from their annual visits to Grandma's house made Dan's already jaundiced eye, all the more so.

In truth, he didn't have a lot to complain about though. Despite factoring in the requisite hassle factor, this trip had actually gone fairly smoothly until now. There had been no major delays. Dan had made all his connections without any difficulty despite long treks up one concourse and down another. He had endured his meetings in L.A. with a minimal amount of suffering and had also had time to read two manuscripts that had been languishing on his desk for weeks. Even the first leg of his return had proceeded on schedule and without any significant hitches, glitches, or snafus.

Over the years he had learned a few tricks to make business travel a bit more bearable. For instance, he never checked his luggage. He always wore a versatile suit aboard the plane and then carried a compact overnight bag with little more than a few toiletries, a change of shirts, ties, socks, underwear, and his jogging gear. In his briefcase he carried the thinnest, lightest laptop on the market and only those few contracts, catalogs, proposals, books, and manuscripts he was absolutely certain he would need once he arrived at his destination. His motto for packing for any trip was, When in doubt, leave it out. To his credit, he had spent a week at the huge Frankfurt international book fair with little more than what he had squeezed into a rucksack.

In addition, he always reserved an aisle seat, preferably on an exit row or bulkhead. His frequent-flier status on four different carriers often enabled him to upgrade to first class for no extra charge—and even when the plane was full, and upgrading was not possible, he was able to board with the first-class travelers to make sure he had room in the overhead compartment for his bags. He always kept a paperback handy in his jacket pocket—to read during all those interminable waits that inevitably accompany air travel—check-in lines, security stations, gate lobbies, and aboard the planes themselves.

Despite all his best efforts though, even the smoothest of trips were just barely tolerable to him. And there was little wonder—he was over six feet tall and weighed two hundred and too much. There just wasn't a whole lot that he could do to ease the discomforts of being on the road and away from home.

Now here he was, nearing the end of this minor exercise in yielding sense and sensibility to the almighty dollar, and what happened? Just when he thought he was actually getting somewhere, he wound up getting stuck on the runway of a connecting airport in a snowstorm.

The woman sitting next to him was evidently as uncomfortable as he was—if not more so. For all her congeniality, she was as nervous as a cat. She had boarded here in Denver just as the flight attendants and ground crew were preparing to close the doors after the final gate call. She was out of breath and bedraggled. And she was also quite large; she practically had to turn sideways to avoid bumping into people on both sides of the plane. As she struggled down the aisle toward him she offered a litany of apologies to everyone within earshot.

"Oops . . . Oh, I'm sorry . . . Excuse me . . . Oh dear . . . did that hit you in the head?" She left a trail of flinching, ducking, and murmuring in her wake. "My, oh, my . . . Are you all right? . . . Ugh . . . Oy vey." The entire plane was in commotion now. "Gee, isn't this plane kind of small? . . . Yikes . . . Oh, sorry . . . Sorry . . . I'm so sorry . . . Excuse me."

She was lugging a suitcase the size of a cello, three shopping bags, and a purse. Airline regulations limit carry-on articles to two per passenger, but apparently no one had the temerity to tell this woman.

As soon as he saw her, Dan knew that her seat was bound to be next to his. It seemed that a trip was never really complete without a kicking, screaming toddler right behind him, a Walkman-sporting teen fully reclining onto his knees in front of him, and a large woman spilling over the armrest beside him.

He braced himself.

Apparently, there is no human ambition more potent than the grim resolve of an airline passenger trying to squeeze an oversized bag into an undersized overhead bin. This woman offered indisputable proof of that maxim. Of course, all the overheads were full. It took the full engineering expertise of two flight attendants and three frequent fliers to rearrange everything and to get all of the poor woman's gear stowed.

Finally, she clambered past Dan and buckled herself into the seat. He steadfastly avoided eye-contact and tried to find his place in the manuscript he had been reading before all the hubbub had begun.

"Boy, I just barely made it, didn't I?" she said more than asked, turning her round face toward him with evident relief. "Whew. Thank goodness they're running a little late. I'm on my way to visit my grandchildren. I haven't seen them for almost eight months. That's an awfully long time to be away from your babies, don't you think? It would have been terrible if I had missed this flight. I don't know what I would have done. I really don't. Just terrible—that's what it would have been."

She spilled open her accordion billfold and proffered an avalanche of snapshots. Her eyes beamed with pride. "I told my daughter and son-in-law that it just wasn't worth it—going off to the big city just to get a job—if it made everybody miserable and split up the family. It just wasn't worth it. Don't you agree? Just for a job? I mean, it's not as if there aren't lots of good jobs to be had right at home, especially for a smart boy like Bob—well actually, he likes to be called Robert now that he's got this new job, but we all still just call him Bob. He looks more like a Bob than a Robert, don't you think?"

She paused just long enough for her next breath. "The way I figure it, there is nothing more important than your family. Certainly not your job. Funny thing is, he really doesn't even like the new job. Bob, that is. My daughter is just worried sick. She says that job is going to give him ulcers. Can you imagine that? Ulcers from a job. And he's only twenty-eight. Now how can a twenty-eight-year-old get ulcers? Tell me that. Well, I'll tell you how—just split up your family, move off to someplace like Chicago for a job you don't even like. Ulcers are probably not even the half of it."

Dan tried his best to be polite. But it took an inordinate amount of effort just to nod and smile perfunctorily. All he wanted to do was to be left alone until the plane had arrived in Chicago where he would bid adieu to this whole woe-begotten affair—the overextended trip, the overcrowded plane, and the overwrought, oversized woman.

Following the announcement from the flight deck, his flight companion was clearly unsettled. "Oh dear. How am I going to let my daughter know that I'm going to be late? She will be so worried. What should I do?"

She began fidgeting. Wedged between the armrests, she couldn't very well move her lower extremities, but her hands were going a mile a minute. She fiddled with the in-flight phone, reading and rereading the instructions but obviously not comprehending how to actually place a call on it.

Dan realized that this was his cue to be a Good Samaritan and explain to her that everything was going to be all right, that there was no reason to worry, that the monitors at O'Hare would let her daughter know the flight status, and that they should all be grateful for the pilot's safety precautions. But instead of doing that, he sat there feeling guilty about just sitting there.

He knew that if Bea were here, she would engage the woman in congenial conversation about the grandchildren. She would look at all the family snapshots, oohing and ahhing appropriately. She would show her how to use the phone and then place the call for her. She might even exchange recipes or gardening tips.

But Dan just sat there. He was in a foul temper and hardly in the mood for a hand-holding conversation. He wished he had it in him to be a little more forthcoming, a little more kind, a little more considerate. But he couldn't. He just wanted to get moving. He stuck his nose in the manuscript and quietly tried to work.

He was trying to work on four different manuscripts at the same time, and they were very different indeed. The first was a delightful cookbook of wildly varied ethnic cuisines from New England, the Northeast, the Southeast, and the Deep South. It was a particular passion for him—both the food and the book. But he didn't really want to work on the manuscript just now because he knew it would just make him hungrier and crankier than he was already.

The second was a book about books. Reading about reading may appear to be a little esoteric to those not particularly inclined to bookishness. But for those of Dan's tribe for whom such arcane habits are perfectly understandable, these tomes are manna for the mind. He was certain that this particular manuscript would prove to be a trove for true bibliophiles. It was full of apt quotations, marvelous anecdotes, and pointed ruminations about the full sensory experience of libraries, bookshops, classrooms, hearthsides, studies, breakfast nooks, and front porch swings—all the places where readers discover the wisdom, insight, comfort, and companionship of books. But at the moment, such things reminded him too much of his father, too much of the long, long ago and the far away, too much of home. So he didn't want to work on it either.

The third manuscript was a contemplative novel. Because it contained only two characters, a very limited frame of reference, and a strict linear plot, it was essentially a novel of ideas. There was hardly any dialogue, virtually no sensory descriptions, no significant character conflicts, and no mystery or intrigue. More than anything, it was an anthology of cultural critiques set upon a modern stage after the pattern of Dante's *Inferno* or Thoreau's *Walden*. If *Seinfeld* had been a television show about nothing, this was a book about everything. Obviously, such a precarious literary experiment required a good deal of intense, uninterrupted deliberation—it was the sort of work that might just as easily succeed quirkily as fail miserably—so he didn't want to work on it while sitting amid a small storm of bustling and yammering aboard the plane on the tarmac.

That left the final manuscript. It was a heavily spin-doctored, ghostwritten, and niche-targeted campaign puff-piece thinly disguised as a serious policy proposal for an up-and-coming congressional leader. Same old, same old. Politics and PR as usual. Since it required the least amount of concentration, Dan had decided to work on it.

After about an hour, the captain notified them that the flight had been canceled and they would have to return to the terminal—no other flights would be departing that night either. As they taxied back to the gate, the passengers were informed that the airline would provide them with meal vouchers and a coupon for one of the airport hotels.

Dan knew this meant standing in one line after another, one to get tickets rerouted, another to get the vouchers and coupons, and another to board the shuttles to the hotels. He looked at his watch. It was already past ten. He figured it would be midnight before he finally got to turn in for a short night of sleep.

True to form, he was being overly optimistic. Once everyone had pried their belongings out of the overhead bins and scrambled off the plane, they had to elbow their way into a single line served by a solitary harried ticket agent who was by all appearances either on her first day on the job or in the throes of a nervous breakdown—or perhaps both simultaneously. It took more than an hour for her to process everyone in line. It took another hour to get to the hotel. And the wait to get checked in lasted another half-hour or so.

By the time Dan fell onto his bed it was nearly one o'clock. Of course, he was so exhausted he had a hard time falling asleep. A nearby ice machine wheezed and rattled and sputtered as Dan's mind wrestled with trivial thoughts so as to avoid contemplating more important matters. His efforts to fall asleep turned into an exercise in futility, an exercise with which he was only too well acquainted.

He gave up, crawled out of bed, and turned on the lights.

First, he tried to do a little more work. He pulled a stack of papers out of his briefcase and booted up his computer and quickly checked his e-mail. But he could hardly face the thought of plowing into one of the manuscripts. His head was full of jangling objections and slights. Bea always said he had the temperament of a toddler when he was hungry or tired. Right now, he was both. He knew that he was in no condition to do any serious editing.

So he decided to try a little light reading. He only had about fifty pages to go in the Ellis Peters medieval mystery he had picked up at the airport. But he was bleary eyed and had a hard time concentrating.

After he realized that his eyes had glazed over and he had been reading the same two paragraphs over and over with little or no comprehension or recollection, he gave up.

He reached for the television remote and began the always-futile endeavor of looking for something interesting to watch. He surfed through the fifty-two channels twice before concluding that his best choices were a rerun of *Xena: Warrior Princess*, an infomercial for a herbal weight-loss program, Geraldo poo-pooing the latest political scandal, or WWF wrestling—a rather depressing commentary on the American entertainment industry.

He finally collapsed in resignation on the crumpled pillow and surrendered to the melancholy.

As he lay there, the woods that once overhung the reaches of the river behind his boyhood home came clearly into view. He saw the steep bank beyond the barn, the high ridge that hid the view from town, and the rapids that turned and hurried below. He smelled the freshly mown hay.

Never before had the image been so clear in his mind. The colors were more vivid than the actual scene. There was hardly a sound but the whistling of the breeze, gusty on the water-meadow banks. He nevertheless witnessed its ruffling force against the stream.

For a moment, soft in the night, he even thought he heard his father quoting Homer—as Dan had done so often himself with an answering heart—"he longed as he journeyed to see once more the smoke going up from his own land, and after that to die."

At last, Dan began to drift off into that peaceful repose conjured by the fairy haunts of long-lost hours.

Suddenly, boisterous voices erupted just outside his door—he awoke with a start and thought he recognized their timbre from the plane earlier in the evening, though he was not certain.

"Can you believe they closed the bar so early?" a raspy, slightly slurred voice asked.

"Early? What do you mean, early? It's past three," retorted the second.

Loud and incredulous, the first responded, "Three? Are you kidding? Whoa, it's really late—or early—depending on your point of view!"

Bursting into uproarious laughter now, the second answered, "Yeah, I'll say."

"Time sure flies when you're having fun."

Both men began guffawing, snorting, and chortling. "You can say that again."

"Well, I guess it's about time to turn in."

"Past three, huh? I guess you're right—definitely time to turn in."

"I don't know about you, but I'm gonna sleep like a rock."

"Yeah, me too. Like a rock."

The men laughed again riotously.

Two doors slammed, and Dan was left with nothing but the wheezing, rattling ice machine sputtering sounds and the certainty that he was going nowhere in more ways than one.

He wasn't the least bit amused.

There are, indeed, many truths which time
necessarily and certainly teaches,
And which might, by those who have learned them
from experience,
Be communicated to their successors at a cheaper
rate:
But dictates, though liberally enough bestowed, are
generally without effect,
The teacher gains few proselytes by instruction
which his own behavior contradicts;
And young men miss the benefit of counsel, because
they are not very ready to believe
That those who fall below them in practice, can
much excel them in theory.
Thus the progress of knowledge is retarded, the
world is kept long in the same state,
And every new race is to gain the prudence of their
predecessors
By committing and redressing the same
miscarriages.

Samuel Johnson

CHICAGO
POPULATION 2,783,726

Bea was a perpetual, eternal, and incurable optimist. She always seemed to have a smile on her face and a sparkle in her eye. She had an innate knack for finding the good in situations that any other sane person might carp bitterly against. Though she was hardly a Pollyanna—she had grown up in a broken home and had suffered through difficult circumstances for a number of years—she always had a ready laugh and a bright outlook. It was as if her world-view was informed by a calm certainty that every new obstacle in life was an opportunity in disguise. Where others gave in to frustration or anger, she nurtured a sense of wonder and anticipation. She was able to find joy in the journey even when faced with dead ends, detours, and one-way signs pointing resolutely in the wrong direction.

"Life is full of surprises," she often quipped, "and I just love surprises."

When she and Dan were first married, they had nothing to call their own except their poverty. Their first apartment was little more than a hole in the wall furnished with scavenged crates and boxes. She said it was decorated in Early American

Poverty. But while Dan worried about their dire straits, Bea reveled in the adventure of it. She just pretended they were camping out.

When she had to spend the last three months of her first pregnancy in bed, Dan fretted and fumed. Bea simply said it was a great chance for her to catch up on her beauty sleep. When Dan lost his job during a major corporate downsizing move, he nearly had a nervous breakdown. She was excited about the possibility of starting a family business or launching out in an entirely new direction. When Dan's new job required him to travel, he moaned and groaned and complained. She really hated the time apart too, but she tried to make the best of it, volunteering her time at a ministry for inner-city poor—and as a result, she not only occupied her time productively, she was reminded daily of her many blessings. When the last of the children left for college, he had mourned, as if it were somehow the beginning of the end of their lives. She rejoiced though, as if it were somehow the end of the beginning of their lives.

For her, sanguinity wasn't a matter of trying to live out the worn clichés of positive thinking—making lemonade when life deals you lemons, blooming where you are planted, seeing the glass as half-full rather than half-empty, or looking at the world through rose-colored glasses. She wasn't impressed in the least by the silly sentiments of pop psychology or chicken-soup moralism. But her perpetually cheerful outlook wasn't a matter of personal discipline or management techniques either—affirming an I'm-okay-you're-okay ethic, putting first things first, developing the habits of highly effective people, or beginning with the end in mind. She was genuinely committed to the notion that life was a blessing, whatever it might bring. She really did believe that inconveniences were just adventures in disguise. She had an authentic and contagious enthusiasm for the present life and an optimistic and expectant hope that transcended it.

As a result, Bea was actually looking forward to jury duty. This despite the fact that she had to drive into downtown Chicago during rush hour and despite the fact that it was jury duty—the prospects of which, either alone might discourage the average suburban soul and both together might bring to dismay even the most stalwart. But Bea was actually atwitter with exultation and expectancy. For reasons known only to her, she could hardly contain herself.

She had never been called for jury duty before—for nearly twenty-five years she had been exempt from service because she still had children at home. But now that they were grown and gone—one was married and beginning a family of her own and the other three were attending college—she was eligible.

Dan warned her that the process was profoundly dull and ought to be avoided. "The judicial system," he complained, "is an imponderable tangle of compromises, constraints, and contradictions. It is an unredeemable mess. And jury duty is an all too painful reminder of that."

"I think it's my duty," Bea retorted with a smile.

Meg Halvers, her good friend from church, said that it was a wretched waste of time—and if there was one thing we are all short of these days, it is time.

"If all the people busy with families, businesses, appointments, and careers failed to show up at the courthouse when they were summoned," Bea replied, "just imagine how bad the judicial system might become—it's bad enough as it is."

"You'll never get picked to sit on a panel," her brother-in-law averred when he called the night before. "The lawyers trying the cases seem to have a knack for weeding out anyone and everyone who seems to think for themselves."

"Nevertheless," she told him, "it'll be a good experience. I'm bound to learn all sorts of new things in the process."

Of course, most people dread jury duty—and for more specific reasons than simply that it is dull, time consuming, and heedless. It often meant losing a week or two of work, which was an extravagance few could afford. And the fact that the system was so bureaucratic, impersonal, and coercive only made matters worse.

But Bea, defying all such logic, was thrilled at the prospect. Armed with an unflappable sunny disposition and braced against the bitterly cold Chicago winds with her favorite wax-cloth Macintosh over a thick Polartec cardigan, she gathered up a hefty stack of books and plunged ahead into what she was sure would be at the very least, a thoroughly enjoyable escapade.

THE VAST Cook County Criminal Justice Building dominates Chicago's Daley Center. It is a proud monument of modern architecture. Built during the halcyon days of the International Style—stark, efficient, and stripped of all ornamentation—it soars up from a denuded concrete plaza on purposefully rusted steel girders and smoky glass curtain walls as a celebration of mechanization, industrialization, and progress.

Architecture has always been a litmus test for the character of a culture. After all, the most valuable things in any human society are those very permanent and irrevocable things—things like families. And architecture comes closer to being very near permanent and irrevocable than any other man-made craft simply because it is so difficult to dispose of. A book may be torn to pieces, a painting may be hidden in a closet, a symphony may be silenced, but a spire flung toward heaven poses procedural difficulties to all but the most fiercely determined suppressors.

In the three decades that followed the fire of 1871, progressive Chicago architects like Louis Sullivan designed buildings with exteriors clearly expressing their innovative steel-frame construction and marked by distinctive three-part windows—large central fixed panes flanked by smaller double-hung sash windows. These so-called Chicago School buildings were praised as the most important precursors to twentieth-century steel-and-glass skyscrapers. And while a number of beautifully ornamented Greek Revival, Prairie Style, and Old Craftsman buildings were also built as the city emerged Phoenix-like from the ashes, the unique vision of the Chicago School's spare modernity ultimately predominated. The Daley Center was the natural progeny of that progressive vision.

Dan had always said that he hated it. To his contumacious sensibilities it was little more than an expensive eyesore, a jarring curiosity, a barren anomaly all out of proportion to human scale—hardly an appropriate symbol of the lofty aims of mercy, truth, and justice. But Bea thought that it seemed to fit right in with the rest of the colossal corporate aeries inside the Loop.

After parking at a nearby garage—at what struck her as scalper's prices—Bea made her way across West Washington and past a massive heap of scrap metal that she presumed was supposed to pass for public art but appeared to her to be more like a memento from a bombing raid on Baghdad or Belgrade. She couldn't help but chuckle at its absurdity.

Traffic was at a complete standstill. Businessmen and women, tradesmen, delivery men, and sundry support personnel, all driven by the tyranny of the urgent, bustled around her. Dirty heaps of snow still made curbs impassable and intersections treacherous. Tempers flared. Street vendors pushed their carts and sold their wares in the midst of the melee. The hawking and wheedling jive of the streets jangled with a bedlam of disquiet, ambition, and agitation. She looked across the broad plaza, named for the city's patriarchal family, and waded into the crowd that teemed there. She almost felt as if she were a visitor from a foreign land—like a stranger in Babylon, an explorer in uncharted territories, or a pilgrim venturing into the howling wilderness. She was amazed.

Bea rarely made her way into town. Even on those few occasions when she actually did venture out of the suburbs, she almost never came in alone. Usually she was with Dan— on their way to a Cubs game at Wrigley Field on the north side of downtown or to a Bulls game at the United Center to the west. So all the sights and sounds that swirled around the courthouse assaulted her senses with a surreal immediacy. She imagined that, like Alice, she had somehow stepped through the looking glass into a whole other world of Mad Hatters and March Hares.

Once inside the building, Bea reported to a clerk outside her appointed courtroom. He checked a computer-generated list of jurors, marked off her name, and told her that there would be as much as a two-hour delay due to a pretrial conference between the attorneys and the presiding judge. He said that she could either wait in the courtroom or go to the cafeteria but she could not leave the premises and would need to check back every half-hour.

Since Bea had a small satchel bulging with good books she had been wanting to read, she decided to find a corner in the courtroom to read.

It was obvious that the architect had designed the room with a specific purpose in mind, but it was an idea that did not take people into account. It was a place of abstraction, not a place of habitation. Despite that—and though it was rather drab and dim and the bench seats were terribly uncomfortable—she curled up and began to page through a recent biography of one of her lifelong heroes, Booker T. Washington.

When she was just a girl, her mother had revealed to her the terribly disreputable fact—disreputable for a white Southerner in the fifties—that she was distantly related to Washington. She got the distinct impression that this was intended to be taken as a mark of shame, but she had always embraced it as a badge of honor. Eventually, as she came to know more about the man and his career, Washington became a very real model for her of honor, integrity, and success.

During her first year of college she had made a pilgrimage to Tuskegee. That spring break, while everyone else was either headed home or to the beach, Bea drove to southern Alabama to visit the university that Washington had built out of little more than sheer pluck, gumption, and diligence.

She discovered that the centerpiece of the Tuskegee campus was a monument to the great man. Upon a grand classical pedestal stood a remarkable bronze statue. Washington himself was portrayed—stately, dignified, and venerable—standing with his eyes set upon the horizon while one hand was extended toward the future. The other hand was pulling back a thick veil—presumably the smothering cloak of Strabo—from the brow of a young man seated at his side. The man was obviously quite poor—he was only half clothed, in stark contrast to the formal and dapper presence of Washington—and was sitting upon symbols of his labor, an anvil and a plow. But he too was gazing into the distance while he grasped a massive textbook upon his knee. The inscription read, "He lifted the veil of ignorance from his people and pointed the way to progress through education and industry."

Bea had always thought that the monument was a perfect tribute to the man. While his life—the long and difficult journey up from the obscurity of slavery to the heights of national influence and renown—was a remarkable testimony of individual achievement and personal sacrifice, she believed that the greatest legacy of Washington was not what he accomplished himself, but what he helped so many thousands of others accomplish—both black and white. He gave everyone a sense of destiny.

Bea loved the fact that Washington never pretended that his noble aspirations would be achieved easily or without great sacrifice. Success would come, he taught his students, only after diligent labor, strenuous industry, and purposeful calling were applied in their lives, their families, and their communities. He once said, "I have learned that success is to be measured not so much by the position that one has reached in life, as by the obstacles which he has overcome while trying to succeed."

She ran her fingers through her long dark curls—she always liked to imagine that they were his gift to her—and lost herself in his inspiring story. She managed to read more than eighty pages of the little hardback before the courtroom began to fill with clerks, lawyers, police officers, prospective jurors, and assorted onlookers.

It was already midmorning when the bailiff finally announced that the court was in session and the judge, the Honorable James Mahoney, made his dramatic ceremonial entrance. After taking care of the few preliminary procedures, Mahoney turned to the officers of the court and offered a few details about the case they would be hearing that day. He outlined his expectations, his standards for courtroom decorum, and the process of jury selection.

"Eighteen of you will be called at random from the pool list." He was young and articulate. His thick shock of coal black hair and his draping robe framed his taut visage and lent a strong, authoritative air. "The prosecution and the defense will then have the opportunity to ask each prospective juror a series of questions. The purpose is to find a group of thirteen men and women—twelve jurors and one alternate—who will be able to fairly, thoughtfully, and without prejudice hear the evidence in this case and then make an appropriate determination of guilt or innocence. What that means is that at least five of those who are called for this first panel will actually be dismissed for one reason or another. This is not intended to put you on the spot—so don't take any of this personally. The fact is that some people cannot make unbiased judgments in certain kinds of cases because of their family backgrounds, or individual experiences, or personal beliefs."

He went on to explain that in the kind of case they would be hearing—a young man was charged with driving while under the influence of alcohol—the jury-selection process was the most time-consuming part of the trial. Each attorney could request a certain number of dismissals and thus would interview prospective jurors very carefully.

As it turned out the case was cut and dry. The young man was a college student. He had been out for a night of binge drinking and was returning to his dorm when he was noticed by a patrol officer. He was driving erratically—swerving in and out of his lane, speeding up and slowing down, and failing to yield to oncoming traffic. He was stopped and given a field sobriety test in the presence of a backup officer who had arrived almost simultaneously on the scene. The young student had failed each component of the test—including basic balance, coordination, and agility tests—and was arrested. Forty minutes later, after his paperwork had been processed, he was given a Breathalyzer test. He failed that as well—registering a blood-alcohol content well above that allowed by law.

It seemed like an open-and-shut case. Bea wondered why it was even going to trial. But obviously the defense attorney felt that he had a good argument for acquittal, and he was determined to make it.

Eighteen names were called and an odd assortment of men and women made their way to the front of the courtroom. Over the next five hours they were interrogated. Bea and the other prospective jurors who had not been chosen for this panel were required to sit through the entire ordeal—and were asked by the judge to pay careful attention to the interrogation process in case they had to be called upon following the dismissal of members from the first panel.

At first, the questions were what Bea had expected. The beefy prosecutor asked each member of the panel about family, education, and any personal connections to law enforcement. He was curt and businesslike. His unadorned rhetoric sank with dismaying velocity toward the pedantic.

But the defense attorney was much more colorful and inquisitive. Even so, he had all the appeal of an overanxious appliance salesman. He asked about personal habits, preferences, idiosyncrasies. Bea began to thank her lucky stars she had not been selected in this first group.

"Do you have any bumper stickers on your car?"

"What magazines do you subscribe to?"

"Are you active in any political or social groups?"

"Do you attend church regularly?"

"Do you believe our current court system is too lenient, too harsh, or just about right?"

"Do you drink socially?"

"Have you ever had a run-in with the law where your perception of the situation was different from that of a police officer?"

He seemed to be all sail and no anchor. His tone was fussical. His manner was fudgical. He appeared to be practicing the juridical concerns of the busybody reformer. And still he carried on his animated inquisition.

"What do you do for a living?"

"Do you like your job?"

"Do you find it fulfilling, satisfying, and enriching?"

Admittedly, most of us do not much care for work. We complain about it. We chafe against it. We will do just about anything to get out of it. Nevertheless, we probably would all reluctantly admit that nearly everything in life worth anything demands a certain measure of labor and intensity. And though this might appear at first glance to be a plight of woe and hardship—perhaps a deleterious effect of the Adamic fall—it is in fact a part of the glory of the human experience.

Bea was struck by how many of these jurors seemed to benefit little more than materially from their jobs. It was evident to her that for the most part, these men and women were doing what they had to do to make ends meet and that was about all. They evidenced little sense of purpose or calling. The ache in their dull voices echoed on the blank terrazzo floor and the spare institutional walls. They were mercenaries, working merely for money with little or no sense of destiny, vision, or calling.

The jury-selection process was painstakingly slow. It was as if the officers of the court had all day to converse and deliberate. Every ninety minutes or so they took a fifteen-minute recess. Just after noon, court was adjourned for a one-hour lunch break.

Bea was taken aback by the fact that there was little interaction between any of the people in the courtroom—even during the breaks. Though there were more than forty prospective jurors in the court, it was as if they were all alone. The only topic of conversation that they seemed to have in common was the recent retirement of Michael Jordan from basketball.

Once upon a time, Chicago was best known as the home of Al Capone and his gangsters. His Airness had changed all that. It was as if Jordan had given Chicago much more than the chance to be home to perhaps the best basketball player ever. He salved its Second City complex, put substance behind its bravado, and even, some people say, allowed Chicago to slip free of the dusty harness of history and create a new sense of itself.

After Number 23 announced his retirement, the city, chilled and submerged under nearly two feet of snow, indulged in a collective eulogy. "It's All Over Now," sniffed a headline in the *Chicago Sun-Times*. "MJ Gone," mourned the *Chicago Tribune*.

Everyone who was anyone across the city added their voices to the requiem chorus. From Studs Terkel to Oprah

Winfrey, from Ann Landers to Andrew Greeley, and from
Sammy Sosa to Saul Bellow, everyone talked about Jordan.

He was a winner. And he had made the city feel like a
winner despite its persistently contrary record. After all, the
losing streaks in this town are legendary: the Bears (who have
been on the fritz since winning the Super Bowl in 1985), the
Blackhawks (whose last Stanley Cup victory was 1961), the
White Sox (who have not won a World Series since 1917), and
the Cubs (who have gone ninety years without winning a
World Series—the home-run heroics of Sammy Sosa notwith-
standing). The only glimmer of hope in Jordan-less Chicago
had been the Chicago Fire, the soccer team that won the
national championship the year before, but alas, too many
people still seemed to have trouble getting all that enthused
about professional soccer.

It was evident to Bea that the Jordan phenomenon was the
result of more than just the sweet wine of victory. There was
Jordan's charm, an ebullient charisma. He had become a cult
in the city because he was such an anomaly—he actually conducted himself akin to a Southern gentleman, one of the few
patricians professional sports had been able to produce of late.
There was no skullduggery when it came to Jordan. There was
no underhandedness. He was not only able to do what he was
supposed to do, he was able to be what he was supposed to
be. He had a clear sense of purposeful calling about him. He
was a man of destiny. Though she really wasn't much of a
sports fan, she had to admit that she loved to watch him
play—and she appreciated him as much off the court as on it.

The jury pool thrown together that day—like so much of
the rest of the city—seemed to admire Jordan because he
embodied the very purposefulness and passion that they all
yearned for. It was as if he were a living portrayal of Booker T.
Washington's work ethic—an ethic that seemed as beyond
their reach as one of MJ's soaring slam dunks.

As Bea listened to her fellow jurors describe the almost painful futility of their lives—both under the defense attorney's interrogation and in the hallways during the breaks—she inevitably thought about Dan. He had always had big dreams—but the harsh reality of simply making a living constrained him, just as it had so many of these men and women. When they first met, Dan was a free spirit. He wanted to live the life of a vagabond artist. He wanted to see the world. He wanted to write, to paint, to make music. He wanted to live a life with no strings attached.

His younger brother, Tristan, had actually done just that—for years he had been one of the mainstays of the folk music circuit in Texas. At one time or another, he had played every nightclub, beer hall, street fair, barbecue joint, dinner theater, coffeehouse, honky-tonk, showcase venue, cocktail lounge, chili festival, rodeo, and fundraiser in the state—and Texas is a big state.

Dan had always envied that life.

Bea had been the sensible one. She had finally gotten him to settle down in Chicago—where job opportunities abounded. She had steered him toward his career in publishing. She had convinced him to buy a house in the suburbs so that their children might have the opportunity to play in their own backyard, ride their bikes on sidewalks, and be a part of a neighborhood.

Dan had always done what he needed to do to take care of her and the children. He had always been a good provider. But she knew that he was as unfulfilled in his job as the pesticide salesman, the air freight driver, and the meter reader sitting in the jury box in the courtroom with her.

Now here he was: middle-class and middle-aged. Over the course of his rather unremarkable career, he had clawed and scraped his way toward a comfortable middle-management position in a midsized corporation in the suburban Midwest. He drove a midsized car and lived in a midrange suburban home.

In a very real sense, he was living the American dream. But he hated it, and she knew that too. He was plagued with the notion that his life had ended up smack-dab in the middle of nowhere.

"One of these days, when the kids are all grown and gone, we're going to sell everything and hit the road," he always used to tell her. "We'll just drive. We'll stop whenever and wherever we feel like it. We won't look at our watches. We'll toss out our Day-Timers. We'll do what we want, where we want, and when we want. And when we finally find a place we can call home—our own Mitford or Lake Woebegone or Fairacre— we'll build our own dream house on the prairie."

"That's the stuff of storybook fantasies and Hollywood romances," she would invariably reply. "I think we've got enough adventure and excitement just keeping up with things right here in our own backyard without having to traipse all over the countryside looking for more. Besides, you never miss an occasion to tell me how much you detest travel."

"There is a big difference between flying all over every-where and going somewhere."

He had always been restless. She thought that it might pass eventually. But it never did. As he became more and more established in publishing, his disquiet only intensified. His reputation in the literary world had taken root, but he never did. He was perennially ready to pull up stakes and move at the mere mention of job openings in New York or Boston or even London. He had the spirit of a vagabond or a gypsy. He was chronically afflicted with the greener grass syndrome. You could almost see it in the distant misty green of his eyes.

She had assumed that this was Dan's reaction to the pres-sure he had always felt to live up to the nearly impossible expec-tations of his father. A brilliant, dominating, and accomplished man, Dan's father was a renowned writer, educator, and social reformer. He was an extremely devout man and had helped to provide the early intellectual foundations for the fledgling Christian Right. The older Gylberd was a leading academic opponent of abortion rights, a stalwart constitutional conservative, and a grassroots political organizer. He cast a larger-than-life shadow whose smothering influence ultimately caused both of his sons to rebel. But Dan, the firstborn, rebelled the most.

Bea had met Dan when he was in full flight from his father's legacy. He had just dropped out of college and was working at a downtown bar. Living without a care in the world, he had no goals, no burning ambitions, no driving passions, and no direction. He had drifted far from his childhood faith—a fact that colored all he was and all he did.

Their relationship was rocky at first—he seemed almost frightened of love and commitment. But ultimately there was no fighting it. They were both smitten. He made a dramatic turnaround after that. She knew that she had brought him stability and a sense of security. Though there never was a substantive reconciliation with his father, Dan had become eminently responsible.

But now Bea wondered at what cost.

She looked around the courtroom. While the lawyers droned on, and despite the discomfort of the bench seats, three people had fallen asleep. Several others were engrossed in magazines, newspapers, or paperbacks. The rest were gazing off into the distance with a kind of zombielike inattentiveness. The proceedings were not exactly enthralling—they had been about as interesting as standing in line at the driver's license bureau.

It was well after four when the defense attorney's long, drawn-out interrogation finally ended and the panel had been pared down to the required twelve jurors and one alternate. The entire day had been consumed, and the trial had not yet even begun. At long last the judge addressed the courtroom—everyone who had not been selected was free to leave.

Bea decided to stay and watch the trial for at least a little while since rush hour had just begun. She knew she would just get stuck in traffic if she tried to go anywhere. After a fifteen-minute recess, Judge Mahoney lowered his gavel and the trial began. No witnesses were called except the two police officers who had made the arrest. The basic facts of the case were reiterated. Copies of the field sobriety and Breathalyzer results were officially entered as evidence. There was a brief period of cross-examination. And then, before she realized how quickly the proceedings had progressed, the attorneys were making their closing arguments.

The jury was sent into an adjacent room to deliberate. Within ten minutes they returned with their verdict: guilty as charged. The entire trial, from start to finish, had taken less than forty-five minutes, and yet it had taken all day just to get to square one. It is amazing what we have to go through—all the delays, the rigmarole, the tortured analysis, the pretense, the shenanigans, and the runaround—just to get to what we ought to have known from the beginning.

Bea had spent half a lifetime trying to cure Dan's wanderlust. She had tried to squeeze him into a mold just as surely as his father had. She was beginning to see that it was just as important for her to encourage him to be what he was called to be as it was for her to encourage him to do what he was called to do. She could not fathom why it had taken her all this time to figure out something so obvious.

Common sense is the most uncommon commodity in all the world. As a result, people spend their lives doing either the expedient or convenient things rather than the veritable or suitable things. They would do what they could rather than what they should.

Bea resolved that she would reintroduce a bit of common sense into her home. She realized that she had been brought to the bar of judgment just sitting there in the courtroom.

She laughed aloud as she made her way out of the building and into the plaza. Twilight was already descending upon the city, shrouding it in a shivering cloak of gray. But Bea was buoyed at the sight of the impinging dusk.

She had been right all along about jury duty. It had been a good experience. She had learned all sorts of new things—about the floundering judicial system, about herself and her expectations, about Dan and his, and about the character of calling and purpose.

Indeed, she mused as she headed toward the western suburbs through the still-dense snarl of downtown traffic, jury duty had succeeded in teaching her about life, the universe, and everything. Or something like that.

Making a decision is easy:
When the difference is big
You know what to choose
And when the difference is small,
It does not really matter
What you choose.

P. G. Wodehouse

3

WHEATON
POPULATION 51,464

THE NEXT DAY, IN the gray hazy moments just before twilight, Bea had just finished shoveling the fresh snowfall from the driveway and front walk when Dan finally arrived home. He came in through the garage, walked straight to his favorite chair in the den, and collapsed—his luggage in a heap in the middle of the room.

"Home again, home again, jiggedy-jig," he called out.

"Well, hey there, weary traveler, how are you doing?" she replied as she hurried down the hallway and into the room, her jacket and mittens still on.

"I feel like I've been roughed up for the last couple of days by the offensive line of the Bears—no, I take that back. It's worse. I feel like I've been repeatedly run over by the Blackhawk's Zamboni."

"That bad, huh?"

"Yeah, well, it's been no picnic. The new Denver airport is a full-service operation—it doesn't just shred your luggage into unidentifiable debris, it somehow contrives to fold, spindle, and mutilate your soul too."

"Yikes. Sorry I asked."

"Life's rough in the big city. So, how about you?"

"I'm great, now that you're home, you cheerful lug." She walked over and greeted him with a kiss.

"Umm. Boy, am I ever glad to be home. Did you know it's supposed to snow again tonight? If I hadn't gotten the flight I did, I might have been stuck in Denver another night."

He looked up at her. She was radiant. After twenty-five years of marriage, he still marveled at her beauty. Her dark eyes were ablaze with vitality. A few long, unruly locks of hair had slipped free of an antique tortoiseshell barrette and had fallen over her ears and across her shoulders.

"I thought you had jury duty. I wasn't expecting to find you home. Is it already over?"

"Well, I didn't get picked—and they released our panel after the first trial."

"So how was it? Boring as usual?"

"Yes and no. The courts are obviously a mess. Everything is so slow and ponderous. It took all day to accomplish what should have been done in an hour. But I'm glad I got to go. If for no other reason than I got a chance to think. Really think."

"Oh? And what was it that you thought about?"

"Lots of things. We'll have lots to talk about in the next few days. I sure hope we get snowed in. That'd be perfect."

"I'll say. I don't think I want to face the office just yet. Let's light a fire and snuggle up for the evening."

"I think you just might be able to talk me into that."

"Good. It's settled then. We'll be homebodies together."

"Are you sure you can sit still that long?" she snickered.

"Absolutely," he responded in mock dismay.

"No sneaking off with your laptop?"

"Nope."

"No checking your e-mail or voice mail?"

"Nope."

"No nervously flipping through your Day-Timer?"

"Nope. I don't even want to think about anything other than being home sweet home." The exhaustion in his voice was obvious.

"Well then, I'm gonna hold you to that."

"Okay. I'm counting on it."

THEIR HOME sweet home was a small, rather nondescript ranch house clad in vinyl siding and a decorative foundational berm of brick veneer. It was set in a fifty-year-old subdivision that backed up to an old weather-stained overpass in a tangle of little streets just off Roosevelt Road—one of Chicago's primary east-west thoroughfares. When they bought it almost two decades ago, the community was already beginning to show the early signs of urban encroachment. But because it was beyond Cicero, Berwyn, Maywood, Brookfield, Oak Brook, Elmhurst, and Glen Ellyn, Dan thought that it might be spared the worst of the encroaching metropolitan kudzu of crime, decay, and overcrowding.

Like all the others in the development, their house had a front porch that was too narrow for furniture and shutters that didn't close or conform to the dimensions of the windows. It had a high gable in the front inset with a false fan window. It sported no other elaboration or affectation except a lone iron carriage lamp on the front lawn that was intended to evoke fond associations with ye olde post road days, or something like that.

What the house lacked in decorative grandeur or structural interest though, Bea had made up for in coziness. Inside, her penchant for warm ambiance, deep-hued natural fabrics, long walls of old books, eclectic artistic contrasts, and a rich patina of antique furniture belied the ordinariness of the utilitarian architecture. A relaxed comfort, akin to the turn-of-the-century Edwardian colonialism, was the keynote in nearly every nook and cranny of the house.

But the marvels she had wrought inside paled in comparison to what she had accomplished outside. Over the years she had created a veritable garden sanctuary all across the front of the house and throughout the backyard. Within a crisp picket fence a redolent palate of colors and textures mimicked the very best of the old English hip pocket conservatories.

In the springtime, flowers and bulbs lined the long walk, surrounded the shade trees, and enfolded the house. Huge herb beds bestowed a complex bouquet of scents, fragrances, and aromas over the entire yard. Several birdhouses and feeders marked the perimeter of this demi-paradise, and a large stone birdbath sat in its center like a brazen oasis of refreshment and delight.

Whenever time and weather permitted, Dan joined her there. They often sat together for long stretches in silence, imbibing the rich libations of beauty and rest that enveloped them. It was about the only time that she could really get him to sit still.

During the summertime, they loved to watch as chickadees and goldfinches fluttered between the branches of the trees and bees buzzed from flower to flower. Dan was particularly wowed by the gentle music of leaves rustling—music that rose and fell in an even, certain, and rhythmical cadence.

Even in the dead of winter, when snow and crystalline frost covered the ground, clung to the prickly shrub stalks, and flocked the stooping branches of the trees, the garden remained a hard-won oasis of rest planted in the midst of the hustle-bustle of life. Though dormant, muted, and glazed over by traces of wintry hoar, it was beautiful, luxuriant, fragrant, mysterious, and rich in surprises.

The Gylberd plot was more elaborate than most of the other yards in the immediate neighborhood. Nevertheless, it fit the ethos of their little community very well. Wheaton had been a picket-fence-and-white-steeple kind of town from its earliest days as a kind of frontier missionary outpost.

In 1859 Jonathan Blanchard left his position as president of Knox College in Galesburg, Illinois, to lead the struggling Illinois Institute that had been founded in 1854 in the countryside due west of Chicago by the Wesleyan Methodists. This able and pious administrator was known widely as a staunch abolitionist and crusader for social reform. It was his desire that the little college commit itself to a combination of intellectual growth and Christian faith. Shortly afterward, a local community leader, Warren L. Wheaton, gave a small parcel of pastureland to the institute, and Blanchard subsequently proposed to have the school renamed Wheaton College.

Touched almost at once by the calamity of the War Between the States, the college said farewell to some sixty-seven enlistees, most of whom never returned. Nevertheless, the school prospered and its reputation grew as it provided students with a liberal arts education undergirded with classical studies and a distinctively Christian emphasis. Eventually, the surrounding village became a quiet enclave of conservative Christian publishing houses, educational suppliers, and evangelistic ministries in the midst of a vibrant metropolitan milieu. Indeed, by the time Dan and Bea moved there, it had practically become the buckle of the Midwest's Bible Belt.

As a result, Wheaton was a great place to raise children. There was always a passel of other kids just around the block with whom they could play. The neighbors were invariably responsible parents. The streets were quiet and safe. There were plenty of excellent private schools—and even the public schools had a reputation for being about as good as public schools might be expected to be. The college sponsored a whole host of special events—concerts, lectures, exhibits, sporting events, workshops, and conferences—so there was always something to do that was spiritually or culturally enriching.

But Wheaton was also a difficult place to have a sense of community. Because so many people were involved in large institutions, ministries, and associations, they often had little time or energy left over for the neighborhood. In addition, such organizations were notorious for a rapid turnover rate. It was difficult for neighbors to get to know one another—much less invest in one another's lives—in that kind of a transitory environment. That genuine sense of connectedness, of accountability, and of covenantal commitment necessary for the intimacy and perpetuity of community never really had the opportunity to develop. Against all reason, the best of men—in the best of circumstances with the best of opportunities in the best of times—had opted for something substantially less than the best.

When the kids lived at home, Dan and Bea had made certain that their house was a hub of the constant activity in the neightborhood. Bea wanted to make sure that her four children and their friends felt welcome and comfortable there—even if they were just hanging out. She understood only too well that teenage boys were essentially walking, talking hormone storms that desperately needed to be kept busy—at least until they graduated from high school and even longer if possible. She had Dan convert the garage into a game room with a Ping-Pong table, a dart board, and a big-screen television equipped with a video library and a game system. She often invited them to help Dan tinker with his perennial project under the carport beside the house—restoring an old VW Bug. At the dinner table, it seemed that there were always a couple of extra places—especially on those occasions when Dan fired up the grill. The fact was there was often so much going on at the Gylberd home, almost everyone jokingly answered the phone, "Grand Central Station."

But now that the kids were off and gone. The house was eerily quiet. Dan and Bea were alone much of the time, but they continued to invest themselves in the neighborhood. Bea was active in a nearby church, serving on several committees and teaching a children's Sunday school class. Dan often volunteered at the college, which housed several fine archives of the works of the authors his father had introduced him to—G. K. Chesterton, C. S. Lewis, Dorothy Sayers, Charles Williams, and George MacDonald. Both served on a Red Cross emergency preparedness council.

Nevertheless, they felt disconnected—as if they were merely sojourners. Their closest friends all lived somewhere else. Bea talked to Sarah in Atlanta and Liz in Nashville nearly every week. When they thought of home, their vision rarely went any further than their own wicket. They had cast their lot like Lot.

ON THIS particular evening though, such thoughts did not disturb Dan and Bea's suburban cloister. If anything, they were glad to be alone together in the happy little shelter they had propped up against the storms of the world.

Dan hoisted himself out of his chair and picked up his luggage. "I'm going to put this stuff away."

Bea shook her head with bemusement. *He is so persnickety,* she thought. He always sorted his clothes and put away his bags as soon as he returned from a trip. He hated disarray and disorder. His closet was as regimented as his schedule—shirts, suits, slacks, and sweaters arranged just so.

She, on the other hand, was much more relaxed about such things—spontaneous and serendipitous, she described it. But she knew he would not relax until he had sorted his laundry, stowed the luggage, and returned his toothbrush to the holder in the bathroom.

"Hey, where's Elvis?" he asked over his shoulder as he headed down the hall.

"I just let him out. He's been shut up in the house all day. He won't be out long though—it's cold and you know what he thinks of snow underfoot. He'll let us know when he wants to come in."

Sure enough, as if on cue, they heard the dog yelp at the back door. He was an aging, overweight black-and-white mutt who had adopted the Gylberd family when he had followed the kids home from school nearly a decade ago. He was approximately the size and shape of a small Hereford and about as genteel—but he thought he was a lap dog. When Bea let him in, he scrambled around her and scampered down the hall to greet Dan.

Elvis pranced around Dan's feet and slobbered a gleeful welcome. Dan was always able to tolerate such insanely joyous receptions not only because they stroked his male ego but also because they were short-lived—Elvis could sustain frenetic activity for only a few minutes before having to retire to a warm spot beneath the kitchen window or beside the living room hearth for a long winter's nap.

Once Dan had everything neatly put away, he made a beeline back to his chair, an old English club high-back enveloped in buttery soft leather. On his way home from the airport, Dan had picked up both of the daily newspapers—the *Chicago Tribune* and the *Chicago Sun-Times*. He liked to compare the two and often discovered hilarious contradictions.

The daily news trade had become notorious for getting things wrong simply by trying so very hard to make things right. Journalists had become activists. And so they saw the events they reported on through the distorted lens of their own bias—skewed according to their own predispositions, prejudices, and presuppositions. It was understandable then—perhaps even inevitable—that two writers seeing the same event at the same time from the same vantage point could report two totally different stories. It was not just a matter of selective quotation or out-of-context citation or slanted research. Complete subjectivity was the norm.

In reality, Dan rarely had the patience to read the newspapers. He usually scanned the headlines and then flipped to Maureen Dowd's column to get his blood boiling. Today the lead headline stories were markedly opposed. The *Tribune* reported, CAMPING ALLOWED FOR DEADHEADS. The *Sun-Times* claimed, DEADHEADS WARNED: NO CAMPING. Similarly, one broadcast, CTA TARGETS CRIME ON TWO LINES, while the other shouted, COPS CALL CTA SAFE DESPITE RISE IN CRIME. Closer to home, Dan saw the *Trib* lament, CHICAGO PUBLISHER LOSES BID FOR CHEEVER BOOK, and the *Sun-Times* report, COURT OK'S PUBLICATION OF CHEEVER BOOK.

Normally such journalistic shenanigans would get him all worked up. "So, *who* are the people of Chicago supposed to believe?" he invariably ranted. "Or more to the point, *what* are the people of Chicago supposed to believe? If even the most basic news events can be interpreted with such dramatically different results, what happens when there are passionate differences of opinion on a particular issue or circumstance? Can the press be trusted to pass on any objective and unbiased information whatsoever? Can we believe even the bare-bones outline of what happened when, where, how, and why?" At the very least, he thought that this ought to give new meaning to the old adage: You can't believe everything you read—or hear—or see.

But that was not the case tonight. He wasn't about to be lured onto one of his soapboxes. He was too tired to think about what was wrong with the world. He tossed the newspapers into the magazine basket next to the ottoman and turned toward Bea, who was shelving several small volumes of poetry.

"All right, now I'm ready to hunker down for a nice boring evening at home."

"Boring? Gee, thanks a lot."

"No, no. I didn't mean it that way."

"Pray tell, what did you mean then?"

"Don't you see? Boring is good."

"Uhh. Right."

"No, really. Boring is what most people are really yearning for—they just don't know it. Boring is having no people to see, no tasks to accomplish, no expectations to meet, no pressures to handle. It's the ideal adventure. People go halfway around the world to find a secluded beach or a remote cabin or a mountain hideaway just so they can do nothing."

"Somehow, that sounds like something your father might have said."

"Yeah, well, maybe so. Whatever. I just know from the dumb certainties of experience that only dull people have to be stimulated constantly. Something has always got to be going on. We're addicted to razzle-dazzle. We want wow. And we want it now. Our whole culture, from popular entertainment to corporate management, is predicated on the idea that our lives ought to be defined by a frenetic go-go-go sense of busyness. There is no time to reflect."

"No time to think."

"No time to do anything at all except be busy obsessing over the tyranny of the urgent."

"It's exhausting just thinking about it, isn't it?"

"It is. But if someone has the temerity to just sit still, they're somehow considered out of step, unambitious, or unmotivated."

"Or boring?"

"Yeah. Or boring. So tonight I think we ought to boldly stand against the tide, against the smothering dullness of busyness for the sake of busyness. Let's just sit in front of our fire and talk."

"Okay, then. Boring it is."

Bea went into the kitchen and began steeping a pot of herbal tea and laid out a platter of fruits, cheeses, sausages, and a wide array of crackers—their favorite light supper. She set the tray on the old steamer trunk they used for a coffee table, pulled a nearly threadbare quilt across her legs, curled up on the plump sofa, and sighed. She couldn't think of anything more ambrosial, more delectable, or more providential than being altogether boring at that particular moment.

She realized that she too was tired of the rat race their lives had become. She had always assumed that once the kids had flown the coop, she would have more time to devote to the things she was interested in. But instead it seemed that she had less time than ever before. And things became more hectic with every passing day. A year ago, Bea began expanding a small consulting company she had started a couple of years earlier—but instead of simply keeping her foot in the door of the computing and software business and providing a little extra income, it was now threatening to take over her life.

Bea had always been good with computers. She bought her first one as a replacement for Dan's ancient Selectric typewriter. She thought that a bona fide word processor might be helpful for his work at home—and that she might be able to do some editorial odd jobs and data entry. To her surprise, she found that she had a knack for understanding how programs worked. Though she had never been mechanically inclined, Bea had a natural ability to recall scores of arcane software commands without having to go back to the manuals more than once or twice. It wasn't long before she began experimenting with a spreadsheet, a home accounting program, a database or two, and dozens of utilities and shareware programs. But these point-and-click, plug-and-play, lowest-common-denominator packages never quite did all the things she wanted—at least not the way she would have liked. So she began tinkering a little with the programs—customizing them with special macros and embedded commands. She became so taken with the possibilities that she signed up for a couple of night classes at Wheaton and taught herself several programming languages. She bought third-party manuals on programming, subscribed to several programming magazines, and traded programming tips through on-line technical forums and chat rooms.

When she started her company, she had only intended to offer a few basic services on an informal basis around the community—software updates, networking solutions, and code remediation. But with the advent of the Y2K scare, she had more business than she knew what to do with. She was making boatloads of money, but she had begun to feel that, like Dan, her schedule was now ruled by a kind of mindless despotism of schedules, agendas, meetings, and devoirs.

Maybe that was why even she had taken to fantasizing about getting away from it all more and more lately—pondering what it might be like to actually do what Dan had always dreamed of doing: selling everything and heading off toward the blue horizon. She read the wonderful bestsellers of Frances Mayes and Peter Mayle—Mayes and her husband left their promising careers and moved to Italy, recounting their adventures in *Under the Tuscan Sun*, while Mayle and his wife had dropped out and moved to France, telling their tale in *A Year in Provence*. She discovered that rather than inspiring her, they left her with a profound sense of yearning as well as a bit of melancholy over her maniac lifestyle. Both books were delightful, witty, stimulating, and well-written jaunts for the heart and soul and senses. They made her heart long, her taste buds tingle, and even gave her a hankering to pack her bags. They made her dream of dramatically downshifting—of dropping all her responsibilities and moving where life was still simple enough to merely rest and laugh and eat and while the time away.

"Why don't we just do it then?" Bea burst out.

"Do what?"

"Take some time off. Sell this house. Do what we want to do for a change."

"Yeah, right."

"No, I'm serious. You always said that, once the kids were grown, we were going to put on the brakes, take time to smell the roses, and travel the world."

"I'm too tired to travel the world. I travel the world for a living. It's lost whatever allure it once had."

"But that's just the point. We're both too tired to do much of anything at all—and we're tired because we're living somewhere we don't particularly want to live and we're working at jobs we don't particularly want to work at. Wouldn't it be wonderful if we were to take a long breather from it all, if for no other reason than to decide if this is really what we want to do for the rest of our lives? Aren't you sick and tired of being sick and tired?"

"We can't afford the luxury of doing whatever we want. We have bills to pay, responsibilities to fulfill. We're just barely making it financially as it is."

"We could clear the decks simply by selling the house. We've got plenty of equity—and we're not in debt."

"I thought it was the man who was supposed to go through the midlife crisis—not the woman. You sure you're feeling okay?"

He walked over to the sofa, sat next to Bea, and mockingly held his hand against her forehead.

"I'm being serious," she insisted. "When I was at the courthouse this week, I saw so many unhappy people in so many unhappy situations. I have never wanted that for us—but as I looked around, I was forced to admit that there really wasn't much of a difference between us and them. Remember when we first met—we used to dream about building a little cabin out in the woods? We were going to break the mold. Whatever we were going to do, we were going to make certain that we were called to it, that it was what we were destined to do."

"That was youthful idealism. That sort of talk was rampant in the sixties."

"Maybe it was. But I think that it was also right."

"Life tends to adjust our expectations, doesn't it? Gradually imposing little compromises?"

"It doesn't have to be that way though, does it? Right now is our window. Now, while we're old enough to appreciate it and young enough to enjoy it."

In truth, Dan had recently begun to think that their unique job situations made the idea of taking some kind of sabbatical feasible, but he had never mentioned it to Bea because he assumed that she would laugh it off as impractical. He could work with his authors from anywhere. The publishing business was conducted almost entirely over the phone and through the Internet already. Most of Bea's client base could easily be managed on-line as well. And as if all that were not enough, he had a friend who owned one of the Chicago arts-and-entertainment tabloids who often asked him to write a series of articles on the rapidly disappearing ethnic food scene across the North and Northeast—he had compiled quite a list of his favorite places during all his travels and had written sporadic reviews over the last couple of years. It was an assignment that might pay their travel expenses for several months. But he had chalked up all such conniving to mere fantasy. He didn't want to hope they would do something like this. So he tried to put it out of his mind.

But now, maybe, just maybe, it was doable. Bea was actually suggesting it herself. Dan allowed himself the luxury of imagining doing what he really wanted to do. An invigorating hope began to stir deep within him.

They talked about these possibilities into the wee hours of the night. As the fire grew cold and a fresh snow began to blanket the ground outside, they both became more and more excited about the idea. Weariness was suddenly banished in a rush of adrenaline and anticipation.

When Dan was thoroughly convinced that Bea was as serious as he was, he retrieved his Day-Timer. It was time to start making lists. What would they need to sell? What did they want to keep? Where would they store it? Who would they need to coordinate with? How would they break this to their respective coworkers, their friends, their children? What would they do about bills, mail, and other business affairs?

Some might imagine that once the decision had been made, all they really needed to do was to pick up their hats and head out the door—or something akin to that. But T. S. Eliot knew better. "Between the idea and the reality," he said, "between the notion and the act, inevitably falls the shadow." Dan and Bea knew better too. Despite the whirling dervishes that their imaginations might have conjured at the thought of rest, relaxation, and time away from the hubbub of the daily grind, they knew that they would have to plan and plan carefully. Not only to keep their constant companion Murphy and his laws at bay, but to prepare for the time when Eliot's shadow would inevitably fall. Thus the ideas, plans, and courses of action poured forth from them both as if a dam had long been ready to burst and at last the torrent was loosed.

It would be a sabbatical. Dan would take a leave of absence although he would continue to work with several of his authors and do some acquisitions work part time from the road. Bea would maintain her relationships with a number of her current clients, especially those who were still in the midst of their ongoing Y2K remediation process. Together the two of them would write a series of food and travel articles as they ate and drove their way across America. They would sell the house—they had wanted to get out of the suburbs and find a place in the country anyway. They would read all the books they had long intended to read. They would study all the music they had long intended to study. They would visit historic sites, great museums, grand homes, stately gardens, and scenic parks. They would eat, drink, and be merry. They would rest. There would be no agenda, no itinerary, no ultimate objective.

As their plans came together, Dan and Bea were amazingly agreed on almost everything. Alas, almost everything is not quite everything.

"We'll sell the Volvo and the Honda and take the VW," Dan suggested, still in full-sprint idea mode.

"No, we will not," was Bea's immediate reply.

"What do you mean?"

"I mean there is no way I'm going to get in that itty-bitty thing—that deathtrap—and break down all across the country. No way."

"Oh, come on. It's not that small. In fact, it has more headroom than the Honda and more legroom than the Volvo. For a long trip, I think I'd actually be more comfortable in it than in either one of the others. And it's about as safe as any other compact car on the road today."

"Absolutely not. No. That's final. We're taking a sabbatical, not trying to recover our sixties roots. It's not like a Big Chill weekend we're talking about here. We're not Deadheads in search of Jerry Garcia's karma." Bea was adamant.

"What could be better than hitting the road in Virgil?"

"Virgil? What are you talking about?"

"Virgil. That's what I've christened the VW."

"You named the car?"

"No. I christened it."

"Now I know you're losing it."

"What do you mean?" Dan pretended to sound hurt. "Look. It's a classic. The Volvo is, well, it's——"

"Safe. That's what it is. It's safe."

"Yeah, but it hasn't got any style. And the Honda is, well, it's——"

"Reliable. That's what it is. It's reliable."

"Right. They're both basically appliances on wheels. Safe and reliable. Ugh. Talk about boring."

"Wait a minute now. I thought you just got through explaining to me why boring was good."

"Well, it is for some things. You want boring when it comes to schedules, to-do lists, and agendas. But not when it comes to cars."

"Boy, that's a stretch."

"Look, the VW is perhaps the most unique automobile ever produced. More than twenty years after the last one was manufactured for the American market, it is immediately recognized and universally loved. It's a symbol. It's an icon. It's simple to maintain, better than a Jeep in bad weather, and loads of fun to drive anytime or anyplace. So where is your sense of adventure? Your esprit de corps? Your joie de vivre?"

"Hey, come on. This trip was my idea. Don't paint me as a spoilsport. I just want to arrive alive——wherever it is we're going."

"I've been working on Virgil for fifteen years just to get him ready for a moment like this. There's no way we can go in any other car. Besides, it runs like a top. It's in perfect shape."

"Dan, let's be practical here. There is no way we are going to be able to get everything we need for a trip like this in that VW."

"Sure we will. We'll just take less. It's just the three of us."

"Three? Now hold on a minute here. You're not thinking of taking the dog too, are you?"

"You'd leave Elvis? Just look at him there."

Elvis was lying on his back, snoring contentedly.

"Tell me you could leave that behind—that bundle of joy, that hunka hunka burnin' love?"

"I just assumed that we'd let one of the kids take care of him while we were gone."

"No way. Elvis is going. You know how much he loves riding. Besides, how would the kids be able to take care of him? Josh and Jacob are still in school. There is no way Jennifer's landlord would allow her to have a dog. Joseph is allergic to dogs and, besides, he barely has time to eat himself while he finishes his thesis. Elvis has to go with us."

"In the VW?"

"In Virgil. He'll ride in the back."

Bea sighed in resignation. She knew she was beaten. She hated to say as much out loud, but she had to admit that the thought of riding across America in a lovingly restored VW with a large dog in the back seat had a bizarre kind of romantic appeal regardless of how impractical it might seem.

"Okay," she relented. "But he sits on your side, and I refuse to call a car by name."

"Fine," Dan pronounced with mock seriousness. "Miss out on all the fun if you want, to say nothing of the profound literary hermeneutical principles you'll be abusing. Revel in your epistemological unconsciousness if you must. See if I care."

"I can't believe this."

"Me either. I feel like I'm walking on sunshine."

Bea smiled. She loved it when he grinned from ear to ear.

Over the next several weeks they began to implement their plan. Amazingly, the pieces seemed to fall into place. Dan's boss was reluctant but willing to give the idea of a sabbatical a try—for a little while at least. Bea's best clients likewise conceded that she could finish up most of the remediation work from the road as easily as if she were on site. The editors of the arts-and-entertainment tabloid were thrilled at the prospect of the series of stories from the road and offered a generous stipend and expense account.

A Realtor thought there would be no problem selling the house—and she was right. There were three serious inquiries the first week it was on the market.

Dan and Bea sat down with each of the children—as well as other extended family members and close friends—and explained what they were doing and why. All with a minimum of grief.

Of course, securing a steady stream of income, ironing out the wrinkles in their personal affairs, and disposing of their house did not occupy most of their time once they decided to actually do what they had been talking about doing for a quarter of a century. Most of their time was spent on the momentous and heart-wrenching task of sorting through three decades of accumulated possessions and organizing a garage sale.

It is astonishing how much junk two relatively sane people can accumulate over a short amount of time. And it is equally astonishing how difficult it is to part with much of it. Clothes that will never be worn again, furniture that will never be used again, gadgets that will never work again—and some that didn't in the first place—have a remarkable ability to attach themselves to one's sentiments once we see strangers rummaging through them.

After three months of feverish planning, preparing, plotting, and packing, they were ready. The house was sold. The bills were paid. The books and antiques were in a storage facility. All their business affairs were in order. Virgil was tuned up, gassed up, and revved up.

Dan and Bea were ready to go.

They were actually going to do it.

Yet they weren't entirely sure where they were going. Or where they might end up. They only had the sketchiest of itineraries. Not that it really mattered. They would figure that out as they went along. What mattered was that they were definitely going.

Somewhere.

BOOK 2

NETHER REALM

A heavy peal of thunder came to waken me
Out of the stunning slumber that had bound me,
Startling me up as though rude hands had shaken me.

I rose and cast my rested eyes around me,
Gazing intent to satisfy my wonder
Concerning the strange place wherein I found me.

Hear truth: I stood on the steep brink whereunder
Runs down the dolorous chasm of the Pit,
Ringing with infinite groans like gathered thunder.

Deep, dense, and by no faintest glimmer lit
It lay, and though I strained my sight to find
Bottom, not one thing could I see in it.

Dante Alighieri

Thanks to the Interstate highway system,
It is now possible to travel
From coast to coast without seeing anything.

Charles Kuralt

CLEVELAND
POPULATION 505,616

THERE WAS A STILL wind in the sky and few clouds shaped to it. Driving in the cold morning, Dan and Bea went up the winding freeway along the shimmering lake and through the leafless woods. Still the road rose until they came to a small town where they thought they might stop for breakfast, having already driven more than seventy miles. And all that way they had hardly said a word to each other.

Dawn had not as yet broken when they guided Virgil out of the Chicago suburban neighborhood and onto the interstate. Even that early on a Saturday morning, traffic was already relatively heavy. The entrance ramp onto the south tollway and I-355 was practically impassable, and speeds near the interchange of I-294 barely crept above forty miles an hour.

"Where can all these cars possibly be going?" Bea asked incredulously.

"I can't even begin to imagine," Dan replied, frustration evident in his voice. He had pictured this scene a thousand times before: leaving his troubles behind, the wind in his hair, a resplendent sunrise peeking over the horizon, and tokens of blessed hope ahead. Somehow, having to negotiate traffic snarls before dawn failed to fit his image of the perfect getaway.

Skirting the southern edge of Lake Michigan, through the gray industrial outskirts of Hammond and Gary, they were practically thirty miles into Indiana before the urban sprawl of metro Chicago began to dissipate into countryside. Just as day broke, they made their way toward the hauntingly beautiful dunes of the Indiana lakeside parks. Finally able to relax a bit—with Virgil humming along nicely—Dan noted the name of the town at the next exit.

"Chesterton. Hmm, that's interesting. I think we're going to have to stop and investigate."

"Sounds good to me. I was beginning to get hungry for breakfast."

Only minutes from the shores of Lake Michigan, Chesterton billed itself as a resort town—offering miles of sandy beaches and the spectacular Sand Creek championship golf course all within easy access of Chicago. Sponsor of the international Wizard of Oz festival and the renowned Great Lakes Art Fair, it was also home to a huge Bethlehem Steel plant.

But it was the name that grabbed Dan's attention.

THOUGH HE was a voracious reader, promiscuously devouring a wide range of books by a diverse array of authors in every imaginable genre, G. K. Chesterton was far and away his favorite author. That had not always been the case though. As a young man, he rashly vowed he would never read a Chesterton book—because his father had so constantly trumpeted his virtues, and Dan had a knee-jerk reaction against almost anything his father had advocated or suggested. But over the years Dan kept running across Chesterton's name, his apt epigrams, quotations, quips, and aphorisms, and he became intrigued. Finally, at Bea's insistence, he broke down and read a collection of the Father Brown mystery stories. He was hooked.

He read a few of Chesterton's other novels. He tried some of the great writer's literary biographies and essays. Then he picked up several volumes on social issues. Dan was amazed at the man's remarkable scope, his scintillating wit, and his paradoxical vision of the world. Indeed, it was Chesterton's writing, even more than Bea's constant pleading and cajoling, that convinced him to explore the foundations of his faith—as well as his doubt—for the first time since he had left home as a rebellious teen.

Chesterton was one of the brightest and most prophetic minds of the first half of the twentieth century—a prolific journalist, best-selling novelist, astute critic, acclaimed graphics artist, beloved poet, popular debater, and profound humorist. He was also one of the most faithful defenders of the traditions of Western civilization against the onslaughts of the emerging neopagan pop culture. The great Christian apologist fired unrelenting salvos of biting analysis against progressive modernists, indicting them for "combining a hardening of the heart with a sympathetic softening of the head," and for presuming to turn "common decency" and "commendable deeds" into "social crimes." If the unfettered capitalism of cultural conservatism was marked by the doctrine of "the survival of the fittest," then, he said, the politically correct "establishmentality" of social liberalism was marked by the doctrine of "the survival of the nastiest."

Long before the bane of television invaded society's every waking moment, Chesterton warned against the dulling of the senses and sensibilities that inevitably results from a sensate society. In his remarkably visionary books, he celebrated the common man and common sense as the most practical, powerful, and palpable rebuke to materialism's mad rush to fuzzy-minded philistinism.

Bea loved his theological works—*Orthodoxy* and *The Everlasting Man*—as well as his provocative literary biographies of

Charles Dickens, George Bernard Shaw, Geoffrey Chaucer, and Robert Louis Stevenson. She felt that he had a knack for making classic literature come to life.

Dan's favorite Chesterton work though was a rather obscure short story about a man who traveled around the world to find his true home—only to end up precisely where he began. The character's name was Thomas Smythe. He had been born, brought up, married, and made the father of a family in a little white farmhouse by a river. The river enclosed the farm on three sides, like a castle. On the fourth side there were stables. Beyond that a kitchen garden. Beyond that an orchard. Beyond that a low wall. Beyond that a road. Beyond that a wood. And beyond that the land gently sloped up to meet the sky. But Smythe had known nothing beyond what he could see from his house. Its walls were the world to him, and its roof his sky. In his latter years, he hardly ever went outside his door. And as he grew lazy, he grew restless, angry with himself and everyone else. He grew weary of every moment and yet hungered for the next.

Smythe's heart was stale and bitter toward his wife and children. His home was drab and wearisome to him. Yet he had a fragment of a memory of happier days, when the thatch of his home burned with gold as though angels inhabited it. It was like a dream to him.

One calamitous day, Smythe's mind snapped under the weight of the contradiction between his fond remembrances of the past and the drab circumstances of his present. He announced that he was leaving to find his home—that better farmhouse by the river. Although his wife and children tried to make him see that he was already there, Smythe's delusion was complete. He would not be persuaded otherwise.

Smythe set out on his epic journey. He crossed hill and vale, mountain and plain, stream and ocean, meadow and desert. He lived a series of existences, but he never diverged from the line that girdled the world. At last, he crested a hill and suddenly felt as if he had crossed into elfland. With his head a belfry of new passions, assailed with confounding memories, he came at last to the end of the world. He had arrived at the little white farmhouse by the river; he had arrived at home. His heart leaped for joy as he saw his wife run to meet him in the lane. The prodigal had returned.

Dan loved the story for a thousand different reasons. It was a powerful parable of the human experience. It was a poignant prose poem of everyman's longing. And it was a stern rebuke to the vagabond spirit that drags all the Cains, the Esaus, and the Lots eastward away from Eden. But he loved it most of all because it was his own story—the testimony of his own, as yet incomplete, pilgrimage home.

DOES THIS town have some sort of connection to Chesterton?" Bea asked.

"I don't know. It is a fairly common English name, but Chesterton did tour America in 1921, visiting this part of Indiana on his way to Chicago. So anything is possible. Let's ask around."

They stopped at a roadside café. Elvis was thrilled to escape the back seat, where he had been squeezed into a small corner beside stacks of luggage, a small ice chest, and a duffle bag filled with books and CDs. While Dan walked him around the back of the small building, Bea went inside to get a seat. By the time Elvis was curled up in the car and Dan had come inside, a cup of steaming coffee was at his place at a booth near the door.

"The waitress said she had never heard of an English author named Chesterton," Bea told him. "She wasn't too sure who the town was named for, but she thought that it might have been an early settler."

They ate a hearty breakfast—scrambled eggs piled high, thick slabs of sausage, hot biscuits with homemade blackberry preserves, and cold corn mush. Afterward, while Dan paid the bill, Bea perused the souvenirs and gifts arrayed on three long counters against the wall. There were mugs, spoons, sweat-shirts, buttons, stickers, post cards, and ball caps emblazoned with images of the Indiana dunes. There were several rows of dusty candy bars. There was an assortment of gaudy trinkets that shamelessly celebrated American kitsch.

"So where are you folks headed?" the waitress asked as she bussed their table.

"Today, Cleveland," Bea responded, looking up from a row of Indiana dunes ashtrays and shot glasses.

"You on vacation?"

"Well, something like that."

"And you're going to Cleveland?"

"Yes."

"So you must have family there."

"No."

"Cleveland doesn't exactly sound like a hot tourist desti-nation, if you know what I mean. Why Cleveland?"

THAT WAS a common question, one that Bea had heard a dozen times already, practically every time she had told anyone about their trip. Everyone asked, "Why Cleveland?"

When Dan first drew up their sketchy itinerary, even Bea had to wonder why, of all places, they would want to make that city their first stop.

Cleveland had very nearly died. Once the fifth largest city in the nation, it no longer ranked in the top twenty. Although once a hub for transportation, a model of industrialization, and a progressive leader in social and cultural reform, it had been in a state of rapid decline. In some ways the city was emblematic of the Rust Belt. Its once busy factories became decrepit, its vibrant communities became depressed, its won-derful setting became spoiled by polluted air and water, and its massive infrastructure became obsolescent. It was an embarrassing blight. The proud metropolis was derisively referred to as the Mistake on the Lake. Population declined by nearly half.

Nevertheless, it had been estimated that there were some eighty ethnic groups in the city speaking more than sixty languages, representing nearly every race, tongue, and tribe on the planet. It boasted the largest mix of Eastern Europeans of any area in America, including the largest concentration of Slovenians, Lithuanians, Slovaks, and Hungarians. That rich diversity was colorfully displayed in Cleveland's neighborhoods and community festivals—and its restaurants.

Cleveland was a great place to eat.

According to Dan, Cleveland was a food mecca, a culinary Shangri-La, an Edenic demi-paradise for the taste buds. So it was the natural place for them to begin. "I can get three or four articles out of Cleveland alone," he had told Bea.

WE'RE GOING there for the food," Bea explained to the waitress.

"Oh," the girl responded. But she clearly did not comprehend. Her dark eyes were clouded with that unmistakable "Did somebody say McDonald's?" look.

Dan beckoned out to the parking lot. They had a little more than two hundred miles to go before they reached their destination for this first day of travel. He was anxious to get back on the road. Elvis was anxious too. He greeted both of his companions with sloppy kisses.

Virgil pulled back onto the Indiana Toll Road. The Gylberds rolled down the windows, put on a Clannad CD, cranked up the volume, and began their pilgrimage eastward through South Bend, Elkhart, and Toledo.

THE INTERSTATE system is a marvel of social order and engineering prowess. Nowhere else on the planet is it possible to travel so far on good roads without going through an international border, risking life and limb at the hands of brigands and banditos, or getting shaken down by the secret police. The ancient world was united more by Roman roads than by Roman armies. Similarly, the nationwide highway grid has made the transcontinental empire of the United States a single navigable geographical entity.

The whole system is nearly as orderly as arithmetic. All east-west routes are even-numbered beginning in the South; all north-south routes are odd-numbered beginning in the West; all triple-digit routes beginning with even numbers are loops around metropolitan areas; and those beginning with odd numbers are spurs into city centers. It follows therefore that I-10 underlies the nation, linking the Atlantic and Pacific Coasts with a line running from Jacksonville to Los Angeles. I-90 links the oceans with a line running from Providence to Seattle. I-95 connects Miami and Boston. And I-5 runs between Vancouver and San Diego. Every road ultimately leads to every other road.

Of course, the great disadvantage of this marvel of uniformity is that the interstate system has imposed a smothering standard of sameness on the wild diversity of the North American continent. Every freeway looks nearly identical, whether traversing the Great Plains or crossing the Appalachians, skirting a major urban center or plunging into a national wilderness area. Scattered all along the system at predictable intervals are copycat tourist traps pockmarked with tacky metal sheds emblazoned with garish neon and selling cheap trinkets and bad food—all comprising a human environment not intended for humans, but rather for automobiles.

Dan noted as they drove across northern Indiana and into Ohio along I-90 and the Shocknessy Turnpike that they could be anywhere. The roadway had no distinctive identity. Although the shores of Lake Erie and Sandusky Bay, just a few miles north, afforded spectacular views, the highway was as blindly and blandly generic as a cafeteria soyburger. He imagined that they were traversing the geography of "nowhere." That eerie notion became more pronounced the closer they came to the Cleveland sprawl.

FIRST SETTLED in 1796, Cleveland remained a sleepy little village at the mouth of the Cuyahoga River on the shores of Lake Erie until the exploits of naval commander Oliver Perry during the War of 1812 highlighted its strategic position. The completion of the Ohio and Erie Canal in 1832 and the arrival of the railroad in 1851 cemented its importance as an avenue to both the coal and oil fields of Pennsylvania and the iron-ore mines of Minnesota.

Following the War Between the States, Cleveland became a political and economic center, giving the nation five presidents during the next fifty years, including Rutherford B. Hayes, James Garfield, William McKinley, William H. Taft, and Warren G. Harding. In addition several of the greatest industrial monopolists had headquarters in the city, including Marcus A. Hannah and John D. Rockefeller.

Cleveland boasted many notable firsts. The first African-American newspaper, the *Aliened-American,* was published here in 1853. The Arcade, built in 1890 in the heart of downtown, was the first indoor shopping mall in the nation. The Negro Welfare Association, the forerunner of the Urban League, was established here in 1917. NACA, the forerunner of NASA, was launched here in 1940. The first black mayor of a major American city was elected here in 1967.

But despite its rich legacy of economic and cultural vitality, Cleveland had fallen on hard times by the end of the sixties. By the end of the seventies it found itself in a full-fledged death spiral. It was only in the last few years that a massive redevelopment program had begun the difficult task of turning things around.

Downtown Cleveland's drab skyline had been festooned with cartoonlike coruscating crenelations erected thanks to billions of dollars of urban renewal investments. These included the multimillion-dollar Gateway Sports and Entertainment Complex—home of the city's professional baseball and basketball teams, the Playhouse Square Center—the nation's third largest performing arts center, the striking Society Tower—the tallest building between New York and Chicago, the one-of-a-kind Rock 'n' Roll Hall of Fame and Museum—which is expected to bring one million visitors a year through the turnstiles, and a whole host of other upscale theaters, luxury hotels, retail malls, lakefront marinas, specialty shops, high-rise apartments, and gourmet restaurants.

As DAN and Bea pulled into town, it was not the glamour and glitz that attracted them. They didn't have the least interest in visiting the newfangled tourist attractions conjured up by the city's eager-beaver marketing gurus. Instead, they had a hankering for hot Polish corned beef, Sicilian brick-fired pizza, and Colombian chorizo-stuffed peppers served up in obscure hole-in-the-wall neighborhood eateries.

Although its rich ethnic neighborhoods were gradually being swallowed up by a smothering urban sameness, Cleveland still had a number of authentic must-see and must-taste attractions. First, for an early supper, Dan planned to visit Mama Santa's in Little Italy, just east of University Circle. That evening he wanted to head over to the Cleveland Flats for a visit to the Flat Iron Café, a blue-collar Irish pub, for a taste of their sweet, crunchy, and addictive fresh-fried lake perch.

Bea wanted to go book hunting. Cleveland has its share of one-of-a-kind shops, and the granddaddy of them all was the mail-order and on-line store of John T. Zubal on West Twenty-fifth Street, in the shadow of downtown. She had been warned to make a list before sauntering among their towering stacks, otherwise it might take her forever to find some great discovery, wandering up and down the stairs and through the warehouse. Since that risk suited her, Bea had determined not to make a list.

In addition, she didn't want to miss Revolution Books on Mayfield Road. It was an all-volunteer, not-for-profit store where fervid conversations about the people's war, feminism, or Maoist theory abounded. Plus it promised books featuring enough ribald left-wing conspiracy theories to make even Oliver Stone's head swim. She had heard that Timbuktu—a quirky ethnic store on Superior—was a must for books on African-American culture and life. She even wanted to check out the Barnes and Noble store on Euclid Avenue. Unlike the white-bread megastores the company had built all over the country, this was a college store for more than just textbooks. Here astute bibliophiles were treated to any number of cerebral and unusual works generally unavailable at the malls of America.

But before they could play, they had some work to do. Bea needed to contact one of her clients on-line for some basic tests of their recently updated network. Dan needed to make a few quick phone calls. So they checked into their hotel near the airport, just off I-71, surreptitiously sneaking a reluctant Elvis up the back stairwell so as to remain unnoticed.

"While you get settled in," Dan said after they were in their room, "I'll make my calls. Then I'll reconnoiter around the Flats and get my bearings. How long do you think you'll need for this network test?"

"It shouldn't take long. Maybe an hour, tops."

"Okay. I'll be back here in an hour or so. And then we'll go out for a dinner sure to knock our socks off."

"I can't wait."

"Me either. I practically have to pinch myself. I just can't believe we're actually doing this. I feel like a kid in a candy store."

"Or a glutton in a deli."

"Yeah, well, that too."

Dan made his calls and left. Bea laid out the laptop, her
Day-Timer, a Java code book, a Windows NT reference guide,
and a copy of her client profile on the credenza next to the
phone. She had already preprogrammed remote access numbers for her Internet service provider into her mail manager.
She was a model of efficiency, ready for a burst of productivity.

But first she had to connect to an outside line and the old-
fashioned bedside phone did not have a data port. Not only
that, but it did not have the typical modular RJ-11 clips from
the unit to the wall, or even from the headset to the base.
Instead, it was hard-wired.

"Oh, brother," she said aloud. "I didn't even know that
phone lines like this still existed." Bea carried an adapter kit
with her for moments like this. It contained a voltage tester,
adapters for pulse and rotary systems, several teleclips, cou-
pler jacks, doubler jacks, and blind dialing decoders. But she
had nothing that would work with this setup.

She scanned the baseboards throughout the room and
crawled under the bed, hoping that she would find some kind of
jack she could use. But all to no avail. Finally in desperation, she
disassembled the phone base and hot-wired a direct courier link.

"Finally, a dial tone," she sighed.

She booted her computer and clicked on the appropriate
desktop shortcut. But when the dial-up sequence engaged, a
message she had never seen before appeared on the screen:
"Please insert data disk to play game."

She was aghast. "To play game? What game?"

To make matters worse, the program would not let her
exit, abort, escape, delete, or reboot. The computer froze.

She powered down the unit, took a deep breath, and tried
again. But she got the same message again. "This is ridiculous!"
she muttered to no one. For most computer users, errors,
glitches, snafus, and crashes are a common occurrence. But
not for Bea. She knew her hardware and software inside out.

Again she powered down. When she rebooted, she bypassed Windows and went into the subterranean code layers of DOS. What she discovered there infuriated her. Apparently someone had loaded a game package of some kind—and it was loaded with corrupted files.

She was furious. "Dante Alighieri Gylberd!" She almost never used his full name. "I'm gonna lambaste you! What were you thinking?"

Despite everything she tried, the system would not permit access to the corrupted data without the program disk. And there was no disk in sight. She riffled through Dan's suitcase. Nothing. She checked his briefcase. Nothing. Stymied, she sat on the edge of the bed and fumed and watched *Oprah.*

Dan meanwhile was having the time of his life driving through the ethnic neighborhoods of downtown Cleveland. He decided Bea probably needed a little extra time—computer programming always seemed to take longer than expected—so he drove to Shaker Heights and back though East Cleveland along Lake Shore Boulevard. He was gone nearly two hours.

As soon as he waltzed back into the room he knew he was hip deep in the Big Muddy. "What? Am I that late? Were you worried?"

"No. I wasn't worried."

"Well, what then? What did I do?"

"Dan, this computer is not a toy."

"I know that," he hedged defensively.

"Apparently not. You loaded some kind of game, and it's corrupted the hard disk. I hope, for your sake, that I don't have to wipe it and reload everything from scratch."

"Umm. A game program?"

"Yes. A game program. Now, where is the disk? I need it to get into the system."

"I think it's in the car with the other CDs—at least I hope it is."

"I hope it is too!"

"Yeah, it's out there, I'm pretty sure."

"Well, don't just stand there. Go get it! I have work to do, and this may take a while."

Dan retrieved the offending disk. "I'm sorry, Bea, I had this on my computer at work and thought it would be fun to have on the trip. It's got lots of good games on it."

Bea glared at him.

"On the other hand," he said sheepishly, "who needs games?"

"Look, I told you before we left that we both ought to have our own laptops."

"I know, but there wasn't enough room."

"There would have been plenty of room if we were driving in the Volvo or the Honda instead of an itty-bitty Volkswagen with an oversized mutt taking up more than half of the available space."

"Look, I said I was sorry. What do you want me to do? Throw myself into the Ganges? Volunteer for an immolation? Sign up for the foreign legion? What?"

"Don't joke. A little while ago, any of those looked good to me." As she set to work rectifying the data-diddling mess he had made, Dan took Elvis out for a long walk.

When he got back, he was braced for another reproof, but Bea was all smiles.

He breathed a sigh of relief. "Did you get it?"

"Yep. All done. I was able to uninstall your games, clean the corrupted files from the hard drive, and get to my dial-up program. It took me three or four tries to get an open line, but finally I got through and ran a quick test on my client's new network and checked my e-mail. It only took a couple of minutes."

"Wow. You're amazing. I am so sorry."

"Just don't pull another stunt like that," she grinned threateningly.

"Don't worry, I won't. Are you hungry?"

"We're good to go."

"Great. I'll just get a jacket."

Mama Santa's was a no-frills mom-and-pop operation in a real neighborhood. People walked around, sat on their porches, and watched their kids play in the parks—even in the dead of winter. It was like a television sitcom sort of community, only uncontrived, unsanitized, and unsentimental.

The food was as good as promised. And the place perfectly fit its surroundings. Everything was about as Sicilian as anything west of Palermo could possibly be. The red-and-white checkered tablecloths, the Chianti-decanter candleholders, the boisterous bebellied waiters, and the rich aroma of sundry spicy sauces gave the establishment a sense of place and purpose.

Likewise, the Flat Iron Café was a raucous neighborhood bar in a raucous neighborhood. Like Mama Santa's, it had none of the artificial atmosphere and faux ambiance that modern designers are apt to decoupage onto the surface of their trendy nightspots. As in so many of the old diners, buffets, saloons, roadside stands, chili parlors, pie palaces, donut shops, barbecue stalls, and corner eateries scattered across the more forgotten and disreputable parts of the American landscape, the Flat Iron Café was distinctive, authentic, quirky, and unmistakably local.

Both places were utterly devoid of pretense; they were extraordinarily ordinary. They simply served great food to common folk.

Dan and Bea loved all of it. They had a wonderful night out. They laughed liked they hadn't in ages. They could feel the icy stress that daily life had wrought begin to melt away. They walked hand in hand back to the car—the streets beneath their feet glistened, the lights above twinkled, and the song in their hearts soared.

Now they were getting somewhere.

Though we travel around the world
To find the beautiful,
We must carry it with us
Or we find it not.

Ralph Waldo Emerson

5

BUFFALO
POPULATION 328,123

Since they had been out late the night before, Dan and Bea decided to pamper themselves a little and sleep in. But they forgot to consult Elvis. He was remarkably patient for a while, but after twenty minutes of sunlight peeked between the curtains, he began to worry that something might have gone wrong. So he crawled up onto the bed, stood over Dan, and began sniffing for discernible signs of life.

Dan awoke with a start. He was disoriented. A huge, wet black nose was inches from his face, and a great weight pinned him beneath the covers. It was not a pretty sight. But then neither was he at that moment. His short salt-and-pepper hair askew, shadowy smudges beneath his eyes, and several days' growth darkened his jowls.

"Arrgh. Get off of me, dog." Flailing from beneath the sheets and blankets, Dan tumbled onto the floor with Elvis. He was stiff and sore. But that wasn't the worst of it. As he tried to rise, he suddenly cringed as if he had been shot. A stabbing pain, centered in the small of his back, radiated down his legs. He shuddered in agony. He tried to walk toward the bathroom, but he was practically doubled over. The dog yelped and scrambled away, dragging the tangle of covers with him.

"What's wrong?" Bea asked groggily. "Are you all right?"

"I must have thrown my back out," he groaned.

"How did you do that?"

"I don't know. I think I must have slept on it wrong or something."

The aging process can be excruciatingly humbling. Dan had always assumed that middle-aged men who hobbled themselves on bad knees or wrenched backs had simply gotten hurt playing a bit too aggressively on the volleyball court or had failed to warm up properly before a little one-on-one at the Y. He never imagined that they might have sustained such injuries in their sleep.

"How can you get hurt sleeping?" he moaned pathetically as he clambered awkwardly toward the vanity.

"You're getting older, Dan."

"I'm falling apart is what I'm doing."

Dan had always been a fine athlete and had taken good care of his body. So he had only recently joined his baby-boomer peers in obsessing over such things as receding gum and hair lines, dietary fiber, and his prostate. His newfound interest in articles about antacids, sleep aids, aromatherapy, and Viagra surprised him as much as it did Bea. It seemed like just yesterday he was a part of that happy-go-lucky mob of Mouseketeers-watching, long hair–growing, bell-bottoms-wearing, Beatles-listening, shoop-shoop hoola-hooping, funky chicken–dancing, peace sign–flashing, and Big Mac–consuming Pepsi Generation. He never imagined that he might actually grow old, and that he might suffer the aches and pains that go along with it.

Who would have imagined that he would wake up in the middle of the night only to toss and turn for hours? Or that he might have to be careful about eating spicy foods? Or that he could predict a change in the weather by the flexibility— or loss of it—in his left elbow? Or regularly read the labels on hemorrhoid products? Or try to keep up with arthritis research? Or use the term "wattle" to refer to something other than poultry parts? Or injure himself doing nothing more strenuous than sleeping?

Dan looked into the mirror. It was a matter of continual consternation to him that he no longer had the resiliency of a twenty-one-year-old college jock. He resisted concluding that his body was changing.

Bea was much more realistic about such things. After all, she had been through childbirth. Four times. She had fought her way back from stretch marks, liver spots, water retention, and Lamaze classes to a remarkable level of vibrancy and fitness. And what her carefully researched regimen of aerobic exercise, good nutrition, and sensible habits was unable to compensate for, expertly applied cosmetic cremes, industrial-strength sun block, and Diet Coke made up.

After Dan had indulged in about as much self-pity as he could stand, he pulled on a pair of sweatpants, running shoes, and a cap. He limped toward the door. "I'm taking Elvis out for a quick jog. I'll be back in a minute." Thankfully, the pain in his back seemed to ease a good bit as he limbered up.

The morning was bright and cloudless. A brisk, late winter wind was blowing off the lake, and so the air was invigorating. Dan was a regular jogger, typically running a leisurely two or three miles a day, focusing more on time than distance. Thirty minutes was generally all the time he could afford. That had always seemed adequate for keeping his heart in shape—until recently. Now it was hardly enough time to get stretched out and warmed up. Even so, the primary reason he ran was for his mind, not his body. He found that this was about the only time he could get away and think.

Elvis fell in beside him as his feet padded a relaxed and regular rhythm. Dan's aching joints and muscles adjusted to the shape of the road—a few gentle hills twisting through an old, hospitable neighborhood on the edge of downtown. A good run never failed to lift his spirits and heighten his sensibilities.

By the time he returned to the hotel, he was ready to tackle the day. He didn't quite feel as good as new, but close enough. Bea was in the shower, so he sat down with her laptop and started writing his first column in an easy stream-of-consciousness style.

When he was a youngster he had always resented his father's insistence that he keep a daily journal. He attempted to squirm out of that exercise whenever and however he could, but his father was unrelenting. The discipline of writing on command, extemporaneously, had been hammered into his daily routine. Now though, he was grateful for the early training. He could sit down at almost anytime, almost anywhere, and compose his thoughts into a reasoned narrative. Sometimes what he wrote might later appear hasty or shallow or poorly conceived, but at the very least, he never had a problem getting thoughts onto paper. He had never experienced the awful barrenness of writer's block.

Dan's prose was smooth, spare, and fluid. He was particularly evocative and sensual. The column practically wrote itself. When he had run the spell-checker and read through it a final time, he yelled through to Bea, "How do I get the e-mail working?"

"Don't ask," she replied as she emerged from the bathroom. "It's not worth the effort."

"But I need to send in my column."

"You're done with it already?"

"It isn't hard to write about food, especially when you're as hungry as I am right now."

"Right," she laughed. "Well, I think it would be easier to e-mail something this afternoon from a different hotel—one that doesn't rely on Flintstones' technology. Your deadline isn't until Friday anyway."

"Okay. Just don't let me forget."

"I thought it was just your body that was falling apart. I didn't realize your mind was starting to go too."

"Very funny. Come on. As soon as I get cleaned up, let's get the car loaded, get some breakfast, and hit the road. I want to get to Niagara Falls before the sun goes down."

"I'm just about ready to go. But I do hope we'll have some time to stop in a couple of bookstores before we zip out of town."

"As if we need more books."

"Excuse me?" she scolded him. "You can never have too many books."

"Right. But just be sure you remember that when you're tempted to complain about Virgil's diminutive profile."

BROWSING IS but one of the many time-honored traditions that have been heedlessly cast aside amid the hustle and bustle of modernity. Nevertheless, it is a habit that seems almost as natural as breathing in a bookstore. Dan and Bea spent more than an hour perusing the cornucopia of legend and lore, tales and traditions, wonder and woe on every shelf in Zubal's.

Before they got on the road that morning, she had discovered fine matching copies of Arthur Quiller-Couch's *Oxford Book of English Verse* and *Oxford Book of English Prose* with Moroccan leather boards and bright gilded edges. She was thrilled! Q's marvelous anthologies had long been her favorites. Dan scrounged a rare copy of *Political Economy* by Thomas Chalmers, the great Scottish nineteenth-century reformer and educator. Both Dan and Bea were smiling from ear to ear, certain they had made off like bandits.

I-90 followed the shores of Lake Erie and from time to time allowed magnificent views of the water. There was a good bit of melting snow and slush along the roadway, but traffic was light. They drove along eastern Ohio, northern Pennsylvania, and into western New York for nearly two hours before making a stop.

Dan filled Virgil's tank with gas, washed the splattered muck off the windshield, and took a quick look under the rear hood to make certain that everything was still in good order. Meanwhile, Bea studied the map.

Their plan was to get into Buffalo in time for a late lunch. Dan had his sights set on the Anchor Bar, the original home of Buffalo wings, where they were properly called Buffalo chicken wings. After that, they would drive toward the Canadian border. Dan had booked what he hoped would be a romantic evening in a honeymoon hotel overlooking Niagara Falls.

Both of them were ravenous by the time they drove past the city limits sign heralding the great metropolis of Buffalo. So they wasted no time in finding the Anchor. The tavern was in a rather disreputable-looking neighborhood near Allentown, at North and Main. Owned and operated by two generations of the Bellissimo family, the Anchor offers a fairly diverse menu, including salads and sandwiches, which are tolerable although not terrific, and a sampling of Italian cuisine of the spaghetti-and-meatballs variety. But most patrons order the house specialty doused in their choice of mild, medium, hot, or suicidal sauce.

According to local legend, Dom Bellissimo was working behind the bar on a Friday night in 1964. It was busy that night, so his mother, Teressa, was working in the kitchen while his dad, Frank, was greeting customers in the restaurant. Just before midnight a group of Dom's classmates came through the door and announced they were starving. Teressa said that there wasn't much left in the kitchen, but that she would try to whip up something for them. She had planned to put the chicken wings in the stockpot for the next day's soup, but when Dom's buddies came in, she requisitioned them for a little make-do experiment. About ten minutes later, she brought out two plates and set them on the bar—the first batch of what would become a world-famous concoction.

Dan and Bea ordered two platters of the fried-crisp, hot-sauced little munchies. Moments later the wings were served with a hefty garnish of fresh celery stalks—to relieve the burning palate—and a bowl of creamy blue cheese dressing for dipping. The portions were immense and both left more than satisfied about thirty minutes later.

Afterward, they drove down Main Street, east of Transit Road, to Aléthea's Chocolatier. It was a wonderful little candy store and soda fountain with a display of delicious pastries. Bea bought a generous bag of pecan-and-caramel turtles—a specialty of the house—while Dan settled for a Dr Pepper float.

BUFFALO, THEY discovered, was a remarkable city with a rich heritage dating back to the French traders and explorers of the early seventeenth century. That prime legacy extended from the opening of the Erie Canal in the 1820s through the heyday of heavy industrialism. Practically within shouting distance of the Canadian border, the city was probably best known for its bitter winter temperatures, abundant snowfall, and perennial almosts on the football field. The downtown area was rather unspectacular aesthetically and architecturally, although the new hockey venue was a notable exception. The city quite obviously had suffered a roller-coaster economy over the past several decades.

Surrounding the downtown area were several lively neighborhoods where people still sat on their porches, talked to their neighbors, walked down their sidewalks, tended their gardens, raised their children, and minded their business. It looked like home. And like any home, it had stories to tell—both happy and sad.

In 1901 a fair was held in the city. At the end of the summer, President William McKinley arrived for a two-day visit of the Pan-American Exposition, hailed at the time as a lavish world's fair dramatizing the great cultural, scientific, economic, and industrial strides taken during the previous century. It was Buffalo's chance to shine before the world.

On September 6, McKinley was greeting well-wishers in a reception line when a young anarchist stepped out of the crowd and shot the president at point-blank range. At first, it appeared that McKinley would recover from the wound. Four days later, Vice President Theodore Roosevelt was encouraged to leave Buffalo so his absence would assure the nation that the crisis was over. But on September 13, the president suddenly took a turn for the worse and died within twenty-four hours.

At the time, Roosevelt and several close friends were climbing remote Mount Marcy, the highest peak in the distant Adirondacks. They were on their way down from the exhausting climb when they were intercepted by a park ranger with the news. Quickly hiking to the nearest telephone—about a dozen miles away—they met with a security detachment and a buckboard for the forty-mile journey to the nearest train station.

Somber and apparently lost in his thoughts, Roosevelt barely spoke to anyone during the arduous passage. His train was mobbed by newsmen all along the way, but he remained in seclusion. He did not speak publicly until after he had taken the presidential oath of office in Buffalo. Then he simply asserted, "The administration of the government will not falter in spite of the terrible blow. It shall be my aim to continue, absolutely, unbroken, the legacy of President McKinley for the peace, the prosperity, and the honor of our beloved country."

At the age of forty-two, Roosevelt was suddenly the youngest president in American history. And though he had arrived at the White House by accident, he had indeed arrived. The event marked the inauspicious beginning of one of the greatest careers in all of American politics. But it also marked the shuddering end of Buffalo's hopes and dreams to take a place among the greatest cities in the world.

Roosevelt had always been a familiar figure to Dan. The larger-than-life figure was his father's hero. Hardly a day went by that the elder Gylberd didn't quote TR or regale him. Teddy—as he called him—became the embodiment of the values and the virtues he yearned to see replicated in the lives of his children and his students.

To be sure, Roosevelt was a remarkable man. Before his fiftieth birthday he had served as a New York State legislator, a U.S. Civil Service commissioner, a police commissioner for the city of New York, an undersecretary of the navy, governor of the state of New York, a colonel of volunteers in the U.S. cavalry, vice president under McKinley, and two terms as the president of the United States.

In addition, he had run a cattle ranch in the Dakota Territories, served as a reporter and editor for several journals, newspapers, and magazines, and conducted scientific expeditions on four continents. He read at least five books every week of his life and wrote nearly fifty on an astonishing array of subjects from history and biography to natural science and social criticism.

Roosevelt enjoyed hunting, boxing, and wrestling. He was an amateur taxidermist, botanist, ornithologist, and astronomer. Roosevelt was a loving husband. His first wife died after giving birth to their first child, and he later married his childhood sweetheart. He was a devoted family man, and they lovingly raised six children.

During his long and varied career, he was hailed by supporters and rivals alike as the greatest man of the age, perhaps one of the greatest of all ages. According to Thomas Reed, Speaker of the House of Representatives, he was a "new-world Bismarck and Cromwell combined." President Grover Cleveland called him "one of the ablest men yet produced in human history." Senator Henry Cabot Lodge asserted, "Since Caesar, perhaps no one has attained among crowded duties and great

responsibilities, such high proficiency in so many separate
fields of activity." After an evening in Roosevelt's company, the
epic poet Rudyard Kipling wrote, "I curled up on the seat
opposite and listened and wondered until the universe seemed
to be spinning round—and Roosevelt was the spinner." Great
Britain's Lord Charnwood exclaimed, "No statesman for centuries has had his width of intellectual range; to be sure no
intellectual has so touched the world with action." Even his
lifelong political opponent, William Jennings Bryan, was
bedazzled by his prowess. "Search the annals of history if you
will," Bryan said. "Never will you find a man more remarkable
in every way than he."

No wonder then that exhortations by Dan's father to
follow in his footsteps and to learn his lessons of leadership
only tended to intimidate Dan. It is a difficult thing to constantly live in the shadow of greatness. Dan knew that only too
well—as apparently, did the city of Buffalo.

IT WAS midafternoon by the time Dan and Bea got back to the
car. Elvis was curled up in the back seat, and rush-hour traffic
was already beginning to pick up.

"We had better get back on the road," Dan exhorted.
"Otherwise, we're going to get stuck in traffic. I'll drive, you
navigate."

"Aye, aye, Cap'n."

They knew Niagara Falls was one of the seven wonders of
the natural world. But it was difficult for them to see anything
natural anywhere around them. A gaudy array of outlet shopping malls, cheap motels, neon, and souvenir shops vied for
the attentions of the estimated eighteen million tourists who
visit the site annually. There were a large number of amuse-
ment parks, several museums, more than two dozen public
golf courses, and nearly twice that many private campgrounds
and fishing lodges. In addition, Dan and Bea noted gambling

casinos, an Imax theater, a clutch of sprawling hotels and motels, a butterfly conservatory, scenic helicopter services, a Marineland park, rental agents for whirlpool jet boats, a daredevil gallery, and a racetrack.

The Gylberds speculated similar fringe towns had grown up near every heavily visited national park, physical wonder, and native attraction. The function of these villages seemed to be to project a gaudy spectacle of dog-eared artifice, unkempt artificiality, and mediocre affectation that subsequently rendered tourists flat-footed for the sucker punch of the natural splendor of the attraction itself.

Something about Niagara Falls appeals to the lover, daredevil, and poet in everyone. Apparently, something also appeals to the gamboling, kitsching, and wayfaring ogler too.

Dan kept driving, hoping that the tawdry would pass and the two of them would be swept into the transcendent glory of the Falls.

No such luck.

To be sure, nature has left an indelible mark on the region. The Niagara River is actually a mere thirty-five miles in length, stretching between Lake Erie and Lake Ontario. But along that short distance are some of the most stunning sights on the face of the earth. The imposing Horseshoe Falls on the Canadian side of the river cascades 177 feet down, and the stupendous Vertical Falls on the American side of the river spills down 184 feet. Together with the thunderous crash of the waters, the rising mist from the pool below, and the wide panorama across the gorge, the Falls create a surreal spectacle of titanic proportions.

Winter brings an added dimension of beauty and outdoor activity to Niagara. Thousands of gulls and terns flock around the Falls and rapids. The clinging spray blankets the nearby trees, rocks, and lampposts, forming luminescent frozen shapes. When Charles Dickens visited in 1841, he wrote, "Niagara was at once stamped upon my heart, an Image of

Beauty; to remain there, changeless and indelible, until its pulses cease to beat, forever."

Over the years though, Niagara Falls has evolved from a stunning natural wonder to strategic military post to a prosperous trade center and finally into a glitzy year-round tourist trap. It seemed an unlikely—and certainly, an unseemly—fate.

IN MAY 1535, Jacques Cartier left France to explore the New World. Although he never saw Niagara Falls, the Indians he met along the Saint Lawrence River told him about it. Samuel de Champlain explored the region in 1608. He too heard stories of the mighty cataract, but never visited.

Etienne Brule, the first European to see Lakes Ontario, Erie, Huron, and Superior, apparently was also the first to behold the Falls in 1615. Later that same year, the Recollet missionary explorers arrived in Ontario. They were followed a decade later by the Jesuits. It was a Jesuit father, Gabriel Lalemant, who first recorded the Iroquois name for the river—Onguiaahra, meaning "the Strait." In December 1678, Recollet priest Louis Hennepin visited Niagara Falls. A few years later, he published the first engraving of the Falls in his book *Nouvelle Decouverte*.

The French soon built a fort there. Later the English made the strategic site their first line of defense against the fledgling American republic's designs on Canada. The Americans followed suit on their side of the river.

During the peace that followed the War of 1812, the region began the slow process of development. In 1820 a stairway was built down the bank at Table Rock, and the first ferry service across the lower river began. By 1827 a paved road had been built up from the ferry landing to the top of the bank on the Canadian side. This site became the prime setting for hotel development, and several early entrepreneurs staked out plots there. Between 1849 and 1962, thirteen bridges were constructed across the Niagara River Gorge. The greatest of these was built in 1855, when John August Roebling, the designer of the Brooklyn Bridge, built the Niagara Railway Suspension Bridge—the first of its type in the world.

Tourism had begun in earnest by 1830, and within fifty years it had increased more than tenfold to become the area's dominant industry. After World War I, automobile touring became popular. As a response, attractions and accommodations sprang up in gaudy, inexpensive strip developments, many of which still survive.

Interestingly, Niagara Falls was established as the ideal honeymoon destination by the French at the beginning of the nineteenth century. Napoleon's brother, Jerome Bonaparte, traveled by stagecoach from New Orleans to spend his honeymoon in Niagara Falls and returned home with glowing reports. It then gradually gained a reputation as the undisputed honeymoon capital of the world.

AFTER WENDING his way through the warren of "Must-See" and "Exclusive" attractions, Dan pulled into the parking lot of the hotel where he had reserved a room for the night. It was a small motor lodge sheathed in pink stucco and aquamarine aluminum with a huge neon sign out front that announced "Honeymoon View Hotel," promising "The Most Romantic View of the Falls" and "Intimate Suites Complete with Champagne Hot Tubs." A paunchy man with slicked-back hair, raggedy black jeans, and a leather jacket stood outside the door of the office, smoking a cigarette.

Dan's heart sank. Somehow it was not quite what he had imagined. He had pictured something a little more along the lines of a country bed-and-breakfast managed by a grandmotherly Martha Stewart aficionado. Instead, what he found was a barely solvent dive run by a guy with possible godfatherly connections.

Bea could see the disappointment on Dan's face. "I'm sure the rooms are fine," she offered. "Besides, we're here for the view."

"I suppose you're right. And we're only here for one night. It's just that I was hoping this would really be special."

"It already is," she smiled as she leaned toward him and kissed him on the cheek. "Come on. I want to see the Falls. It's been so long since we were here. Let's get checked in."

The paunchy man took his time sorting through the complex matter of assigning them a room and giving them a key. But finally they were able to retrieve Elvis from the car and carry their bags up the wrought-iron stairs around the back of the building and to their room.

After unlocking the door, the two of them just stood there on the landing. Aghast.

It was obvious that the effect was supposed to be something akin to that of Kublai Khan's pleasure dome. But it came off as little better than a cheap Cracker Jack surprise.

"Oh my," Bea couldn't help exclaiming.

"It's worse than I thought," Dan concurred.

The room was vast. The bed was in one corner; a Jacuzzi occupied another. There were mirrors on almost every available surface of the room. A small love seat and two reclining chairs were placed around a small coffee table, facing a television off to one side.

The drapes over the single small window, the upholstery on most of the furniture, and the bed linens were all fashioned of crushed red velvet. The ancient shag carpet was a dark industrial gray, as were the Formica surfaces on the dresser, the vanity, and the coffee table. The love seat had a fake fur rug hanging across the back—a bad imitation of leopard hide. Several large abstract oil paintings dominated by swirling blacks and amoebic reds—apparently culled from the remainder bins at some starving artists sale—adorned the few spans of wall space not occupied by mirrors.

Dan sighed and entered the room. Bea came in behind him. For the longest time, they just stood there and stared.

Even Elvis was briefly disturbed, distracted by so many reflections of himself.

To top it off, the bed was round.

"How do you know where to put the pillows?" Dan asked.

"I don't know," Bea responded, a bit incredulous. "More important, how do we know which side is yours and which side is mine? We've slept on our sides of the bed for a quarter of a century. I'm not about to change now—at least not if I can help it."

The Jacuzzi was bright red and heart-shaped. It was the only tub in the room.

"I think we're going to have to use this."

"Yeah, I'm afraid you're right."

"Why is it sitting out in the middle of everything?"

"I think someone thought that it might be sexy that way."

"I can think of a lot of things that are sexy, but staring at myself in a red-and-black room full of mirrors with the bathtub in the middle of everything is not one of them."

"Especially at our age, and especially after having driven in a Volkswagen all day. I feel swollen, tired, and achy. It's just not a sight I want to see reflected on a half dozen mirrors before turning in for the evening."

They stood there, bags in hand, for a little while longer. Then Bea started giggling. At first, Dan failed to see the humor, but finally he started to chuckle too.

"This place is so tacky," he groaned.

"And there's no reading lamp."

"For some reason, I get the impression that the designers didn't anticipate anyone might want to thumb through Q's *Oxford Book of English Verse* while they were here."

"Hmm. You may just be right."

There are three ways to view such places as this Taj Mahal. They can be dismissed as a glut of awful piffle, plastic, and polyester—cartoonish environments attractive only to tasteless nitwits, shallow dunderheads, or hopeless philistines. Or they could be legitimate expressions of popular sentiment and thus worthy of respectful consideration. Or they can be taken at their own level, regarding such schmaltz as little more than the kind of harmless junk—relics of pink flamingos, velvet paintings of Elvis, avocado appliances, greasy cheeseburgers, plastic paneling, Day-Glo, op art, hubba-hubba culture—that could only have been produced by the sole remaining super-power and the greatest democracy on the face of the earth.

Dan and Bea realized that, like most Americans, they had reacted to kitsch in all three ways at one time or another. She believed that such ambivalence is probably best accepted rather than railed against. He believed that it should be properly addressed with jeremiads and anathemas—and then quietly imbibed like so many other secret pleasures.

After they had acclimated themselves to their digs for the night, they decided to retreat to the Falls. They set out along the Rainbow Bridge toward customs on the Canadian side, stopping along the rail from time to time to take in the splendor of the crashing waters. As the sunlight caught the unending spray, a perfect rainbow formed over the American Falls. The magnitude of the scene was arresting. Hand in hand they marveled at the sights and sounds and senses of eternity that gripped them. And suddenly every distraction faded from view as Niagara worked in them a sense of absolute wonder.

"Do you remember the first time we were here?" she asked.

"Uh-huh," he murmured, apparently lost in the memory of their Yuletide honeymoon.

"Do you remember the lights and the chime tower?"

"Yes."

"Do you remember what Christmas carol the chimes were playing?"

"Was it 'Silent Night'?"

"No."

"'Joy to the World'?"

"You don't remember, do you?"

"Well, sure I do," he hedged. "It was 'O Come All Ye Faithful.'"

"Nope."

"Okay, what was it?"

"If you don't remember, I'm not telling you."

"I'll remember—just give me some time. You see, the mind's going too."

"I love you anyway, Dan Gylberd," she whispered into his ear, standing on her tiptoes.

He drew her close. "I love you too."

About an hour later they wandered back over the bridge. They strolled along the American side of the gorge to the historic Red Coach Inn, where they were seated in a cozy nook for two. The sky—streaked with the brilliant rose, violet, and crimson hues of the setting sun—provided a perfect backdrop for their view of the upper rapids of the Niagara River as the water rushed to a precipitous fall. The ambiance was splendid, their meal superb. After dinner, they meandered back toward the hotel. They looked in a few shop windows. They walked. They talked. They laughed. They enjoyed themselves.

When they finally came back to the Honeymoon View Hotel, they were exhausted and ready for bed. Although they had a little difficulty figuring out where—and how—to lie on the round bed, they finally turned out the lights and plopped into place. Even Elvis seemed to have made his peace with the place.

That was when they first noticed that there were mirrors on the ceiling over the bed and the glitter in the textured paint. The effect was the same as if a spinning disco ball hung over their heads. The place was dazzling and sparkling like a house afire.

They began to laugh all over again as they snuggled into one another's embrace. Their honeymoon suite had become a theater of the absurd. Like so much of the rest of life.

And they just couldn't help but enjoy it.

All I really need to know I learned from Noah and his
adventure on the Ark.

First, plan ahead. It wasn't raining when Noah began
construction.

Second, be at the ready. When you're old and gray you
may still have a big job to do.

Third, don't listen to the critics. Time will prove that
they're the ones who're all wet.

Fourth, there are no lone rangers. It is always wise to
traverse perils in pairs.

Fifth, speed isn't always an advantage. The cheetahs
and impalas made it aboard.

But then, so did the slugs and snails.

Sixth, don't forget that we're all in the same boat.

Seventh, remember that the ark was built by amateurs,
the Titanic was built by pros.

Eighth, don't miss the boat—you may not get a second
chance.

Ninth, the stench on the inside is infinitely preferable to
the deluge on the outside.

And tenth, no matter how bleak life looks there's a
rainbow beyond adversity.

Tristan Gylberd

COOPERSTOWN
POPULATION 2180

Normally, DAN AND BEA communicated very well—as beloved friend and cherished lover, as life partner and soul mate, as dear husband and helpmeet. They had fallen into the trap of talking past one another as gruff male and genteel female, as brute logic and raw emotion, as iron bludgeon and porcelain vessel, as unfeeling haste and sensitive hesitation. Their words slipped unheeded past the other like ships passing in the night.

They were having a full-blown Mars-and-Venus moment.

It started when Bea called the children the next morning. Dan had already been out for a run with Elvis, taken his shower, gassed up Virgil, repacked the trunk and back seat, revisited the American side of Niagara one last time, paid the motel bill, bought coffee and pastries at the local café next door, and plotted that day's journey.

He was anxious to get on the road.

Bea was in no hurry. She was telling Jennifer about everything they had seen and heard and done the previous day—all in excruciating detail. "Of course, the hotel looks like something out of a trailer-park bordello. We laughed and laughed and laughed . . ."

Dan wasn't laughing now though. He was pacing. Impatiently. But Bea pretended she didn't notice.

"We had a wonderful dinner out. Your father had all these wonderful places picked out. Of course, they were little more than holes in the wall. But the food was great . . ."

Dan tried to speed things up. He pointed to his watch. He gestured toward the door. But Bea continued to chat.

"What's that? . . . Oh, yes, I talked to each of the boys. They're all fine. You ought to give Josh a call though. Just to encourage him. He's really bogged down this semester . . ."

Dan had a big day planned. And the morning was nearly gone. He couldn't imagine how anyone could talk on the phone as long as Bea could. He huffed and puffed. He mumbled and grumbled. Bea was cheerfully undisturbed.

"All right, dear, I'd better go. Your father is having a conniption here. . . . Yes, I love you too. Okay, I'll call you later. Maybe tomorrow night. It depends on how far we get. . . . Uh-huh. I love you too. Bye bye."

"Well, it's about time," Dan sighed.

"About time?" Bea snipped.

"You've been on the phone all morning."

"I have not."

"You most certainly have. I've done half a dozen things already—and you're not even ready to go yet."

"I was talking to your children."

"I know who you were talking to. I didn't say I didn't want you to touch base with the kids. I just didn't think you would want to fritter away the whole day on the phone."

"Fritter?"

"Yeah, fritter."

"Is that what you call maintaining good communications with your family? Frittering away the day?"

"No, of course not. It's just that—"

"That's just typical. Just typical. Getting to the next sleazy motel or greasy spoon is more important to you than your own family."

"I didn't say that."

"You didn't have to. Not in so many words."

"But—"

"Are they so unimportant to you that you can't even invest a little time talking to them? And you begrudge me the few moments I have with them? Here I am, traipsing around with you. And I can't even call the kids without getting a bunch of guff?"

"No. It's just that we've got a schedule to keep."

"A schedule? Why? I thought that was the whole point of this trip. No schedule. No deadline. No agenda. And no pressure. We're on sabbatical. We're supposed to be taking it easy. We're supposed to be relaxing. We're supposed to be enjoying ourselves. Remember?"

"And you're not?"

"Well, I was. Until now."

Dan threw up his hands. "Do you really want to spend all day here?"

"It's not even ten o'clock. I'd hardly call that all day."

Dan sighed. He tried to change the subject. "So is that what you're going to wear?"

"What's wrong with what I'm wearing?"

"I didn't say there was anything wrong with it."

"Yes, you did."

"No, I didn't."

"I know what you're thinking."

"Obviously not."

"You were using that tone of voice."

"What tone of voice? I don't know what you're talking about."

"Oh, yes, you do."

"I don't."

Both were getting exasperated. Dan tried one more time. "Can we just go now?"

"Fine."

"Okay, fine. Let's go."

They harrumphed out to the car, clambered in with Elvis, and puttered away still muttering under their breaths.

They hardly said a word leaving Niagara, through Buffalo, onto I-90, and eastward along the shores of Lake Ontario.

"Men," Bea complained, "are impossible."

"Women," Dan responded, "are incomprehensible."

There were other times when Dan and Bea felt that they both understood one another almost too well. It seemed as if they had known each other since before time. They were so familiar with each other's thoughts that often their conversations tended to be random phrases that used to drive the kids crazy.

"Bea, I was thinking that maybe tonight—"

"Remember, we've got that deal."

"What deal?"

"You know, the deal over at the—"

"Oh, yeah, right. That deal."

"And even if we didn't, there was supposed to be—"

"I almost forgot about that. But didn't—"

"No, he had to go out of town."

"Really? So soon?"

"Well, he didn't want to, but—"

"Budget restraints?"

"That and the time of year."

"Right."

It was as if they could finish one another's sentences, fill in one another's blanks, and read one another's thoughts. They knew everything that there was to know about each other— every annoying habit and irrational opinion, every twitch and tic, every bad joke and hidden weakness. Jennifer used to say that after a decade of marriage some sort of a mind meld must have occurred between them. It did seem as though they had a pretty good lock on their relationship.

But every so often, just when everything seemed to be hunky-dory, something would intrude upon their harmony to remind them that, like all other couples, they were from entirely different planets.

And so they drove on in tense silence, wondering who would be the first to break down and apologize. They stared out the window at the passing scenery, and despite the fact that they were sticking to the interstate, there was a good deal of interesting scenery to stare out at.

THEY WERE following the route of the famed Erie Canal through the rolling hills and wide fertile valleys of upstate New York. It had been the superhighway of antebellum America. When the canal opened in 1825, it was a marvel of engineering and human labor. From Albany to Buffalo, it opened up the American frontier and made westward expansion inevitable. It turned New York Harbor into the nation's number-one port and shaped social and economic development throughout the region. With branches crisscrossing the state, cities and industries developed along the canal and flourished. Chief among these were Rochester, Syracuse, and Binghamton.

Until the American colonies declared their independence in 1776, European settlement of the New World was largely confined to the eastern seaboard. The Appalachian Mountains were a formidable obstacle to westward movement. Only the Mohawk River Valley in New York offered both a land and a water passage through the barrier.

By 1817 plans for a man-made waterway fed by the Mohawk River and bypassing its waterfalls and rapids had been made. This canal was to traverse New York State, connecting the Hudson River in the east with the Great Lakes in the west. When it opened, vast parcels of land became accessible for the first time. Shipping costs dropped dramatically. Immigrants to America crowded the canal boats in search of new lands and new opportunities in the West. The westward movement of the nation had begun.

By the late twentieth century, the importance of the Erie Canal had shifted to recreation. It still connected the Great Lakes and inland waterways to the Hudson River and the Atlantic. But the old shipping and transport barges made up little of the modern-day traffic. Instead, pleasure craft of every size, dinner cruises, and intrepid canoeists kept the canal and its locks busy.

BY THE time they arrived in Rochester, Dan and Bea were famished. It was practically lunchtime, and their timing could not have been better. Dan decided that, given the circumstances, they would have to visit Nick Tahou's world-famous hot dog stand on Lyell Street.

The ramshackle place looked more than a little dubious to Bea despite the long line that stretched out the front door and around the corner. But her fears were quickly allayed.

Western New York is the heart and soul of America's sausage and wiener center, and Nick Tahou dishes out some of the finest to be found anywhere. Upstate franks are not slim aristocrats like those found at Nathan's at Coney Island in New York City, nor are they crowned with the baroque bouquets of condiments like the all-beef dogs from Eli's at Watertower Place in Chicago. The tube steaks in this part of the world tend to be bare and spare but irresistible.

Tahou's place is an around-the-clock eatery where the air is redolent of pungent spice and rich porcine variety. The menu boasts several meaty treats—Yankee hots, red hots, pork hots, Texas hots, and the house pink hots. Note the emphasis on the word *hot*. Each hot dog Nick serves radiates fiery jalapeño, habañero, Tabasco, or cayenne peppers. They are split down the middle and grilled to attain maximum character before they are loaded into fresh-baked buns and heaped with a fine-grained chili. The famed house special, the pièce de résistance, the *especialté de la maison* is what Nick has dubbed the Garbage Plate: baked beans, fried potatoes, macaroni salad, a pair of grilled dogs, raw onions, and a large ladle of chili—all amassed upon a thick cardboard platter.

The inimitable Samuel Johnson once asserted: "The way to a man's heart is his stomach." It is amazing what a good meal and a full stomach can do to improve a man's attitude and temperament. Halfway through their meal, Dan and Bea were talking and laughing again, their Mars-and-Venus moment all but forgotten.

DAN'S FATHER used to say that there was a direct connection between food and the joy of life. In fact he often quipped that there was little more revealing of a person's ultimate concerns than what he or she ate and how it was eaten. He claimed he could tell a great deal about anyone's theology by examining what they ate. As crazy as it sounded, Dan believed his father had been right about that just as he had been about so much else.

Generally, people tend to think of faith as an otherworldly concern while we think of food as a thisworldly concern. It is difficult to see how the twain could meet, but in fact, food and faith are inextricably linked.

Dan once undertook a study of the subject. He was editing a book about the culture, manners, and habits of the ancient Near East, and he needed to verify some details. What he discovered was, to say the least, fascinating.

The word *faith*, he discovered, is used less than three hundred times in the Bible while the verb "to eat" is used more than eight hundred times. He could hardly read a page of

Scripture without running into a discussion of bread and wine, milk and honey, leeks and onions, glistening oil and plump figs, sweet grapes and delectable pomegranates, or roast lamb and savory stew. He encountered images of feasts and celebrations throughout. Even the themes of justice and virtue were often defined in terms of food, and the themes of hungering and thirsting were inevitably defined in terms of faith. Community and hospitality were evidences of a faithful covenant. Righteousness and holiness were evidences of a healthy appetite. Worship—in both the Old and the New Testaments—did not revolve around esoteric discussions of philosophy or ascetic ritual enactments, but around a covenant family meal.

To underscore this, he came to the startling realization that nearly all of the resurrection appearances of Christ occurred during meals. On the road to Emmaus, in the Upper Room, and at the edge of the Sea of Galilee, Jesus supped with His disciples. He did not say, "Behold, I stand at the door and knock. If anyone opens the door, I will enter in and discuss theology with him." No. Jesus said, "I will come in and sup with him."

Food is the stuff of life. And it seemed to Dan that Christian doctrine regularly and intentionally reminded believers that Jesus came to give life. Indeed, He came to give His followers "abundant life." As a result, Dan concluded that it was not surprising for Jesus and all the other biblical teachers, writers, apostles, and prophets to utilize food as a primary image in describing theology. It amazed him that the church was practically mute on this subject about which the Bible seemed to be so articulate.

A few years later, Dan saw a little plaque in a kitchen supply store that read, "A good theology will invariably produce a good meal." At first he just chuckled and quickly dismissed the maxim as just another bit of gourmet hyperbole. But the more he thought about it, the more he began to realize that the epigram conveyed a substantive and healthy world-view.

Like a fine feast, a good theology ought to be more than the sum of its parts. While it may be composed of certain essential dogmas and doctrines, each of those essentials ought to also be carefully related to all the others. Dan clearly saw the crucial connection between the profound and the mundane. While a good theology might wisely attend to the minutest detail, it must also remain fully cognizant of how those details affect the bigger picture. It necessarily will place as much significance on the bits and pieces as it will on the totals, and vice versa.

A good theology ought to be good for the soul. But it also ought to be good for the world. Its spiritual vision should give vitality to all that it touches—from herb gardens and table settings to nation states and cultures—simply because the integrity of that vision ultimately depends as much on a balanced perspective of everyday life as it does on a solid comprehension of our highest aspirations. Its attention to heavenly concerns ought to be integrally bound to its fulfillment of earthly responsibilities. It seemed to Dan that a good meal, a joyous family celebration, or a well-kept seasonal feast effectively portrays that truth in a tangible and very profound fashion.

Of course, Dan realized that making that kind of integrated connection between heavenly concerns and earthly responsibilities is never easy—in either a mealtime or a lifetime. Everyone is constantly tugged between piety and practicality, between devotion and duty, between spiritual communion and worldly calling. Like blending sundry recipes into a cohesive meal plan, honing a balanced world-view involves both the drudgery of daily labor and the high ideals of faith, hope, and love. But the results are always worth the effort.

Dan was convinced that a good theology with a comprehensive world-view inevitably cheered the heart like a sumptuous dish. Conversely, a bad theology with a fragmented world-view could only leave a bitter taste in the mouth.

Yet whenever the subject of world-view came up in the limited circles in which Dan was active—at the publishing house, at the local church Bea used to attend, or in conversation with the authors he dealt with, his friends, or his neighbors—everyone generally thought first and foremost about philosophy, not cooking. They thought of intellectual niggling. They thought of the brief and blinding oblivion of ivory-tower speculation, of thickly obscure tomes, and of inscrutable logical complexities.

In fact, Dan was convinced that one's world-view was as practical as potatoes. If there was anything he had learned from his father, it was that a world-view is less metaphysical than understanding marginal market buying or legislative initiatives. It is less esoteric than keying a book on a computer or sending a fax across the continent. It is as down to earth as grinding condiments for a savory sauce. A world-view, he always used to say, is simply a way of viewing the world. And a balanced view of the world will inevitably be fraught with a sort of cook's paradox: an appreciation for both the potentialities and the liabilities of fallen creation.

Dan supposed that the problem boiled down to the fact that most people tend to hammer out their philosophy of life in isolation from life. They disconnect their world-view from the world, and that inevitably leads to imbalance. In the words of the old saying, either they become so heavenly minded that they're no earthly good, or they become so earthly minded that they're no heavenly good. It was no easy feat to be "in the world" and not be entirely "of it."

As Dan could testify from personal experience, a world-view was a difficult ideal to visualize, much less implement in daily life. Without tangible models, it was bound to remain an unrealized ideal.

As he sat there in Nick Tahou's hot dog stand, he thought that is just what a healthy appreciation of the connection between food and faith does. Dan contemplated that this sense of being "a part of" and "apart from" was a paradigm of the connection between food and faith. By vitally connecting the head with the hand with the heart with the palate, by placing emphasis on the whole of life—relationships, traditions, simple joys, family celebrations, tastes, pleasures, and expressions of thanksgiving—the high ideals of a biblical world-view were happily instituted in the warp and woof of culture.

His father invariably began mealtimes by quoting the psalmist: "Taste and see that the Lord, He is good." At this particular moment, eating the junkiest of junk food with Bea, Dan almost thought he could.

AFTER THEIR lunch had restored their hearts and minds, Dan and Bea continued to follow the length of the Erie Canal eastward toward Syracuse. Both were happy and even giddy. Their earlier spat seemed absurd.

As they drove they were somehow able to conjure up, from the recesses of their memories, the old boatman's folksong. The "Erie Canal Song," also known as "Low Bridge," was first published in 1913. It was composed to protest the coming of mechanized barges to replace the mules that had been used previously.

Dan and Bea had both sung it as schoolchildren. They were amazed that they could actually remember most of the words and were even able to croak out some semblance of the tune:

> I've got an old mule and her name is Sal
> Fifteen miles on the Erie Canal
> She's a good old worker and a good old pal
> Fifteen miles on the Erie Canal
>
> We've hauled some barges in our day
> Filled with lumber, coal, and hay
> And every inch of the way we know

From Albany to Buffalo

Low bridge, everybody down
Low bridge for we're coming to a town
And you'll always know your neighbor
And you'll always know your pal
If you've ever navigated on
The Erie Canal

We'd better get along on our way, old gal
Fifteen miles on the Erie Canal
'Cause you bet your life I'd never part with Sal
Fifteen miles on the Erie Canal

Git up there mule, here comes a lock
We'll make Rome 'bout six o'clock
One more trip and back we'll go
Right back home to Buffalo

Low bridge, everybody down
Low bridge for we're coming to a town
And you'll always know your neighbor
And you'll always know your pal
If you've ever navigated on
The Erie Canal

The Erie Canal Museum is in Syracuse at the 1850 Weighlock Building, a National Historic Landmark. The building, the only remaining structure of its kind, was designed to weigh canal boats and collect tolls at the confluence of the Erie and Oswego Canals.

Bea wanted to stop, but Dan convinced her that they needed to press on. He was still harried by a sense that they needed to keep to an itinerary. Bea thought he was just being bullheaded. They passed through town and veered toward the south through the congestion that clogged I-81.

It was hard for either of them to imagine Syracuse as a shipping and industrial center. Today the metropolitan area is better known as home to more than fifty thousand college students, the third largest concentration in the nation. That makes Syracuse a young, vibrant, energetic place and a place with a long history of nurturing entrepreneurs, innovators, and inventors.

Syracuse is also a prime tourist destination. The Finger Lakes, Onondaga Lake, Oneida Lake, Lake Ontario, and a host of rivers, streams, and canals make the surrounding area a boating, fishing, skiing, and sightseeing paradise.

The traffic around them reflected that kind of privileged demographic. Sports utility vehicles towed recreational trailers, students navigated land yachts, and tattooed motorcyclists weaved across the lanes. The freeway was as dangerous and as raucous as swing dancing in a crowded gym.

At the junction of the Susquehanna and Chenango Rivers, about sixty miles south of Syracuse, is the city of Binghamton. The place is a melting pot of ethnic communities and traditions. As a result, it is a culinary adventure. From Ethiopian, Ukrainian, Greek, and Polish to Italian, Mexican, Indian, and Chinese cuisine, there is something to suit practically anyone's desire in the low-slung downtown hugging the riverbanks.

But Dan had something very particular in mind for their brief stop in Binghamton. Nothing short of an authentic Spiedie would suffice. A culinary concoction of chicken, pork, beef, or lamb marinated in oil, oregano, and Italian spices, Spiedies are cooked on a skewer over a charcoal fire and served sandwich-style on Italian bread. It is a rare and exotic dish—served and savored nowhere else on earth but Broome County, New York.

The S&S Charpit on West State Street in Binghamton is a rather undistinguished and commonplace fast-food restaurant. With seating for approximately a hundred customers, a bevy of plastic signs, and Formica-covered tables, the hasty and efficient architecture hardly betokens promise. Nevertheless, it is there that the Lupo family has been selling their Spiedies for nearly half a century to appreciative customers who often have to endure long lines and crowded parking.

Spiedies are worth the wait, as Dan and Bea quickly discovered. The delicacy—pronounced "speedies"—are apparently derived from an old Italian tradition. But how and when Spiedies came to this country remain a mystery.

Little matter. Suffice it to say that the Gylberds savored them with unfettered relish and abandon. The succulent marinated cubes of meat infused with wood smoke, the chewy Italian bread, the creamy Sicilian coleslaw, and the deli pickle garnish were a feast for the senses.

It was twilight by the time they bid the Lupos good-bye and headed back toward the highway. Dan was determined to make it to Cooperstown before they stopped for the night. And they had a good seventy or eighty miles to go by his best estimate. As Dan glanced into Virgil's rearview mirror to check the flow of traffic, he had the strangest sense that he was being followed—not just by the normal queue of vehicles as they merge, but followed. He checked the mirror again, saw nothing, and decided he was imagining things.

As they drove, the sun disappeared behind the hills, splashing golden hues across the road in front of them. For a day that had begun with such pique, things had turned out markedly better.

About halfway between Binghamton and Albany, just off I-88, Cooperstown is set in the magnificent rolling hills west of the Hudson Valley. The home of the Baseball Hall of Fame, it is an American mecca. Already a charming community, Cooperstown is made even more so by the magnetic attraction of the nation's greatest pastime.

ACCORDING TO baseball lore, the first scheme for playing the game was devised in 1839 by a local athlete, Abner Doubleday, who would later attain glory as a Civil War hero. Although historians doubt the authenticity of the story, the significance of Cooperstown has hardly been diminished. The Doubleday story is not a legend in the sense that the Shoeless Joe Jackson story may be a legend; that is, in the sense that it may possibly be a lie. Rather it is a legend in the broader and more human sense. Legends are the most important things about baseball, just as they are about history.

In Cooperstown, these legends come to life. The Hall of Fame's museum is rather what one might expect. With a Smithsonian sense of completeness, it documents nearly every phase of the game, displaying the mementos of the greatest players, managers, and teams that have ever played. Visitors speak in hushed tones of sanctified wonder as they saunter from one exhibit to another—Babe Ruth's bat, Ty Cobb's glove, Jackie Robinson's warm-up jacket, and Honus Wagner's tobacco trading card, Hank Aaron's uniform, Walter Johnson's locker, Mark McGwire's seventieth-home-run ball, and Sammy Sosa's cleats.

Just down the street from the museum, however, is a site of equally mythical proportions. It is the real field of dreams. Situated where Doubleday supposedly invented the game, the old-time ballpark was constructed by the WPA during the Great Depression. The red brick façade and white wooden trim make for a fine setting for the annual Hall of Fame game each July. The bleachers, the wrought-iron backstop, and the Victorian details seem to exude the tradition, dignity, and drama that baseball once epitomized. The scene in the half-light of the moon made Dan want to pull out bat and ball and hearken back to the days when sandlot games and pickup ball were among his greatest joys.

Around the corner from Doubleday Field, Dan and Bea found a delightful bed-and-breakfast hotel. Built in 1812 as the family home of James Fenimore Cooper, the famed American novelist, the grand Georgian mansion was practically empty during the off-season. Its seven guest suites and three parlors provided a luxurious ending to a day unabashedly devoted to heartburn-inducing foods.

After the Gylberds had settled into their room, they took Elvis for a walk along Main Street, which was lined with theme bars, convenience markets, memorabilia emporiums, fast-food restaurants, and junk shops. Bea noted what appeared to be an antiquarian bookshop, Willis and Mony's, next door to a baseball card trading center, Mickey and Babe's.

"We'll have to come back and check this out in the morning. Look——," she pointed to a row of faded hardbacks in the small display window. "Those look like first-edition Mencken volumes. And look at all the Cooper sets. Wouldn't it be nice to have an old leather-bound copy of *The Last of the Mohicans* or *The Deerslayer*?"

"What time do they open?"

"Ten."

"Uhh. Well, do you think we'll still be here then?"

"Oh come on, you're not going to start that nonsense again are you?"

"No. No. Of course not."

"Yes, you were."

"No, I wasn't. Honest. I was just hoping that we might get an early start. We've got a long way to go tomorrow—especially if we're going to get into Vermont."

"You're hopeless."

Dan smiled a broad, sheepish, guilty smile. "I know. I guess I am."

"You guess?"

"It's going to take some getting used to, this relaxing business. I haven't had much practice."

"So I've noticed."

"Okay then. The new plan is to get off to a slow start. Maybe wander over here after breakfast and browse for that leather-bound Cooper. Then we can go through the museum. Dawdle a bit. Whatever."

"How about having no plan at all?"

"No plan? No plan at all? Well, all right. That will work. My revised plan then is to try to have no plan."

"You're really hopeless, aren't you?"

"What? What did I say now?"

Bea just laughed as she turned back up the street toward their hotel.

"No, really. What?" Still clueless, Dan followed along, scratching his head.

Nonconformists travel as a rule in bunches.
You rarely find a nonconformist who goes it alone.
And woe to him inside a nonconformist clique
Who does not conform with nonconformity.

Eric Hoffer

MONTPELIER

POPULATION 8247

SOMEHOW OR OTHER, BEA convinced Dan to spend a couple of days in Cooperstown before they headed on. A summer sight-seeing destination can be delightful in the waning days of winter. The thickly shellacked surface of kitschy bric-a-brac and gaudy gewgaws that is so much a part of American tourism fades at the onset of winter, and a remnant of the authentic place begins to bleed through. Much of the town was closed up until the season began, but to Dan and Bea those were the least interesting parts of the town.

Dan was able to write several columns, e-mail them back to Chicago, and follow up on several projects at the publishing house. Bea was able to spend two afternoons helping several clients track down pesky glitches. But the bulk of their time was spent relaxing. Really relaxing.

Together they strolled down Main Street for a leisurely morning of window-shopping. They ate at the Doubleday Café, an upscale diner that offered a particularly good breakfast menu. They had a quiet dinner at the Tunnicliffe Tap Room,

where innumerable baseball heroes of the past had carved
their names into the vintage tables and where the steaks were
genuinely worthy of the Hall of Famers who frequented the
place. They went for long runs along the shores of Lake Otsego
with Elvis. They slept late. They talked. They downshifted.

Best of all, they spent hours on end at Willis and Mony—
the finely stocked bookshop Bea had noticed the first night
they were there. It was a wonderful place to while away a
winter afternoon. The shop offered four snug rooms laden
with books. Against each wall stood huge oaken cases, neatly
arranged. In the center of the largest room was a long, low
table, also crowded with books and surrounded by several
comfortable leather club chairs.

According to Aristotle and Aquinas, list making is the
essence of true literature—a notion only recently violated by
the bare bones prose of Hemingway amd his modernist kin. It
seemed to Bea that a bookstore was therefore a uniquely
medieval place—one that turned her mind to long, satisfying,
and arcane lists. Thus this store was for her an earthly Ely-
sium. In some strange way, it represented so much of what
she aspired to, and it embodied so much of what she yearned
for. A good bookstore, to her, was like a well-stocked library.
It provided a sort of nexus of piety and sensuality, holiness
and seduction. She always imagined that such sanctuaries
from the hustle of everyday life were in some sense cenacles
of virtue, vessels of erudition, arks of prudence, towers of
wisdom, domains of meekness, bastions of strength, thuribles
of sanctity, crucibles of dissipation, throne rooms of desire,
caryatids of opulence, repositories of salaciousness, milieus of
concupiscence, and trusses of extravagance.

When she was a child, bookstores had afforded Bea a
refuge from the turbulence of her broken home, a shelter from
the storm of her troubled relations. But even now, in much happier days, she found them redolent with security and solace.

The rich fragrance of hand-oiled Moroccan leathers, the visual panoply of deep natural hues, the effluvium of fine vellum, the hollow ring of sequestered silence, the sacred spectacle of light filtered through high, dusty windows, and the hush of monkish thoughtfulness, combined to grant such places an air of amplitude. The total effect was of a concert of alluring terrestrial beauty and majestic supernatural signals.

Bea had learned long ago that the creative arts consisted of signs. Thus if images were, as Aristotle asserted, "the literature of the layman," then books consisted of signs of signs and bookshops were signs of signs of signs. They were therefore the truest of all the creative arts, combining rhythm, tone, structure, progression, logic, melody, heft, texture, redolence, perspective, cipher, harmony, balance, epic, symbol, emblem, saga, craftsmanship, hue, lyric, form, function, ballad, and sanctity. Bookshops were united in their variety and varied in their unity, unique in their diversity and diverse in their apt assembly. They were sustained by a law at once heavenly and worldly.

Willis and Mony was well stocked in both breadth and depth. Bea found several first editions of H. L. Mencken's biting critiques of American life. She loved the way he thumped the tub of the folks he called "the booboisie" who traded the glorious inheritance of Western civilization for the mess of potage currently found on prime-time television and sold at local strip malls.

At the same time, Bea also found a couple of volumes of G. K. Chesterton's supremely buoyant essays on the common sense of the common man. She loved his sane vision of a quiet world where folks minded their business and raised their children and tended their gardens and cared for their neighbors unencumbered by the expectations of the rich and glamorous or the expert and meticulous. Mencken and Chesterton were in some ways world-view opposites, but both represented well her conflicted thinking about the world and the ways of the world.

Dan found several first editions of the old traditional mysteries he loved to read. Over the years he had become an aficionado of the genre. To his mind—and this notion was supported by academic criticisms of the detective novel, such as Umberto Eco's work on popular semiotics—the best mystery protagonists were generally dissatisfied outsiders.

The theory is that detectives like Sherlock Holmes, Hercule Poirot, Father Brown, Adam Dalgliesh, Owen Archer, Miss Marple, Matt Scudder, Nero Wolfe, and Brother Cadfael connect with the reader because they are somehow set apart from the society they investigate and thus are able to observe more objectively. Sometimes they are not aliens to their worlds, but their behavior may be unusual, and as a result they are able to look at people clinically, as if they were specimens.

Often they distance themselves slightly from their fellows with their own peculiar moral code. And it is that strong sense of immutable ethics that often allows them to use solutions beyond the mere letter of the law—as when Holmes lets someone walk away or Poirot stays silent. As a result, readers get a bit of moral commentary that urges them to think about the implications of society as it is portrayed. And sometimes the standard of ethical value helps the reader see the crime or the criminal differently.

Always wrestling with such issues himself, Dan found the well-crafted traditional mystery aesthetically satisfying on any number of different levels. He found several first editions of P. D. James and Ellis Peters mysteries and was thrilled at the prospect of curling up over the next several nights to read and reflect.

WHEN THEY were finally ready to load Virgil and tool out of town, they were both thoroughly refreshed. Their route took them north and east through Albany, across the Hudson Valley, and through western Massachusetts toward Vermont. A light dusting of fresh snow made the countryside even more pristine. The small farms, clapboard outbuildings, little red barns, stone fences, and squat silos distinctive of rural New England were cloaked with an ethereal elegance.

They followed I-90 east into Springfield and then I-91 north into historic Northampton. Dan had pulled another sure-fire restaurant from his little black book, but Bea was more than a little skeptical.

"This kind of cuisine doesn't travel well. You know, Dan."

"Well, normally, I would agree with you. But I think this place is an exception. I've got a strong hunch it'll be great."

"Isn't it generally true that the farther you get from the source, the worse food gets? You wouldn't order Gulf shrimp in Nebraska. You wouldn't want Chicago-style pizza in Louisiana. You wouldn't even think about trying lobster in Montana. You wouldn't ask for lox and bagels in Utah. And you wouldn't want to eat Mexican in New England. I think this is a no-brainer."

"I know. I know. It doesn't seem possible. But you're going to have to trust me on this. I've heard that the food is fabulous."

"You're serious? You'd eat Mexican in western Massachusetts? Aren't you just a little afraid of Tacos à la Alpo?"

"It's going to be great. Just wait and see."

Dan had that little-boy-on-a-grand-adventure look in his eyes again. Bea knew there was no use in arguing with him. She sighed in resignation and hoped for the best.

Her fears were quickly laid to rest. La Cazuela was indeed a rare treat, defying all odds. The fashionable second-story restaurant is in the heart of downtown Northampton on Old South Street. With décor reminiscent of upscale Santa Fe, it is a colorful and succulent outpost of sizzling red-hot salsas, savory blue corn enchiladas, pungent pollo verdes, tangy chipolte chilis, zesty pico de gallo, and smoky roasted poblanos. Even Dan was pleasantly surprised.

Northampton is the cultural center of a vibrant academic community. Five eminent institutions—Amherst, Hampshire, Smith, Mount Holyoke, and UMass—create an atmosphere that is a cross between Harvard Square and Santa Cruz, with a little Greenwich Village thrown in.

As Dan and Bea walked back to their car, passing eyebrow-pierced punks, tattooed earth mothers, spaced-out skaters, aging hippies, lunar New Agers, and tie-dyed thrashers, it was difficult for them to imagine that just two hundred years ago Northampton was the center of America's greatest spiritual revival. It was here that Jonathan Edwards, perhaps the most brilliant theological mind America has ever produced, taught and preached for nearly a quarter century. But these days it was more likely that the Gylberds might run into folks like Kevin Eastman and Peter Laird, who created the Teenage Mutant Ninja Turtles out of their tiny Northampton comics bookshop and who donated some of their earnings to set up a cartoon museum downtown.

THE STEADFAST political correctness of Northampton today belies—and perhaps even betrays—its historical roots. The town began as a Puritan settlement purchased from the Nonotuck Indians in 1654. For the price of something like a hundred fathom barrels of wampum, ten coats, and a few trinkets, the Puritans acquired the area of rich farmland. Throughout its first century of existence, Northampton remained a strict New England Christian community.

It was within the bounds of that staid and upright cultural context that the ministry of Jonathan Edwards took place. He was not a particularly enthralling master of pulpit theatrics or hermeneutical technique. Instead, he won his reputation as a thinker. He was highly regarded as a precise dogmatician and also widely admired as a careful systemizer and a cogent preceptor. His books were among the greatest achievements of human intellect. He was to prove himself, according to many accounts, superior to Locke, Newton, Descartes, and a couple of Pascals combined.

But as a preacher, he apparently left a little to be desired. He read his densely theological and tautly philosophical sermons from painstakingly researched longhand manuscripts, often in a flat, monotonous voice. Only rarely did he make eye contact with his congregation. Although not unpleasant in demeanor, he hardly cut a dashing or charismatic figure.

Nevertheless, it was here that he read what was perhaps the most famous sermon delivered in American history. Entitled "Sinners in the Hands of an Angry God," this sermon was an exposition of the imminence of judgment and the horrors of perdition. It was real hell-fire-and-damnation stuff.

Later described by literary and historical critics as a rhetorical masterpiece, Edwards's sermon was astonishingly gripping and terrifyingly vivid. It caused an immediate sensation. Even before Edwards had finished delivering the sermon, people were moaning, groaning, and crying out. In fact, there was so much distress and weeping that Edwards had to quiet and calm the people several times so he could conclude. The fervor of the Great Awakening, which had thus far bypassed the region, now swept through it with a white-hot intensity. Suddenly the people were bowed down with an awful conviction of their sin and its consequences.

The sermon not only won for Edwards even greater renown than he already enjoyed, but it provoked a further awakening among its distant readers. Since then it has been reprinted hundreds of times, perhaps thousands. To this day it is not only a standard text for the study of great preaching, it has passed into the realm of classic literature, making it the most anthologized sermon in the English language.

In later years Northampton would gain renown as the epicenter of the Shays Rebellion in 1789—America's first tax revolt—which significantly influenced the outcome of the Constitutional

Convention that had just convened. Still later, Daniel Webster gained fame here in 1847 in a successful lawsuit before the Northampton bar. Ralph Waldo Emerson and Sojourner Truth stirred the passions for war at the Free Congregational Society here in 1861. Famed soprano Jenny Lind gave a concert here in 1851 and proclaimed the city the paradise of America; she liked it so well that she honeymooned in Northampton two years later. Sylvester Graham, the eccentric Utopian and inventor of the graham cracker, owned the brick house on Pleasant Street that is now home to Sylvester's Bakery and Restaurant. President Calvin Coolidge practiced law in the Main Street building that today houses Fitzwilly's Restaurant. Coolidge served as Northampton's mayor for two years and swiftly rose to state senator, governor of Massachusetts, and vice president of the United States before becoming president in 1923.

ALL TOO little of this venerable legacy was evident to Dan and Bea as they made their way out of the little town and northward into Vermont. The fact that the town's heritage was obscured by the relentless march of terminal trendiness and smothering hipness was more than a little depressing to them. Despite the wonderful meal they had enjoyed at La Cazuela, they found the quaint artifacts of New England's past subsumed in the septic sea of New England's present. They were hoping to leave behind the oppressive ingratitude and relentless tackiness of modernity. But they were still far from that goal.

A historical awareness is essential for the health and well-being of any society. It enables communities to know who they are, why they are here, and what they should do. Just as a loss of memory in an individual is a psychiatric defect calling for medical treatment, so too any community that has no social memory suffers from illness. The venerable aphorism remains as true today as ever: "He who forgets his own history is condemned to repeat it."

It seemed to Dan and Bea that in this awkward new epoch, many communities were afflicted with a malignant contemporaneity. Their morbid preoccupation with themselves—and thus their ambivalence and ignorance of the past—has trapped them in a recalcitrant present.

Surely Vermont would offer a welcome respite for them. After all, the Green Mountain State is hidden in the northeast corner of the United States, so hidden that most Americans hardly know where it is. Similarly, most of the residents of Vermont don't seem to realize that they are supposed to be Americans. There is nary a Wal-Mart in sight. There is not a single mega-mall. There are no interstate loops around the large cities, primarily because there are no large cities. And it is possible to drive for several days without seeing a McDonald's. You can't even do that in Paraguay.

The capital of the state, Montpelier, would hardly constitute a subdivision in most other places in America. In fact, there are several minor attractions at Disney World bigger than Montpelier. To be sure it is a quaint and picturesque and congenial place. But that hardly qualifies most towns to be a county seat, much less a state capital.

To complicate matters further, it is not possible to simply stumble upon Montpelier. You have to be going there to get there. And even then, you have to be very determined. It is cut off from most of New York by the beautiful Adirondack wilderness. The city is isolated from direct interstate access by the imposing length of Lake Champlain. It is separated from much of New Hampshire, which is itself rather out of the way, by the White Mountains. It is even detached from the rest of Vermont by the Green Mountains.

None of this seems to bother Vermonters in the least. Indeed, they seem to be inordinately proud of the fact that they march to the beat of a different drummer. A fierce sense of independence has been an undeniable hallmark of Vermont's history from its earliest days. All of this made a trek through Vermont practically irresistible to Dan and Bea.

Originally populated by a variety of diverse tribal peoples from the Algonquin, Iroquis, and Abenaki nations, the land now known as Vermont was first discovered by European explorers in 1609, when the French adventurer Samuel de Champlain sailed across the lake that now bears his name. It is obvious that the French paid their first visits during the warm summer months, because when they later described the mountains that form the spine of the state, they named them Les Verts Monts, or the Green Mountains. Montpelier also got its name from the French; it means "the naked mount" or "the mountain without trees." As so often happens with place names, Les Verts Monts was transliterated into Vermont over time. And as so often happens with explorers, Champlain laid claim on everything he saw for the king of France.

Following the Seven Years' War—a global conflict known in the Americas as the French and Indian War and celebrated in our folklore by the tales of Washington Irving and James Fenimore Cooper—the Treaty of Paris warded England the entire region. From 1763 until the outbreak of the Revolutionary War, the land would be claimed by the colonial governors of both New Hampshire and New York. The fiercely independent residents, however, always maintained their autonomy. In fact, that was a large part of the reason why, when they joined the spreading rebellion against British rule in 1775, Vermonters chose to go it alone rather than join forces with the thirteen Atlantic Coast colonies.

Ethan Allen and his Green Mountain Boys did not fight for American independence, rather they fought for Vermont's freedom. The great victory at Fort Ticonderoga was not won by American forces but by the militias of a sovereign Vermont under the authority of President Thomas Chittenden and the national legislature convened in Windsor. Even after the other colonies had confederated into a single American nation, the small state of Vermont remained an independent republic. It was not until 1791, some fifteen years after declaring its autonomy, that Vermont joined the United States as that fledgling nation's fourteenth member state. Even then, Vermonters retained the right to secede at any time by a simple majority vote of its legislature, the only state to continue to have that statutory privilege.

To this day, the people of Vermont remain stalwartly independent. Indeed, the state's sole congressional seat is held by the House of Representatives' only independent, the irascible cultural curmudgeon, Bernie Sanders.

Vermont boasts a number of important firsts. Besides being the first state to join the original thirteen colonies in the new Union, its constitution was the first to outlaw slavery. The first patent, signed by George Washington, was issued to Samuel Hopkins of Pittsford in 1790 for a process he had developed for making potash, a vital contribution in launching the state's soap manufacturing industry. The first U.S. postage stamp was printed in Brattleboro in 1846. In 1856 Charles Orvis of Manchester invented the ventilated fly-fishing reel, which proved to be so successful that the company he founded remains one of the most well-known suppliers of fishing and sporting goods.

In southern Vermont, the Springfield Telescope Makers makes its home on a high hilltop backed against a southern shield of tall spruce trees and facing north Mount Ascutney. The oldest association of citizen scientists in the country, the community group is devoted to building and using astronomical telescopes and other scientific instruments.

A two-story house, known as the Orange Smalley–Thomas Davenport Shop, stands on the east side of the road that leads from Brandon to the village of Forestdale. It was built around 1830 as the workshop of Orange Alfonso Smalley. There, adjacent to the fields of his father's farm, his experiments with electromagnetism led to the development of the first fully functional electric motor. The shop is now a monument to Yankee ingenuity and American creativity.

Vermont has always been a pioneer in the arena of education as well. It built the nation's first land-grant college, its first agricultural college, its first normal school, its first private military academy, and its first school specifically established for the college training of women.

The tiny state has given two sons as presidents, Chester Arthur and Calvin Coolidge. It was also the birthplace of the founders of the Mormon church, Joseph Smith and Brigham Young. The Green Mountain State also produced John Deere, the inventor of the plow that broke the plains, and Norman Rockwell, whose best-loved illustrations of small-town America invariably included the settings and people he found in and around the quintessentially New England towns of Arlington and Manchester.

DAN AND Bea were appropriately impressed. The drive northward along I-91 followed the winding course of the Connecticut River into some of the most magnificent ski country anywhere in the world. Even from the whizzing efficiency of the freeway, the view was picture-post-card perfect.

Twilight began to encroach on the landscape shortly after the Gylberds got past the Green Mountain National Forest. So they decided to stop for the night in Weston, a quaint New England village off the freeway on Highway 100.

Famed the world over for its Vermont Country Store and the adjacent Bryant House Café, Weston was everything they had hoped for and more. After they settled into a nearby hotel, they walked over to the restaurant's beautifully restored colonial buildings, which boasted a mahogany barroom and an antique soda fountain.

Most of America's great regional cuisines have enjoyed a certain fleeting vogue in recent years—Cajun, Tex Mex, California Chic, Gulf Coast, Southern Country, Western Ranch, and Comfort Food. One that never has been trendy, and likely won't be, is old-fashioned Yankee home cooking. The rather fuddy-duddy ways of the New England kitchen do not lend themselves to the highfalutin' interpretations of fashion-setting chefs. But the parsimonious habits of the proper Yankee cook can be richly rewarding, as the folks at the Bryant House demonstrated only too well.

On the menu were the most delightful treats of the region. Boiled New England Dinner consists of corned beef boiled with a combination of vegetables—cabbage, beets, carrots, new potatoes, onions, turnips, or rutabagas. Brown Betty is a cracker-crumb pudding sweetened with molasses or pure maple syrup. Doughboys are essentially Yankee donuts concocted for strolls at the Grange Fairs—disks of quick-fried dough topped with cinnamon sugar or confectioner's sugar. Grape Nuts Pudding is a sweet custard in which the cereal softens to create streaks of grain. Johnnycakes are little corn cakes made from hard-flint corn, generally eaten for breakfast like pancakes. Red Flannel Hash is made from leftover boiled dinner and takes its name from the deep hue left by the blush of the beets. Indian Pudding is a mixture of cornmeal and molasses, cooked for hours to become a dark, spicy samp, like a breakfast cereal, but eaten for dessert and served hot with a scoop of ice cream. And Whoopie Pie is a snack cake made of two disks of chocolate cake with the most delectable sugary white goo between them.

Bea ordered crackers and milk: good old cracker-barrel crackers, a bowl of milk to crumble them in, and a hefty hunk of cheddar on the side. Dan had a richly aromatic chicken potpie topped with a broad flaky biscuit and an apple crisp on the side.

Afterward they walked over to the store, renowned around the globe for making the accouterments of New England country life available via a mail-order catalog. There they found a bonanza of such local culinary peculiarities as five-pound bags of mush cereal, cans of fiddlehead greens, and penny candy by the piece. They found everything from Monkey Brand black tooth powder and Hoof Quencher bag balm to Flexible Flyer snow sleds and Buford's pickles in a barrel. There were also rugged clothes, sensible shoes, shrewd farm implements, and other efficient tools. The place was a jamboree of common sense and practicality.

The next morning Bea called the kids while Dan took Elvis for a long run through the woods. Then together they went back to the restaurant for a hearty New England breakfast, complete with corn mush dripping with Vermont maple syrup and zesty wild turkey hash smothered in creamy salt pork gravy.

They fueled the car and returned to the interstate, plunging deeper into Vermont ski country. Each town they passed seemed to be an odd conflation of open village greens, white-spired churches, and neat picket fences thrown together with hippie craft stores, New Age crystal shops, and roots-and-berries health-food restaurants. The combination of a staid and restrained colonial conservatism with Birkenstock, ponytail, and nose-ring ultra-hipness was an anomaly they could not easily reconcile.

As the Gylberds approached the capital, traffic intensified. At one point a large number of motorcyclists roared past them. There must have been twenty-five or thirty Harleys, and nearly all of them had two passengers astride the wide leather saddles. Bea shivered at the thought of hurtling through the cold mountain air at seventy miles an hour perched on an open bike.

"They're all in uniform," Dan quipped.

"What uniform?"

"They're all wearing the same thing. They think they're bold because of their black leather jackets, black jeans, long chains dangling from their wallets, Wellington boots, and silly half helmets."

"Yeah. So?"

"They've probably all got the same Harley-Davidson T-shirts, the same tattoos in the same places, the same beards, the same everything. They're wearing a strictly enforced uniform."

"And your point is?"

"I just think it is kind of funny that America's most avid mavericks, freethinkers, rebels, and iconoclasts are so fiercely, obstinately, and unswervingly orthodox in their heterodoxy."

Bea chuckled. "You're just an old crank."

"That I am."

As they made their way into Montpelier, they began to see why the highway had become so congested. Apparently they had stumbled upon a gay pride march at the state capitol—a magnificent building topped with a gleaming gold dome, local granite columns, and a stately portico. Crowds thronged in and around it. Dan and Bea were agog at the bacchanal unfolding before them.

IN ANCIENT Greece and Rome, the festival of Bacchus was held each year to celebrate the spring harvest. It was always a chaotic and raucous affair. During the obstreperous weeklong festivities, the normally sedate city-states of the Peloponnesians and the Etruscans succumbed to unbridled passions and compulsive caprices. The people profligately indulged in every form of sensual gratification imaginable, fornication, sodomy, intoxication, and gluttony. It was an orgy of promiscuous pleasure.

Bacchus was the god of wine, women, and song. To the ancients, he was the epitome of pleasure. His mythic exploits were a dominant theme in the popular art, music, and ideas of the day. Chroniclers of the age observe that the annual carnival—called the bacchanal—commemorating this legend was actually the bawdy highlight of the year. In fact, it dominated the Helleno-Latin calendar then even more than Christmastide does today.

But a wild picture of immorality that only poets and mobs can describe is always simultaneously a wild picture of melancholy that only parents and emissaries can understand. Thus, even as they reveled in the streets, the ancients were troubled by a sublime sadness. It was like an ache in their hearts or a knot in their stomachs, but it was essentially an abscess in their souls. Even as they celebrated their gaiety, they were forced to acknowledge their unhappiness.

Ultimately, it was the bacchanal's smothering culture of sexual excess that proved to be the undoing of Greco-Roman dominance in the world. Historians from Thucydides and Herodotus to Himmelfarb and Schlossberg have documented that the social collapse of Greco-Romanism was rooted in the moral collapse of Greco-Romanism. The reason is as simple as it is universal.

Just as liberty and equality are opposite extremes often contrary to freedom, so sensuality and satisfaction are opposite extremes often contrary to happiness. There is no real connection between the pursuit of happiness and the pursuit of pleasure. Happiness and pleasure are, in a sense, antithetical sensations since happiness is founded on the value of something eternal, while pleasure is founded on the value of something ephemeral.

Sadly, the lessons of history are all too often lost on those who most need to learn them.

THIS WAS the first time Dan and Bea had ever actually witnessed a gay pride march. They were astonished. Although they thought of themselves as open-minded, accepting, and well-informed, they were reminded instantly of the ancient bacchanals. The raucous revelry, the perverse promiscuity, the orgiastic opulence, and the apollyonic abandon that they saw in Montpelier seemed almost identical to the descriptions they had read of the Greeks and Romans on the precipice of their demise. The malevolent scene before them could have easily been transported three thousand miles and three thousand years to the bustling Plaka under the shadow of the Acropolis without missing a beat. The sights and sounds would have been no more alien there than here.

It was not the march itself that proved to be disconcerting to Dan and Bea. Both of them were veterans when it came to the jangling discontent and roiling umbrage of street demonstrations. Dan had seen his parents organize regular Saturday morning pickets at an abortion clinic, rallies at the steps of city hall, or protests at pornographic theaters. Although his father had been a genuine academician, Dr. Gylberd was certainly not the typical ivory-tower book-sniff. Instead he was one of those rare idealists who was also a passionate activist. Dan often characterized him as "a rip-snortin', rootin'-tootin', ride-to-the-sound-of-the-guns, talking-out-loud-to-yourself-in-broad-daylight kind of intellectual." So for Dan it wasn't really the idea of public protest that bothered him; he was quite accustomed to that. And as for Bea, she had been a regular participant during the heady days of the Vietnam War protests on her college campus.

Their problem was not so much the so-called awareness march itself, but the tenor and character that it seemed to take. It was on that disorienting day in that discordant place that they first encountered the despondent distress of unbridled eros.

The exuberant participants in the day's festivities, cavorting in the aura of libertine excess, apparently had come to Montpelier from throughout the region. Burlington and Middlebury were college towns just up the interstate a few miles, and both boasted large and active gay and lesbian populations. The kids all seemed so cocky, idealistic, and tragically self-sure.

Bea noticed one girl in particular as she walked past. She was strikingly attractive and reminded Bea of Jennifer. But she seemed to have gone to extraordinary extremes to hide her natural beauty from the world. She wore baggy cargo jeans, an oversized lumberjack flannel shirt, a surplus pea jacket, and high-laced, waffle-stomper Doc Martins. Her hair was bobbed painfully short, and she wore no makeup or jewelry, except for a ring of silver studs piercing the entire ridge of her right ear and a small silver loop through her nose. She was also gaudily adorned with a bevy of buttons bearing the slogans of various lesbian activist groups: "Refuse and Resist," "I'm a Lesbian. Get Used to It," "I'm a Mother-F#%@er," "Abortion on Demand and Without Apology," "Queens, Queers, and Quays," and "Dykes on Bykes." They were pinned willy-nilly all across the back of her haute gauche khaki photojournalist's vest.

Bea shook her head. It was beyond her comprehension what extremes people would go to for the sake of fashion. Bisexuality, lesbianism, and any number of other once unspeakable passions had been the very epitome of chic and hip in the American campus Zeitgeist. The students before her now seemed to have bought into a plague of terminal trendiness, lock, stock, and barrel. She reeled at the implications of such a rheumy-eyed and tyrannosexual "kulturesmog."

Apparently, the march had been organized by Queer Nation, a radical breakaway faction of the equally radical ACT-UP homosexual activist organization. Recently relandscaped and renovated, the park around the capitol was normally crowded with brown-baggers, strollers, and a few joggers— even in the dead of winter. But by the time Dan and Bea arrived, it had been abandoned into the hands of the rally organizers. A small platform had been erected and a makeshift sound system and podium had been installed.

At first there were only a few hundred activists. They were milling around, tending to a few last-minute details, rechecking the schedule of events, and generally making merry. Representatives from several renowned "fellow-traveler" organizations began to unfurl their banners and to set up long folding tables loaded with pamphlets and paraphernalia around the perimeter of the park. Three or four burly members of the local Women's Action Coalition were raising a giant black-and-blue display that announced "High-Octane Anger." Meanwhile, two volunteers from Planned Parenthood were laying out the necessary supplies for a "Condom-Fest" scheduled for later in the afternoon.

As the crowd began to swell, a full complement of the vaunted minions of the American Left made appearances. There were representatives from the ACLU, People for the American Way, NOW, Fund for the Feminist Majority, NARAL, Greenpeace, NAMBLA, Sierra Club, CISPES, the Children's Defense Fund, the NEA, and the Audubon Society. Even the slightly less reputable partisans of the Left's many obsolete "lost causes" circulated among the protestors: the New Symbionese Liberationists, the American Maoists, the Trotskyites, the Weathermen, the Neo-Jacobins, and the Black Panthers.

Before long, the park was a carnival of inflated rhetoric, exaggerated emotions, and excited hormones. They tended to be a rather colorful lot, though were it not for the odd sado-masochistic twist that the protestors proudly flaunted, the crowd might have been indistinguishable from the typical hippyish rent-a-crowds that populate such things as Earth Day celebrations, Amnesty International benefit concerts, or Pro-Abortion photo-ops. Absolute conformity is never so certain as among absolute nonconformists.

In recent years the haunting and emaciated figures of men on the threshold of death have become regular fixtures at local Gay Pride parades and protests. This one was no exception. From across the square, orderlies were helping several wheelchair-bound AIDS patients make their way toward the rally. They were residents from a neighborhood hospice. The anguish of uncertain eternity was etched on their faces.

As the rally got under way, one of the organizers was at the podium leading an angry chant, "We're here and we're queer." The crowd was working itself into a cathartic frenzy. Fists were raised. Curses were hurled. Tempers flared.

The beautiful girl Bea first noticed stood at the edge of the crowd shaking her head in cadence with the crowd. Over and over again she repeated the chant, her face red, her veins bulging. "I'm your worst nightmare," she shouted. "I'm America's worst nightmare. I'm a mad fag with nothing left to lose."

Bea had always attempted to abide by the pious truism that admonished her to "separate the sin from the sinner." But like so many other truisms, she found that it was easier said than done. It was easier said than done because, nine times out of ten, sinners were too mad, too adamant, and too proud to allow it.

As soon as they could extricate themselves from the snarl of traffic around the capitol, Dan and Bea wove their way through the oglers and protestors toward the outskirts of town. Dan was especially frustrated that they had been prevented from finding a place to stop. He had hoped to visit the shop where his father had always ordered his trademark bow ties.

For many years—really from the time that he was a teenager—Dan had disdained what appeared to him to be his father's recalcitrant and unabashed eccentricity and his deliberate defiance of fashion convention. Only recently had he begun to understand his father's bold and individual resistance to the slavish conformity of fads and fancies, a resistance that so defined his father's life and career.

The stylish throng swarming through the New England village streets made a visit to the shop all but impossible. It struck Dan as the height of paradox. It was an irony that he might have missed just a few years ago. Indeed, it was an irony that he seemed to have missed all his life up until now.

The more things change, the more they stay the same.

For a long time the Gylberds sat in silence, reflecting on the demonstration they had just witnessed, as they negotiated Virgil around the capitol crowd and back toward the freeway.

Dan routinely performed the act of merging into interstate traffic as he had hundreds of times before, and there it was again—the same feeling he'd experienced on the way to Cooperstown. This was too weird. He looked around, checked all of Virgil's mirrors, and drove on, chalking up the déjà vu experience to the emotional beating they had taken at the capitol.

About twelve miles outside of town Bea noticed a road sign noting the Robert Frost Wayside Trail. In the odd melancholy of the moment she quoted her favorite Frost verses from *The Road Not Taken* and *Mending Wall*, both of which seemed entirely apt at that juncture. She remembered bits and pieces of *Pan with Us*, particularly the lines about the "pipes of pagan mirth" and a world in search of "new terms of worth." But particularly vivid were the brooding stanzas of *Reluctance*:

> Out through the fields and the woods
> And over the walls I have wended;
> I have climbed the hills of view
> And looked at the world, and descended;
> I have come by the highway home,
> And lo, it is ended.
>
> The leaves are all dead on the ground,
> Save those that the oak is keeping
> To ravel them one by one
> And let them go scraping and creeping
> Out over the crusted snow,
> When others are sleeping.
>
> And the dead leaves lie huddled and still,
> No longer blown hither and thither;
> The last lone aster is gone;
> The flowers of the witch hazel wither;
> The heart is still aching to seek,
> But the feet question "Whither?"
>
> Ah, when to the heart of man
> Was it ever less than a treason

> To go with the drift of things,
>   To yield with a grace to reason,
> And bow and accept the end
>   Of a love or a season?

Dan looked over at Bea as she whispered the final phrase. He thought he saw a tear fall across her cheek as he drove toward Boston.

Nothing is more common
Than for men to make partial and absurd distinctions
Between vices of equal enormity,
And to observe some of the divine commands
With great scrupulousness,
While they violate others, equally important,
Without any concern, or the least apparent
    consciousness of guilt.
Alas, it is only wisdom which perceives this tragedy.

                                    Samuel Johnson

BOSTON
POPULATION 574,283

THE *MAYFLOWER* WAS NOT the first ship of colonists to arrive in the New World. It was not even the first in the English domains. Yet it retains a place of first importance in the lore and legend of this land. In telling the story of that little ship, one generation of Americans after another has been able to catch a glimpse of the faith, resolve, and bold sense of providence that its passengers brought with them from across the Atlantic, which they then endowed upon all those who would follow them.

Likewise, Boston was not the first settlement established in New England by the Puritans and Pilgrims. Yet it quickly assumed a place of preeminent importance, a place it maintained throughout the next century and a half as the straggling little colonies flung along the jagged Atlantic coastline were forged into a vibrant national power.

In the spring of 1630 eleven small cargo vessels set sail across three thousand perilous miles of ocean. On board were seven hundred men, women, and children who were risking their lives to establish a godly, Puritan community on the shores of Massachusetts. John Winthrop, the leader of the group, composed a lay sermon, "A Model of Charity," during the journey, which he probably read to the assembled ship's company. The sermon expressed his intention to unite his people behind a single purpose, the creation of a new form of government, ecclesiastical as well as civil, so that their community would be a model for the Christian world to emulate. Theirs was to be, he said, a "City upon a Hill," a genuine model of Christian civility, graciousness, charity, and prosperity.

As a result of such soaring ambitions—and the grand achievements that such ambitions ultimately secured in the succeeding generations—the city of Boston is the very crossroads of American history and myth. The largest and most important city in New England to this day, it is a place of stark contrasts. Granite-and-glass towers now stand where once only rutted village lanes were cleared. Monuments of high finance and higher technology stand side by side with old civic landmarks and worn national icons.

Oddly, for most of the last decade, Boston has been a massive construction site. In an effort to ease the city's strangling traffic congestion, transportation authorities have undertaken the single largest rerouting of a freeway system anywhere at anytime. Tunnels for I-93, U.S. 1, and several multilane spurs have created the world's most expensive hole in the ground. It has also created the world's biggest mess. During certain times of the day, the area around Logan Airport is practically impassable. The tranquillity of the historic North End has been sundered by blasting crews, semipermanent traffic detours, and massive construction depots.

It was into this maelstrom of old and new, historic and histrionic, ancient fortitude and modern decrepitude that Dan and Bea were thrust.

After their disappointing visit to Montpelier, they crossed over into New Hampshire and drove southward through Concord, Manchester, Nashua, and Salem. They spent the night just across the Massachusetts border at a freeway motel.

The next morning they slept late, took care of some on-line business from their room, and waited until commuter traffic into Boston cleared before making their way into town. Dan's plan was to get a historic bed-and-breakfast in Beacon Hill then walk the length of the Freedom Trail and make a few strategic stops along the way for lunch and dinner.

The Freedom Trail is the central feature of the Boston National Historical Park. It includes a self-guided tour set up by the National Park Service along nearly three miles of the city's labyrinthine streets. A painted red line on the sidewalk guides visitors from site to site through almost three centuries of Boston's history, from the colonial and revolutionary eras right up to the present.

Navigating the warren of streets was no easy feat. Neither was finding a parking space. After nearly an hour of circuitous driving around detours, diversions, and dead ends, Dan found a public lot—designated by a massive sign declaring Blue Zone Parking—just two blocks from the Cambridge bed-and-breakfast where he had made reservations for the next three nights.

The Gylberds checked in, carried their luggage into the room, and settled Elvis under a warm beam of sunlight streaming from a bay window. Dan and Bea then walked over to the southernmost terminus of the Freedom Trail.

From there they walked out onto the Boston Common. The venerable site was America's oldest public park, originally purchased in 1634 by the Puritan settlers as a militia training field and for the feeding of cattle. During the battle of Bunker Hill, the British embarked for Charlestown from the common. At the northeast corner of the park is the new State House. Designed by Charles Bulfinch, it was built in 1795 on land that originally belonged to the John Hancock family.

The cold wind zipping across the city from the inner harbor and around Beacon Hill was bitter and biting, but Dan and Bea were actually fortified by it. Dan was bundled up in his Scottish Barbour waxed coat, a tartan muffler wrapped around his neck, and a University of Tennessee football national championship ball cap pulled down low and tight. Bea wore her L. L. Bean expedition down parka, flannel-lined jeans, and insulated hiking boots. But it was the sites and sights that warmed them more than the clothes they wore. Purposeful travel was in itself invigorating.

From the end of the fifteenth century to the beginning of the twentieth, it was expected that all the members of high-born families, aspiring artists, poets and historians, prospective members of the diplomatic corps, and young bon vivants would undertake an extended pilgrimage to the great cities of the Western world. It was considered an essential part of a well-rounded education. In many elite circles, such a journey was believed to be the capstone of a classical curriculum. Many of the most eminent people in history thus set out on what became known as the Grand Tour just before they entered into public life. Traveling to the great centers of culture, history, and influence, they sought to take in as much of the art, music, literature, architectural sites, historical monuments, social revelries, and culinary delights as they possibly could. Taking anywhere from just a few weeks to several months, the Grand Tour was intended to help the next generation of leaders to learn the languages, customs, and more of far-flung lands and societies. They desired to broaden their horizons, test the practicality of their book learning, and to deepen their social and academic awareness. It was to enable them to eventually do all they were called to do and be all they were called to be.

These travelers accepted the dictum of Saint Augustine, "The world is a book, and those who do not travel, read only a page." It seemed to these world rovers that travel's greatest purpose is to replace an empty mind with an open one.

Even today, many of those who travel for pleasure rightly associate with such travel the pleasure of history—for history adds to them, giving them a great memory of things stretched over a far longer span than one life. If such travel fails to make them wise and great, it at least allows them to commune with wisdom and greatness.

The richness of this experience is enhanced when these travelers realize that they stand on or near a historical site. Heady moments occur as they emerge from the Old West End of Boston, by Cambridge Street, and gaze not only upon pleasant neighborhoods but also the place in which the fate of American liberty was decided. Dan and Bea felt it to their very bones as they followed the Freedom Trail.

Around the corner from the State House was the Park Street Church. William Lloyd Garrison gave his first antislavery speech in this church, built in 1809.

Adjacent to it is the Granary Burying Ground, where many notable Americans are interred, including Revolutionary patriots John Hancock, Robert Treat Paine, Paul Revere, Samuel Adams, and several victims of the Boston Massacre, among them Crispus Attucks. Dan and Bea wandered through the cemetery, reading headstone inscriptions and identifying the final resting places of some of the nation's greatest heroes.

Two blocks north, on Tremont Street, they came to the King's Chapel and Burying Ground. The first Anglican congregation in Boston was founded here in 1688, although the present structure was completed in 1754. In colonial times the church was presented with gifts of silver and vestments by Queen Anne and King George III. After the revolution, it abandoned Christian orthodoxy and became the first Unitarian church in America. The burying ground next door was the first in the colony. Governor John Winthrop is buried here. William

Dawes, who joined Paul Revere on the famous midnight ride, is also buried here, as is Mary Chilton, the first Pilgrim to touch Plymouth Rock in 1620.

A little farther down the street is the famous Franklin Statue. Designed by Richard S. Greenough, this portrait statue, the first erected in Boston, commemorates one of the city's most versatile sons. The bronze tablets depict Benjamin Franklin's career as a printer, scientist, and signer of the Declaration of Independence and the peace treaty with Great Britain.

Next came the Old Corner Bookstore. Originally built in 1712 as the home of Thomas Crease, this building was the center of literary Boston in the late eighteenth century and throughout the nineteenth. Such noted authors as Henry Wadsworth Longfellow, Ralph Waldo Emerson, Henry David Thoreau, Nathaniel Hawthorne, Herman Melville, and Oliver Wendell Holmes often gathered here to exchange ideas, share their work, and read their books. Today it is a museum, but it still inspires those with literary ambition.

Around the corner was the Old South Meeting House. Built in 1729 as a Congregational church, it was the largest building in colonial Boston and often served as a community gathering place whenever attendance grew too large for Faneuil Hall. Town meetings were frequent at Old South, especially in the years prior to the Revolution.

The most famous meeting at Old South took place on December 16, 1773, when Samuel Adams met with members of the Sons of Liberty and several of the surreptitious Committees of Correspondence to consider the new tax on tea. After the meeting, several of the patriots disguised themselves as Indians. They left Old South for the waterfront, where they boarded three ships and dumped their cargoes of tea into the harbor. The Boston Tea Party caused the English Parliament to close the port of Boston, bringing the colonies one step closer to rebellion.

According to G. K. Chesterton, "The real hero is not he who is bold enough to fulfill the predictions but he who is bold enough to falsify them." By all accounts, Samuel Adams was a real hero. He upended every expectation, confounded every prophecy, and falsified every prediction. And thus he laid enduring foundations of greatness in his own life and in his beloved nation.

Adams was a most unlikely revolutionary. As was the case with so many of his fellow patriots—Patrick Henry, John Hancock, Richard Henry Lee, George Washington, James Iredell, Henry Laurens, Samuel Chase, and John Dickinson—he was profoundly conservative. Adams was loathe to indulge in any kind of radicalism that might erupt into violence—rhetorical, political, or martial. He was the faithful heir of the settled colonial gentry, and as such he was devoted to conventional Whig principles: the rule of law, noblesse oblige, unswerving honor, squirey superintendence, and the maintenance of corporate order. Adams believed in a tranquil and serene society free of the raucous upsets and tumults of agitation, activism, and unrest—hardly the stuff of revolution.

His initial reticence to squabble with the crown was obvious to any casual observer. He desired to exhaust every lawful recourse before entertaining the resort to armed resistance. For more than a decade he supported the innumerable appeals, suits, and petitions that colonial leaders sent to both Parliament and king. Even after American blood had been spilled, he refrained from embracing impulsive insurrection. Adams, at best, was a reluctant revolutionary.

Why then did he finally throw in his lot with the rebellion? Why did he become the Revolution's most articulate champion? What could possibly have overcome his native conservatism? Apparently, the answers were to be found in his traditionalism, his commitment to those lasting things that transcend the ever-shifting tides of situation and circumstance.

He urged his fellow patriots to fight against king and mother country in order to preserve all that which king and mother country were supposed to represent.

Adams asserted that only a grave responsibility that the leaders held to God and countrymen could possibly compel the peace-loving people of America to fight. He believed that the combined tyranny of the politicalization of matters of commerce and legislative despotism and the politicalization of matters of conscience had ensured that an appeal to arms and the God of Hosts was all that was left to them.

It was appallingly evident to Adams that the colonial charters had been subverted or even abrogated, citizenship rights according to English common law had been violated, and freedom of religious practice and moral witness had been curtailed. Thus rule of the colonies had become arbitrary and capricious; it had become supra-legal and intolerable. Under such circumstances a holy duty demanded a holy response.

Adams's reluctant conclusion—that ideological and political encroachments upon the whole of society could no longer be ignored—was shared by many of those who faithfully occupied American pulpits across the land, including the pulpit of the Old South. The very conservative colonial pastors certainly did not set out to "stir up strife or political tumult at the cost of the proclamation of the Gospel," as Charles Lane of Savannah put it. On the other hand, "The Gospel naturally mitigates against lawless tyranny, in whatever form it may take," said Ebenezer Smith of Lowell. Indeed, as Charles Turner of Duxbury asserted, "The Scriptures cannot be rightfully expounded without explaining them in a manner friendly to the cause of freedom." Thus, "Where the spirit of the Lord is, there is liberty" was a favorite pastoral text, as were "Ye shall know the truth and the truth shall make you free" and "Take away your exactions from my people, saith the Lord God." The leading churchmen of America were generally agreed with

Adams that "where political tyranny begins true government ends" and the good Christian "must needs be certain to oppose such lawless encroachments, however bland or bold."

It was not a love of firebrand Enlightenment rhetoric, a passion for political upheaval, or even a restless vision for social reform that drove Samuel Adams from hearth, home, and pub to the forefront of the American Revolution. It was the certainty that God had called him to an inescapable accountability. It was the conviction that he was covenantally honor-bound to uphold the standard of impartial justice and broadcast the blessings of liberty afar. It was the firm conviction that it was his Christian duty to vindicate the cause of freedom.

In the end, he was forced to arms by a recognition of the fact that "resistance to tyrants is obedience to God." Thus was birthed an unflinching stalwartness. And thus an unlikely boldness burst forth from the Old South church doors, and a reluctant revolutionary stirred the land toward liberty.

Old South remained a church until the 1870s, when its congregation moved to a new church in the Back Bay. The Old South Association, a private organization, was formed to preserve the building. The association remains active as a hub of revolutionary ideas through lectures, exhibits, and publications. Dan and Bea noticed posters announcing meetings endorsing a bevy of save-the-starving-third-world-lesbian-codependent-whales causes and concerns.

A block north of Old South sits the Old State House. Built in 1713, this was the seat of colonial government in early Massachusetts. Here in 1766 the first gallery from which the public could watch the government in action was opened. A circle of cobblestones in the street outside marks the site of the Boston Massacre. On March 5, 1770, British soldiers killed five agitated patriots armed only with sticks and snowballs.

By the time Dan and Bea arrived at Faneuil Hall, they were famished. They had planned to eat at Durgin Park—but they

almost decided to go elsewhere when they saw the long line
snaking out of the restaurant and into the street. The line was
moving quickly, so they decided to suffer the wait. In the end
they were glad they did.

Durgin Park is an antique Yankee mess hall mobbed by
tourists and locals alike who line up for unaffected Yankee fare
dished out by brusque Yankee waitresses. It is a rather raucous
place where food is slapped onto plates without a concern for
looks or presentation, then slammed down on long communal
tables with no regard for etiquette. But this was little matter to
the customers. The food makes up for everything. Beantown
standbys, all served in abundance, include blocks of down-
east corn bread, oyster stew made with milk and cream, stone-
crock baked beans, thick, dark, and sticky Indian pudding,
and strawberry shortcake made with plump, fresh berries on a
sweet biscuit.

Dan ordered a prime rib. It came as advertised, thick as
the Boston Yellow Pages and dripping with juices. Bea had a
steaming potter's crock of clam chowder. Afterward they
shared a hot apple pandowdy topped with a scoop of vanilla
ice cream and a small taster's cup of Durgin Park's special concoction of coffee Jell-O.

Faneuil Hall is a marvel of colonial architecture made even
more marvelous by the unfolding drama of its history. Peter
Faneuil donated the building to the city in 1742. It was enlarged
in 1806 and extensively remodeled 150 years later. The lower
floor has always been a market. The second floor provided a
meeting hall and was dubbed the "Cradle of Liberty," because of
the protests against English policy voiced here. The third level
houses the Ancient and Honorable Artillery Company Museum.
Faneuil Hall formed the heart and soul of Revolutionary Boston,
and it still holds a tenured place in the life of the city.

A long hike above, around, and through the horrors of
the freeway and tunnel construction ultimately led Dan and

Bea to the Paul Revere Home. This house, the oldest in Boston, was built about 1680. Revere owned it from 1770 until 1800. While living here he produced his famous Boston Massacre engraving and from here, on the evening of April 18, 1775, he began his historic ride to warn Lexington and Concord of approaching English troops. After Revere's time the house was used variously for commercial shops, mercantile stores, and tenement housing. Its restoration by the Paul Revere Memorial Association in 1908 was a landmark event in the historic preservation movement. The adjacent Pierce-Hichborn House was the home of a cousin, Nathaniel Hichborn, and is one of the earliest brick houses in the city.

It was the window display that captured Bea's attention. "Look, Dan, what a beautiful tea set."

"Tea set?" Dan was obviously focused on the trail of freedom, not window-shopping.

"Oh, and look at the name of the shop—The Boston Tea Party—how cute!"

The tiny gift shop near the Revere home sold all kinds of gifts, books, and—in homage to the first stirrings of freedom from tyranny—tea sets, loose teas of every variety, and related items.

Bea was captivated. Dan was anxious to keep moving.

"I'd like to go in and have a look around."

"What for?"

"I want to get a closer look at that tea set. It's darling."

"Honey, we're tooling around the country in Virgil, who is already stuffed to the gills with a chubby canine and the rest of our stuff. What would we do with a tea set?"

"Well, when we get to wherever it is we're going, this tea set would be a delightful way to begin to make a house a home."

"Uh-oh."

"Come on. What harm will it do to go in and look?"

"All right."

But as Dan knew the moment they walked through the door of the shop, they were not leaving without that tea set.

"Oh, Dan, see how fine the china is? And the bluebonnets—they look so real. And it has eight cups and saucers. Most sets only have four. It's perfect!"

"But Bea, we don't need a tea set."

"Okay, okay. I'll make you a deal."

"Oh boy."

"No, it's up to you. If you can remember the carol the chime tower was playing in Niagara when we were on our honeymoon, I won't get the tea set. If you can't, then I'll have it wrapped and sent back to the bed-and-breakfast. Deal?"

"Okay, deal." He knew he was sunk.

"So? What was it?"

"'The First Noël'?"

"No."

"Umm, 'Good King Wenceslas'?"

"Nope. I'll give you one more guess."

"All right, all right, I know this. It was 'Hark the Herald Angels Sing'!"

"I'll have them wrap it up."

Bea bustled off to the counter to arrange for the delivery, and Dan turned to browse through the rest of the shop. He wandered through several aisles until a Christmas display caught his eye. He glanced over several of the items then picked up a book entitled *Christmas Spirit*. It was an anthology of stories, songs, and seasonal traditions, observances, and rituals that capture the true essence and joy of the season. As he flipped through the book, he paused in the section of Christmas carols and found it—"Of the Father's Love Begotten." He couldn't believe it. How could he have forgotten? He wandered over to the counter where Bea was making the delivery arrangements, added the book to their order, and whispered the title to their Christmas carol in her ear. She turned, grinned, and said, "How? . . . So the mind's not so bad after all, huh?"

They headed out of the shop and back onto the Freedom Trail. A few blocks farther into the North End, they came to the Old North Church. Built in 1723 as a house of prayer for all people, Old North, or Christ Church, is the city's oldest standing and continuously used church. From its steeple two lanterns were hung to warn Charlestown that the English were crossing the harbor on their way to Concord.

For several years both Dan and Bea had been fascinated students of the early years of American life and liberty. Admittedly, separating fact from fiction, exactitude from nostalgia, and actuality from myth are often more than a little difficult, but they had found it to be worth the effort. Although they did not have anything like an idealized perception of that great epoch, they were nevertheless constantly amazed by the breadth and depth of the fledgling American culture and by the substantive character of the people who populated it. Living in a day when genuine heroes are few—at best—and far between, those pioneers and the times they vivified provided a startling contrast.

Colonial America produced an extraordinary number of prodigiously gifted men. From William Byrd and George Wythe to Thomas Hutchinson and William Stith, from Robert Beverley and Edward Taylor to Benjamin Franklin and John Bartram—the legacy of the seventeenth-century's native-born geniuses was unmatched. Their literary, scientific, economic, political, and cultural accomplishments were staggering to consider. According to historian Paul Johnson, "Never before has one place and one time given rise to so many great men."

As a child, Dan's attentions were naturally drawn to such men as Washington, Hamilton, Adams, Lee, Laurens, Hancock, and the other leaders of the Revolution. His father's influence was especially evident in that bent. But as he grew older—and especially as he and Bea began to read about the period together—it was the men who preceded the so-called Founding Fathers that most captivated his interests. Men like Cotton Mather, perhaps the most prominent of the many extraordinary pastors of the Old North Church.

Both Dan and Bea had often reflected on the cruel irony of history that Mather was generally pictured unsympathetically as the archetype of narrow, intolerant, severe Puritanism, proving his mettle by prosecuting the Salem witch debacle of 1692. In fact, Mather never attended the trials. He lived in the distant town of Boston and actually denounced them. As for his Puritanism, it was of the most enlightened sort. Mather was a man of vast learning, prodigious talent, and expansive interests. He owned the largest personal library in the New World, consisting of some four thousand volumes and ranging across the spectrum of classical learning. He was also the most prolific writer of his day, producing some 450 books on religion, science, history, philosophy, biography, and poetry. His style ranged from *Magnalia Christi Americana*, dripping with allusions to classical and modern sources, to the practical and straightforward *Essays to Do Good,* long considered to be one of the most influential books ever written in this hemisphere.

Besides being the pastor of the most prominent church in New England—as the Old North Church certainly was— Mather was active in politics and civic affairs, serving as an adviser to governors, princes, and kings. He also taught at Harvard and was instrumental in the establishment of Yale. Mather was the first native-born American to become a member of the scientific elite in the Royal Society. And he was a pioneer in the universal distribution and inoculation of the smallpox vaccine.

His father, Increase Mather, was a president of Harvard, a gifted writer, a noted pastor, and an influential force in the establishment and maintenance of the second Massachusetts Charter. In his day he was thought to be the most powerful man in New England and was elected to represent the colonies before Charles II in London. But according to many historians, Increase Mather's obvious talents and influence paled in comparison to his son's.

Likewise, both of Cotton Mather's grandfathers were powerful and respected men. His paternal grandfather, Richard Mather, helped draw up the *Cambridge Platform*, which provided a constitutional base for the Congregational churches of New England. And with John Eliot and Thomas Weld, Richard Mather prepared the *Bay Psalm Book*, which was the first text published in America, achieved worldwide renown, and became a classic of ecclesiastical literature. Cotton Mather's maternal grandfather was John Cotton, who wrote the important Puritan catechism for children, *Milk for Babes*, as well as drawing up the *Charter Template* with John Winthrop as a practical guide for the governance of the Massachusetts Colony. The city of Boston was so named to honor him; his former parish work in England was at Saint Botolph's Boston.

These men laid the foundations for a lasting spiritual dynasty in America. Even so, according to his lifelong admirer, Benjamin Franklin, "Cotton Mather clearly out-shone them all. Though he was spun from a bright constellation, his light was brighter still."

Two blocks from the church, overlooking the mouth of the Charles River Basin, sits the Copp's Hill Burying Ground. Begun as a cemetery in the 1660s, this site was used by the British a century later as an emplacement for the cannon that fired on the colonial soldiers on Bunker Hill. Buried here are the eminent members of the Mather family as well as Edward Hartt, builder of the USS *Constitution*. From the crest of Copp's Hill, Dan and Bea could see the Charlestown Navy Yard on the opposite side of the river—the next stop along the Freedom Trail.

The navy yard opened in 1800 to build, service, and supply ships for the U.S. Navy. For 174 years, dry docks, ropewalks, and shipways were part of the scene at the navy yard. The facility reached peak operation during World War II, when its work force numbered fifty thousand. Damaged ships were repaired and a record number of vessels built.

Today the yard is the proud home of the *Constitution*, the oldest commissioned warship in the world. "Old Ironsides" was launched at Boston in 1797. She sailed against the Barbary pirates and later fought the British during the War of 1812. She never lost a battle in her long career. The adjacent museum tells the story of her years under sail and the story of the navy yard.

The last stop on the Freedom Trail was the Bunker Hill Monument. The obelisk, which served as the model for the Washington Monument in the nation's capital, commemorates the June 17, 1775, battle of Breed's Hill, the first major engagement of the Revolution.

In 1825, to commemorate the fiftieth anniversary of the battle and to dedicate the site of the monument, Daniel Webster, the venerable senator from New Hampshire, delivered one of the most eloquent orations in American political history. Long studied both for its rhetorical brilliance and its civic perspective, the address outlined the basic principles and precepts of the nation's extraordinary experiment in liberty. Bea read aloud Webster's stirring concluding words from a nearby plaque:

> Let our age be the age of improvement. In a day of peace, let us advance the arts of peace and the works of peace. Let us develop the resources of our land, call forth its powers, build up its institutions, promote all its great interests, and see whether we also, in our day and generation, may not perform something worthy to be remembered. Let us cultivate a true spirit of union and harmony. In pursuing the

great objects, which our condition points out to us, let us act under a settled conviction, and an habitual feeling, that these twenty-four States, are one country. Let our conceptions be enlarged to the circle of our duties. Let us extend our ideas over the whole of the vast field in which we are called to act. Let our object be, Our Country, Our Whole Country, And Nothing But Our Country. And, by the blessing of God, may that country itself become a vast and splendid monument, not of oppression and terror, but of Wisdom, of Peace, and of Liberty, upon which the world may gaze with admiration for ever.

Dan and Bea sat outside the monument museum, the shadow of the obelisk aiming a pointed finger toward the bustling minions of Boston. They reflected on all that they had seen that day—a compressed panorama of America's founding era. Both were sober in light of where the nation had been and where it had gone.

"Call me naive," Bea said, "but I actually thought that this would be a really inspiring day."

"Yeah, me too," Dan sighed.

"But I feel more depressed than anything."

"Ditto."

"I thought that perhaps I might get a better sense of what blessings we've gained because of American liberty. Instead, I have a higher sense of the virtues we've lost because of American license."

"Boy, isn't that the truth?"

"And the worst of it is, I can't really point a finger of blame anywhere—my own complicity is as blatant as that of anyone else."

"I'm not sure I'd go that far—"

"No, really. I've been as heedless about our legacy of freedom as anyone. I have just taken so much for granted for so long."

As the afternoon twilight began to soften the shadows and dull the wintry colors into monochrome, they sat in contemplative silence. Finally, Dan stood and said, "Look, I think what we really need right now is a good meal. I used to think my mother was crazy when she offered food as the solution to every problem from moodiness to nuclear proliferation. But now I'm becoming a believer. What do you say? Want to join me for some Boston clam chowder?"

Bea offered a wry smile, took his outstretched hand, and stood. "I love you."

"You must. Because I know you're not hanging around for the fame, the fortune, or the fabulous adventures."

"Oh, now, I wouldn't be too sure," she said as she hugged him tightly. "This day isn't over yet. Adventure could be right around the corner."

"Lord have mercy. Let's hope not. I'm too tired for an adventure. And besides, my feet hurt."

"Well then, let's catch a cab. That way if adventure awaits, we'll have had a few minutes to rest along the way."

"Sounds like a winner."

They took a cab over to the Fish Pier, on the other side of the North End. Dan wanted to try the food at a little unnamed luncheonette that had been the haunt of fishmongers and mariners for years. It was an old lunch room on the pier among the fish warehouses and lobster companies that expanded into a large commercial restaurant. But the owners have never gotten around to giving the place a name. The locals just call it No Name.

It was still open when Dan and Bea arrived. The menu was surprisingly varied, but they decided to stick to the basics. Dan ordered a cup of chowder and broiled scrod. Bea selected a dinner plate of fried clams, scallops, and shrimp. Both platters were served with a milky coleslaw and an especially tasty tartar sauce.

They felt immensely better as they headed back through the darkening streets. Dan had the cab driver drop them both off at the hotel even though he needed to retrieve a couple of things from the car before he went in. Bea went upstairs to get Elvis and a leash. Dan cut across the street, around the corner, and up the block to the lot where the car was parked.

When he got within sight of the lot, he began to feel a dizzying sense of disorientation. The lot was empty. Completely empty. And it was barricaded off.

Virgil was gone.

He checked and double-checked, just to make certain that he was at the right lot. He circled the block. Just then a police cruiser came into sight. Dan started waving his arms madly.

The officer pulled up beside him. "What seems to be the trouble, sir?"

"Well, I think my car was stolen. Or maybe it was towed. I don't know."

"When did you last see the vehicle?"

"This morning."

"And where was it parked?"

"Right over there," Dan pointed toward the lot. "In that public parking lot."

"Well, sir. Your problem is that's a Blue Zone lot."

"A what?"

"Blue Zone. That means it is available for public parking only between the hours of ten and five."

"Between ten and five?"

"Yes, sir. See the sign that says Blue Zone Parking?"

"Sure. It's as big as day."

"Well, that's what it means. You should have parked in a Red Zone lot. You can park there from ten to eight. Or even a Green Zone lot, which is available for public parking twenty-four hours a day."

"Why doesn't the sign say that? All it says is Blue Zone. How is anyone supposed to know what that means?" Dan's tone was beginning to get a little heated.

"Well, sir. All the regulations are printed in the newspapers."

"A lot of good that does a visitor. Why don't they print the rules on the sign?"

"That I can't answer, sir."

"I can't believe this. I don't think I have ever heard of anything more absurd than this."

"I'm sorry, sir. All this construction has taken its toll on everyone."

"So Boston has sacrificed sanity for a freeway tunnel?"

"I'm afraid we've sacrificed far more than sanity for that, sir."

"Great. So where is my car?"

"That I can't answer either. I'm sorry."

"So how do I find out?"

The officer reached into a satchel and pulled out a card. "You'll have to call this number."

"This is just dandy. Spend a day recalling why the American Revolution had to be fought, and then get a reminder that it probably needs to be fought all over again."

"Again, I'm sorry, sir."

"I appreciate it, but at this point sorry doesn't help me a whole heck of a lot."

Dan went back to the hotel. Bea, out in front with Elvis, had begun to worry. He explained the situation and quickly made the call. It seemed that Virgil had been towed to Quincy, a historic township south and east of Boston. The towing company informed him that he would have to pay $120 to reclaim the car.

He got directions to the impound lot in Quincy, but the Jerry-Springer-educated-dyslexic who was working the night shift got most of the turns backward and out of sequence. The cab driver thought he knew where the lot was. And so they drove. And drove. And drove. Somehow they ended up on a nameless highway in a dismal marine industrial area outside of Quincy that reminded Dan of *The Twilight Zone,* only scarier. The sky above the horizon was a spooky shade of purple and the highway stretched on forever, and they were stuck on it because the median was one of those unbroken concrete safety barriers.

They stopped at three businesses trying to ask directions, evidence that it was getting late and they were beginning to get desperate. It was nearly midnight and no one had a clue where the impound lot was. Dan reasoned, when in doubt and lost in the middle of the night, find the nearest truck stop.

Bingo.

Finally armed with the proper directions, they set out again. After a few more twists and turns, they found the lot. Dan paid the cab driver an inordinate sum and walked into a tiny mobile home propped up on cinder blocks. It smelled like a wet dog. Two college girls were already waiting ahead of him. The woman behind the desk didn't pay attention to any of them until the *Montel* rerun broke for a commercial.

The girls were obviously upset and fidgety. They nervously looked at Dan. He just smiled and stood in line behind them.

The woman at the desk finally coughed up a few words in a rather holier-than-thou irritated voice, "Can I help you?"

One of the girls stepped forward. "I'm here to pick up the Explorer."

"Driver's license?" the woman barked.

"It's in the car," the girl replied.

"Your total is $120."

"My money is also in the car."

"All right," the woman responded with a huff. "I'm going to open the gate and you can walk around the back of the building."

"Oh, okay. Should I pull my car up to the gate?"

"No," she countered, as if the girl had suggested that she was looking for a string of felony offenses. "Just retrieve your belongings and return for a release." She opened the gate and both girls meekly walked into the night.

A few minutes later they returned and handed her a Visa. The woman took it, sneered at its surface, flicked it back at the girl indignantly, and said, "Cash only. I told you on the phone. Cash only."

The girl's voice had an obvious tremor. "No, you didn't. You didn't say anything about cash."

"Yes, I did. That's the policy. Everyone is told, right off the bat. Cash only."

"Umm, no," the girl replied, flustered. "I think I would have remembered if I was going to have to come up with $120 cash in the middle of the night."

Dan volunteered his two cents' worth, "I spoke to you earlier this evening and you didn't say anything about cash to me either."

The woman glared at him. "This, sir, is none of your business. Butt out and wait your turn."

At this point the girl began trembling. Her face was flushed. She looked like she was about to cry.

Dan turned to the girl and asked if she had a checkbook.

The woman cut in, "Cash only, I said."

"Excuse me." Dan had had about enough of this woman now. "I wasn't talking to you. This is none of your business. Butt out and wait your turn."

Both girls snickered. In a huff the woman turned back to her television.

"I've got enough cash to bail out both of our cars. If you'll write me a check, I'll take care of this bottom-rung bureaucrat's hankering for petty tyranny."

The woman was none too pleased. But within fifteen minutes they had taken care of their transactions, paid the woman the prescribed fines and towing fees, and retrieved the vehicles.

As he headed back toward downtown, Dan pondered the lessons he had learned throughout in this cradle of liberty. When it became too depressing an exercise, he flipped through the radio dial until he found a classical music station. He leaned back as the strains of Bach's "Jesu, Joy of Man's Desiring" poured over him, smoothing his furrowed brow.

*Today's mass culture would not know an idea,
subversive or otherwise, if it met one. It traffics instead
in sensibility and image, with a premium on the
degrading: rap lyrics in which women are for using and
abusing, movies in which violence is administered with
a smirk and a smile. Casual cruelty, knowing sex.
Nothing could be better designed to rob youth of its
most ephemeral gift: innocence. The ultimate effect of
our mass culture is to make children older than their
years, to turn them into the knowing, cynical pseudo-
adult that is by now the model kid of the TV sitcom. It
is a crime against children to make them older than
their years. And it won't do for the purveyors of
cynicism to hide behind the First Amendment. Of
course they have the right to publish and peddle this
trash to kids. But they should have the decency not to.*

Charles Krauthammer

9

NEW YORK
POPULATION 7,322,564

HARTFORD, SITUATED MIDWAY BETWEEN New York and Boston, is the capital of the state of Connecticut. The city is a center of government and a wide range of commercial, social, and cultural activities. But it is perhaps best known as the insurance capital of the world. Aetna, Cigna, ITT Hartford, Phoenix Mutual, and Travelers are some of the larger insurance firms that make their corporate headquarters here.

At the turn of the century, Mark Twain also called Hartford home. He once quipped, "Of all the beautiful towns it has been my fortune to see, this is the chief." Most people probably think he was looking out over the wide twists and slow turns of the muddy Mississippi as he wrote his most popular books. In fact, he wrote a good number of them while looking out over the Park River here in central Connecticut.

Twain defined a literary classic as "a book which people praise and don't read." Alas, by that standard much of his own work has achieved classic status. Certainly, if anyone were actually to pay attention to the noisy multicultural debate over *The Adventures of Huckleberry Finn*, it would be obvious that those with the loudest opinions could never have read the book.

Be that as it may, it is likely that most people today know Mark Twain from his sparkling, dead-on, humbug-piercing epigrams rather than his more extended writing. He once wrote, "The difference between the right word and the almost-right word is the difference between lightning and the lightning-bug." And he knew that finding just the right word could be a mighty struggle. In a notebook page from the last decade of the nineteenth century, he left evidence of his great labor to breathe life into a new wisecrack: "The man that invented the cuckoo clock is no more," he began.

Then come several attempts—all heavily scribbled over—in an effort to construct a suitable punch line: "This is old news but good." "As news, this is a little stale, but some news is better old than not at all." "As news, this is a little old, but better late than never." "As news, this is a little old, for it happened sixty-four years ago, but it is not always the newest news that is the best." "It is old news, but there is nothing else the matter with it."

Finally, he must have concluded that no amount of polishing was going to make that particular material shine, for at the bottom of the page he wrote, resignedly, "It is more trouble to make a maxim than it is to do right."

But he did take the trouble, and most of the time he got it right—which is why we still quote Twain today, nearly a century after his death. In fact, to get a respectful hearing for just about any statement, a speaker need only preface it with the magic words, "As Mark Twain said . . ."

A few years earlier Bea had taken on the project of filling an entire notebook with some of Twain's pithiest and wittiest quips. And ever since she had quoted the best of them *ad nauseam:*

> It is agreed, in this country, that if a man can arrange his religion so that it perfectly satisfies his conscience, it is not incumbent on him to care whether the arrangement is satisfactory to anyone else or not.

All you need is ignorance and confidence; then success is sure.

It is better to keep your mouth shut and appear stupid than to open it and remove all doubt.

When in doubt, tell the truth.

By trying we can easily learn to endure adversity. Another man's, I mean.

We all do no end of feeling, and we mistake it for thinking.

Always do right. That will gratify some of the people, and astonish the rest.

Grief can take care of itself, but to get the full value of a joy you must have somebody to divide it with.

The political and commercial morals of the United States are not merely food for laughter, they are an entire banquet.

It could probably be shown by facts and figures that there is no distinctly native American criminal class except Congress.

The man who does not read good books has no advantage over the man who can't read them.

If you invent two or three people and turn them loose in your manuscript, something is bound to happen to them—you can't help it; and then it will take you the rest of the book to get them out of the natural consequences of that occurrence, and so first thing you know, there's your book all finished up and never cost you an idea.

It is by the goodness of God that in the West we have those three unspeakably precious things: freedom of speech, freedom of conscience, and the prudence never to practice either of them.

After the frustrated paradox of their visit to Boston, Dan and Bea were hoping that the bucolic environs that had spawned *Tom Sawyer, Huck Finn,* and all those witticisms might reinvigorate their flagging affections. Indeed, Bea wanted to spend all day at the Twain house, a wonderfully colorful brick Victorian mansion built in the midst of a famed artists' colony. It bristled with creativity. The place was like a tonic of inspiration in the same way that a visit to Winston Churchill's Chartwell, Teddy Roosevelt's Sagamore Hill, Hilaire Belloc's Kings Land, William Faulkner's Rowan Oak, William Butler Yeats's Thoor Ballylee, Vita Sackville-West's Sissinghurst, or Walter Scott's Abbotsford had been for her.

Dan wanted to stay too. He could have spent hours perusing Twain's massive library or just looking out at the spectacular views from the billiard room's tall turreted windows. And besides, there were several other homes in the little colony he would have liked to visit—for instance, the home Harriet Beecher Stowe bought with the enormous royalties from her controversial novel, *Uncle Tom's Cabin,* was right next door at Nook Farm.

But they both knew that they really needed to get on the road. Dan had made arrangements for them to be in New York City that evening. In fact, they were supposed to be there sometime before seven, when they were to meet some old friends from the publishing business who would give them the keys and the run of a Lower East Side townhouse for a week-long visit to Manhattan. Their friends were going to spend the week in Paris and needed to catch a plane from LaGuardia Airport. Needless to say, Dan and Bea could not afford to be late.

So reluctantly they pulled away from Hartford and its rich literary and artistic ambiance, steering Virgil toward the Big Apple.

CONSIDERED BY many to be the single greatest city of the single greatest country in the world, New York is, without doubt, a marvel to behold. And it always has been, it seems. From its earliest days in the seventeenth century as a Dutch settlement and its subsequent British colonial ascendancy to its early American prominence and its current status as an international cultural and business center, the city has always aspired to larger-than-life pretensions of glory and visions of grandeur. By all accounts it has essentially achieved them. The city is surprisingly compact yet absurdly gargantuan. It is unique unto itself yet wildly varied. It is a jumble of contradictions yet carefully organized and codified. It is a world city that no land can entirely claim as its own, but it is, as a result, steadfastly American. It is a kind of towering Babel where, nevertheless, every nation, tribe, and tongue has found a way to cohabit peacefully—at least, somewhat peacefully.

According to author George Bernard Shaw, "New York is a place halfway between America and the world." Architect Le Corbusier asserted, "New York is a catastrophe—but a magnificent catastrophe." And critic John Ruskin quipped, "New York City is absolutely and wretchedly awful. Yet it remains somehow triumphant and thus absolutely glorious in its wretched awfulness."

Indeed, New York City's unique and defining charm is that it offers a dazzling variety of everything, a cultural smorgasbord for the entire globe. Jorge Borges said, "New York is as Latin as any of the great Latin American capitals." Flan O'Brien retorted, "I love New York. It is so Irish." According to Umberto Eco, "New York is as Italian as Rome is—perhaps even more so." David Ben-Gurion asserted, "New York is nearly as Jewish as Jerusalem." And somehow, all of them were right. The nations of the earth find that only here are they altogether at home together.

Manhattan is a relatively small but precious stretch of land only thirteen miles long and less than three miles wide, yet it is home to one and a half million people and host to more than four million daily commuters. And while Manhattan is actually only one small part of the city—the other boroughs like Brooklyn and Queens are nearly as huge—it still exceeds the populations of Vermont and Wyoming combined, while it comprises just over twenty-two square miles. If you were to include all of the five boroughs, New York's total population is nearly eight million. And if you were to take into account the surrounding metropolitan area—combining all the New Jersey, Long Island, Connecticut, and upriver suburbs—nearly twenty million people make New York their home.

It has been asserted that Manhattan has used more marble in churches, building lobbies, and façades than all of Rome. The city boasts as many French restaurants as Paris, offers more museums and art galleries than London, and has more than one thousand skyscrapers—at least three times as many as any other city in the world. There is hardly anything about New York that is not exaggerated beyond the capacity of rational belief.

From the Connecticut border all the way into the city, a distance of some seventy miles, I-95 wends through a dense urban landscape of Babylonian proportions. The area is all solid city, stretching as far as Dan's and Bea's eyes could see in any direction. The view boggles the imaginations and strikes awe in the hearts and minds of first-time visitors and frequent travelers alike.

Dan and Bea had been to New York many times. Nevertheless, they never ceased to be amazed by its density, its enormity, its variety, and its urbanity. Even as long-time residents of Chicago, New York represented an almost alien landscape. And as was always the case for them, once they navigated the tangle of freeway cordons into Manhattan itself, the ethos appeared to them to be, if possible, even more mythic, even more puissant, even more intimidating, even more solitary, even more extravagant, even more axiomatic, and even more sensational than they could have possibly remembered.

Dwarfed by the vast monoliths of glass and steel, New Yorkers bustle about apparently unconcerned and unaware; their hive of activity, although bound in a kind of cosmopolitan captivity, is hardly an issue in their magnificent Vanity Fair. It seems that everything is concentrated here—population, theater, art, writing, publishing, importing, business, murder, mugging, luxury, poverty. It is all of everything. It goes all night. It is tireless. Its air is charged with energy at all times, in every place.

Dan and Bea threaded their way through the grand canyons of uptown toward the even grander canyons of downtown and into the Lower East Side. They were appetent at the spectacle unfolding before them and hardly said a word to one another.

Just beyond the famed Cooper Union, between Astor Place and Tompkins Square, they maneuvered through the dense traffic of vying taxies into an odd little neighborhood affectionately dubbed the East Village by its residents. Like so much of the city, it is a community of violent contrasts: historic Stuyvesant Street is lined with stately landmark homes while shabby boutiques, disreputable tenements, and shooters galleries dominate the surrounding blocks; homeless people sleep in the doorways of chic art galleries and along the sidewalks in front of fashionable lofts and condominiums; impeccably tailored Wall Street moguls and would-be moguls hurry to work amid peddlers hawking their dilapidated wares; petition gatherers for every imaginable cause desperately distribute their leaflets to world-weary commuters and gawk-eyed tourists; fly-by-night hucksters vie for sales outside vintage establishments like the Strand, the Yiddish Theater, and Pageant Book and Print.

Like so much in this poor fallen world, this community had a checkered past. For more than two hundred years it had remained a fairly comfortable and quiet literary neighborhood where writers from James Fenimore Cooper and Willa Cather to W. H. Auden and Allen Ginsberg all lived and worked. But by the middle of the twentieth century, the area had begun to go through a series of fairly dramatic transformations.

Just after the Second World War, it had become rather dilapidated and run down—in fact, the Bowery section became known for its poverty and depravity. In the fifties, though, it became a popular bohemian and beatnik nexus of coffeehouses, poetry dens, and countercultural cabals. In the sixties it became a haven for the dropped-out and tuned-in hippie drug culture. In the early seventies, big-time rock 'n' roll came alive at the Electric Circus on Saint Mark's Place and at Fillmore East on Second Avenue. Then when Greenwich Village rents began to soar in the early eighties, gentrification began in earnest, and the substantial Jewish, Polish, and Ukrainian populations that had survived these changes were gradually displaced by uptown yuppies. By the nineties the area had become a thriving, vital, and varied neighborhood of prosperous shops, exclusive lofts, and vast new developments.

The architectural centerpiece of the neighborhood, Saint Mark's Church-in-the-Bowery on Tenth Street, had been built in 1660 as a Dutch Reformed chapel on Gov. Peter Stuyvesant's farm—*bowery* or *bouerie* literally means "farm." Late in the seventeenth century the chapel became an Episcopal parish church for the emerging community of small freeholders and yeomen and has been in continuous use ever since. In the late seventies the church helped to launch the famed Poetry Project, and by the early eighties it had become the neighborhood's center of avant garde radicalism, activism, and dissent. But the continuing evolution of the East Village has made even its most adventurous forays into the uncharted realms of multicultural political correctness seem terribly tame in comparison.

Just around the corner from the old church on Saint Mark's Place—three doors down from the site of James Fenimore Cooper's last knickerbocker home—Dan and Bea's friends lived in a converted loft above an old butterscotch factory. It was vast but comfortably appointed with Shaker antiques, quilts, and Early American arts and crafts. The original oak-plank floors and post-and-beam construction still smelled faintly of sweet confections. From here Dan and Bea would make their forays into the heart of the city over the next several days.

AFTER DAN and Bea saw their friends off to the airport, they decided to grab a late-night pastrami on rye at the Katz Deli, a vintage Lower East Side line-up-and-order delicatessen that had been serving customers in the same location since 1888. The pungent meat was piled high; the bread was sliced thickly, soft and chewy inside but crisp and flaky outside. It was a perfect way to start their week in New York.

Afterward they decided to go for a walk. Walking is one of the most delightful aspects of New York, they thought; people actually walk here. Unlike most American cities where automobiles define every aspect of life, New York's sidewalks, parks, promenades, jogging trails, and neighborhoods are always filled with people on foot. And the public transportation system is so good that when they need to travel longer distances, many New Yorkers still avoid their cars. Indeed, a large proportion of them do not even own cars. Dan had long ago determined that New York is easily one of the most agreeable cities in the world to live in, despite its vastness. He often told his friends in Chicago that New York is a city where a civilized person can still lead a civilized life against a civilized background and consider it, not a feat of escapism, but as something amounting to total immersion. He was convinced that the reason for this is simply that it is easy to get about in the city and also easy to get out of, and he also noted that each neighborhood retained something of its individual character.

The next day, Dan and Bea got an early start. It was a dismal gray New York morning. A wintry witchery hung in the air.

They walked up Broadway toward Madison. Although it was hardly past dawn, the streets were already beginning to bustle with hurrying crowds and the shops were abuzz with activity. Young women clad in the latest fashions, but wearing the city's obligatory tennis shoes instead of pumps or heels, made quick stops at the bakeries, the druggists, and the espresso stands on their way to work. Hot dog, pretzel, and falafel vendors were beginning to roll their freshly stocked carts toward their staked-out corners. Harried executives ducked into local newsstands and tobacconists on the way uptown. Street musicians began to take their places amid the throng. Buskers and panhandlers rattled their cups and pleaded their cases. The happy cacophony bore testimony to the profound fact that despite all the ills of this world, the ordinary affairs of life go on.

Dan and Bea ducked into a Chock-Full-o-Nuts coffee shop for some fresh pastries and a couple of tall lattes. As usual, Dan had the entire day carefully planned out. There were several bookstores he wanted to visit, which suited Bea just fine. But he also had a whole host of historic sites he wanted to try to get in: the Statue of Liberty and Ellis Island, the Empire State, Woolworth, and Chrysler Buildings, Columbus Circle, Washington Square, the Theodore Roosevelt birthplace museum, Trinity Church, Central Park, the Cloisters, and Columbia University.

"You think we're going to be able to do all that in one day?" Bea asked him incredulously as they stepped out into the cold, damp streetscape.

"Well, I think I've got it pretty well timed out. Why? Do you think we need to cut something out?"

"Yeah, about half of it—if not all of it."

"No way."

"We've got a week to enjoy New York. There's no hurry."

"But there are so many things that we will surely want to see and do and experience. If we don't keep up a steady pace, there's no way we will get it all in. There's the newly renovated New York Public Library Reading Room and all the museums—the Met, the Guggenheim, the Frick, the Morgan. Then there are the shows we will want to see, the Lincoln Center, Radio City Music Hall, and the Ed Sullivan Theater. And then there's—"

"Well, we may just have to come back if we can't fit it all in a sane, relaxing, and enjoyable schedule. I will not be frantically dragged around New York just so we can keep some sort of crazy itinerary. And that's that."

"Oh."

"I mean it." And with that, Bea grabbed Dan's carefully outlined to-see-and-do list, crumpled it up, and tossed it into a trash can chained to a corner post. Dan moped but he knew that Bea was probably right. She usually was, after all. They walked along in silence.

After a few moments they came to a little antiquarian bookshop that was just opening its doors. The dim and quiet literary nook—its etched-glass door emblazoned with the words *Tattered Muse*—specialized in poetry and serious belles-lettres. Bea found several gems right away, including a beautiful Moroccan leather-bound edition of Hilaire Belloc's *The Four Men: A Farrago*—one of her favorite novels—and a rare small-press edition of the collected stanzas of Dan's brother, Tristan.

Bea was signing the receipt for her purchase when the young clerk noticed that she had never signed her name on the back of her credit card. He informed her that he could not complete the transaction unless the card was signed.

"Oh? Why?" she asked. The card was nearly two years old and she had never had any problems before—in fact, no one had ever even noticed the signature strip before.

He explained that it was necessary to compare the signature on the credit card with the signature on the charge receipt.

"It is a safety precaution to try to cut down on the use of stolen credit cards."

So Bea dutifully signed the credit card in front of him. "Okay, here," she said.

He carefully compared that signature with the one she had signed on the receipt just a moment before. As luck would have it, the two signatures matched and the clerk's objections were now satisfied. He smiled with a look of triumph and handed her the little package of books.

Dan had slipped out a moment before to explore a couple of the other shops on the street. When Bea came out of the bookstore, he had just emerged from an eclectic emporium across Broadway that specialized in comics, cybernetics, and other assorted science fiction bric-a-brac.

A woman with a shaved head and a plethora of ominous tattoos was carrying on an animated discourse with a man dressed in a fine Brooks Brothers suit. Dan caught a few snatches of their conversation that seemed to indicate that the two of them had gone to high school together. A light drizzle began to fall. A bag lady stood nearby, singing loudly—show tunes, perhaps from *Porgy and Bess*. Meanwhile, shoppers continued to whirl past, as if in a dizzying dervish dance.

Ah, New York, he thought. *There's no other place like it.*

He looked down the block where a huddle of shoppers were riffling through the sidewalk overstock bins in front of several boutiques and haberdasheries despite the fact that the rain was starting to come down harder. A homeless man dangerously dodged traffic in the center of Broadway, tracing imaginary designs above his head with a ragged umbrella. A young Hasidic couple hurried along, strange archaisms draped across their frail frames. A small group of teens, oblivious to everything else around them, bopped along to the syncopated beat that blared from their gargantuan boom box, apparently on their way to school. Two elderly women compared the vari-

ous virtues of cucumbers at a vegetable market with all the
fervor of bond traders. A tall, distinguished-looking man,
dapper and dashing, walked behind a pair of perky Pekinese
who were clearly relishing their regular morning jaunt.

Dan took all this in with obvious satisfaction. He smiled.
New York is, indeed, utterly amazing. It is a cosmopolitan city,
but it is not just a city of cosmopolitans. Most of the masses in
New York have a nation whether or not it happens to be the
nation to which New York ostensibly belongs. And their Babel-
like swarming defines the place in a dramatic fashion that
utterly baffles the mind and dazzlingly assaults the senses.

Apparently it has always been so, as Alexis de Tocqueville
affirmed more than a century and a half ago. Of course, much
has changed in New York since the famous two-week-long
visit of de Tocqueville and his friend Gustave de Beaumont in
1831. They described the city then as a rather disagreeable
provincial town with badly paved roads, garish arts, teeming
confusion, pretentious architecture, and bizarrely rude manners. While some critics might well still make such charges
against the city, clearly New York has come of age in the inter-
val between then and now. Regardless, the city struck a chord
with its famous visitors then, even as it does today.

The two aristocratic travelers were at the beginning of
what would be a nine-month tour of the fledgling United
States. They had a mandate from the French government to
study the land's criminal justice system, but they were actually
interested in seeing far more than America's courts and jails.
They wanted to explore the essence of the American spirit, discover the secret to American ingenuity, and plumb the depths
of the American soul.

Eventually they visited nineteen of the country's then
twenty-four states, stopping in more than fifty towns and villages, from the thronging urban centers of the East to the rough-
and-tumble frontier settlements of the West. They covered more

than eight thousand miles, mostly by foot, on horseback, in steamboats, and on stagecoaches. As de Tocqueville later wrote, "I confess that in America, I saw more than America; I sought there the image of democracy itself, with its inclinations, its character, its prejudices, and its passions, in order to learn what we have to fear or to hope from its progress."

New York was the young republic's thriving banking and trading center. Although it had spread across only about half of Manhattan Island—the rest was still divided between country estates, a few farms, and a bit of wild forestland—the city had already become densely populated and was growing rapidly. It was shot through with the great American optimism of the Jacksonian Age. It was already the nation's largest city, and it hummed with commerce. Of course, there was no Empire State Building, no Statue of Liberty, no Times Square, no Central Park, no Radio City Music Hall, and no Rockefeller Center—each of these landmarks would come in the succeeding decades. Nevertheless, much of what would ultimately give the city its unique character and culture was already in evidence.

Essentially what de Tocqueville discovered was that America was the only modern nation in the world that was founded on a creed. Other nations found their identity and cohesion in ethnicity, geography, partisan ideology, or cultural tradition. But America was founded on certain ideas about freedom, human dignity, and social responsibility. It was this profound peculiarity that most struck him. He called it "American exceptionalism."

De Tocqueville simultaneously concluded that if this experiment in liberty, this extraordinary American exceptionalism were to be maintained over the course of succeeding generations, then an informed patriotism would have to be instilled in the hearts and minds of the young. Not surprisingly then, de Tocqueville has oft been quoted—perhaps apocryphally but nevertheless true to the basic tenets of his evident opinion—as saying:

I sought for the greatness and genius of America in her commodious harbors and her ample rivers, and it was not there; in her fertile fields and boundless prairies, and it was not there; in her rich mines and her vast world commerce, and it was not there. Not until I went to the churches of America and heard her pulpits aflame with righteousness did I understand the secret of her genius and power. America is great because she is good and if America ever ceases to be good, America will cease to be great.

His remarkable chronicle of the trip, *Democracy in America*, was offered to readers in the hope that the ideas that made America both great and good might remain the common currency of the national life. He felt that the world needed to know those things because the world needed to share those things.

New York was the starting place of his great journey, both physically and intellectually. It was here that he first observed all that was right and all that was wrong with America. It was here that he first caught a glimpse of liberty's great power, great promise, and great purpose. It was also here that he first felt the gnawing certainty that something so great could greatly disappoint.

DAN REJOINED Bea across the street and together they walked toward the Strand, one of the world's largest bookstores. It is the place where the Bass family has served the literary needs of New Yorkers since 1929. Featuring more than two million books on eight miles of shelves in a thirty-two thousand square foot space on four floors, the Strand makes the modern Barnes and Noble or Borders megastore look downright dinky. For the next several hours both of them browsed from section to section completely agog at the range of selection.

When they finally emerged from the Strand, it was nearly time for lunch. Dan had picked out a little falafel stand near Bryant Park. Although it was still sprinkling and gray outside, Dan and Bea were having a glorious time.

After a hefty street-stand lunch—falafel from the southern and eastern shores of the Mediterranean is the healthiest and most filling junk food in the world—they walked toward Rockefeller Center, stopping at a few more bookstores and antique shops. Having dispensed with the rigors of Dan's sightseeing list, they ambled about until dark when they headed to the theater district to take in a show and get dinner.

Book shopping in New York is an incredibly satisfying experience—indeed, it is the greatest book town in the world, with the possible exception of London. More publishers have made their mark here than anywhere else: Appleton, Dodd Mead, Dutton, Harper Brothers, Holt, Doubleday, Scribners, Putnam, Frarrar, Brentano, Houghton Mifflin, Simon and Schuster, Bantam, Knopf, and Viking. Likewise, an astonishing array of poets, journalists, novelists, historians, critics, and playwrights have made this city their home: Philip Freneau, William Cullen Bryant, Samuel Morse, Alexander Hamilton, Walt Whitman, Washington Irving, Herman Melville, Edgar Allan Poe, Henry James, O. Henry, Joseph Pulitzer, Jacob Riis, William Randolph Hearst, Stephen Crane, Horatio Alger, W. E. B. Du Bois, Sinclair Lewis, Willa Cather, E. W. Scripps, Hart Crane, James Thurber, E. B. White, and Tom Wolfe. It is not surprising then that the hundreds of bookshops that seem to pop up in every neighborhood and section of the city are fraught with sundry literary associations.

By the time they had visited the Gotham Bookmart, Argosy Bookstore, Blakemore Galleries, Rizzoli Shop, and Fedulki Antiquarian Market, it was nearly dusk and they were both loaded down with several heavy parcels. They decided that they had better take the subway back to the townhouse, take care of Elvis, and freshen up before they ventured into the theater district.

Arms full of packages, they headed for the nearest flight of subway stairs. As they descended, the hair on the back of

Dan's neck stood up. He whirled around, knocking several bundles from Bea's load.

"What on earth? Dan!"

"There it is again!"

"There what is again? What are you talking about?"

"That feeling—like we are being followed."

"Well, we are in New York, you know—lots of people all around."

"No, Bea, I'm serious."

"This really has you rattled, doesn't it?"

"Yeah, this is the third time I've had this feeling—on the way to Cooperstown and then again when we were leaving Montpelier."

"Don't you think it's because we're in the city, Dan? You're already on alert—trying to keep us safe," she attempted to soothe and reassure.

"I don't know, maybe it is all just a coincidence."

ABOUT AN hour later, having taken care of their various errands, Dan and Bea were standing in the center of the bright glare of Times Square. During the first half of the nineteenth century, the area was a very exclusive residential neighborhood, Long Acre Square, developed by the Astor family. But around the turn of the century, Adolph Ochs, the new proprietor of the declining *New York Times,* bought the corner of Forty-second Street and Broadway. There he built a spacious office building for his paper—from which the place derived its new name. In 1907, as a publicity stunt, Ochs decided to host a New Year's Eve party for the city outside the building. Thus was born a legend, a tradition, and a cultural icon. For all the world, Times Square became synonymous with New York.

Over the years, theaters, showcase clubs, pubs, restaurants, and specialty shops burgeoned there. Times Square became the social axis upon which the entire metropolis turned.

During the sixties and seventies the area declined precipitously. Bordellos, brothels, pornographic theaters, and strip clubs moved in and gave the area a seedy, run-down reputation. But then in the eighties and nineties, a massive rejuvenation program led by such entertainment corporations as Marriott, Disney, Virgin, and Sony transformed it into an ostentatious showpiece, once again the pride of the Big Apple.

The area had always been rather gaudy. Adorned with bright lights and neon, glamour and glitz, bravado and brazenness, gargantuanism and aggrandizement, fantasy and audacity, it was everything about New York blown up large. At the beginning of the twentieth century, G. K. Chesterton visited Times Square and commented, "When I had looked at the lights of Broadway by night, I made to my American friends an innocent remark that seemed for some reason to amuse them. I had looked, not without joy, at the long kaleidoscope of colored lights arranged in large letters and sprawling trademarks, advertising everything, from pork to pianos, through the agency of the two most vivid and most mystical gifts of God: color and fire. I said to them in my simplicity: What a glorious garden of wonders this would be, to anyone who was lucky enough to be unable to read."

In every way, from the vast Jumbotron monitors—literally covering the sides of buildings—to the stunning fireworks display of flashing lights that adorned every available surface, Times Square bore testimony to the place New York has claimed, not just as the book capital, but as the media capital of the world.

The driving business and creative forces behind the globally dominant American entertainment industry—network television, movies, theater, video, computer imaging, broadcast journalism, cable distribution, content production, sports development, real-time software applications, and electronic gaming—are all at home in New York.

At the corner of Forty-third and Broadway, just beneath a huge three-story-tall digital screen broadcasting the NBC network news was a video game parlor, the likes of which neither Dan nor Bea had ever seen. While it seems that every mall in America has a game arcade, this one was different from those not only in size but in character. There were hundreds of game machines to choose from and thousands of adolescents and teenagers, mostly boys, thronging around them. There was an intensity about the place that might have rivaled a Dow-Jones trading floor. It was a pleasure dome the likes of which even Kublai Khan could not have imagined.

But as immense and jangling as it was, Dan and Bea probably should not have been so dramatically taken aback by the sight. After all, American teens take their prowess at video consoles quite seriously. Indeed, Bea commented as they stood there staring that she had read somewhere that a recent survey found that the average American teenager spends as much as twenty hours a week killing, maiming, and destroying, or punching, shooting, and stabbing, or flying, driving, and navigating, or climbing, plumbing, and slogging through their beloved video games.

"You're kidding, twenty hours a week? That's practically a part-time job," Dan quipped.

"And apparently," Bea went on, "when they're not playing their gory video games, they're watching murder and mayhem on television, tramping off to see more of the same in the movies, listening to vivid lyrics about destruction, devastation, and despair, or surfing the Internet's virtual village of sex, lies, and videotape."

She said it without a hint of hyperbole. Television has become America's drug of choice, a kind of electronic valium. And virtually everyone is using it. In fact, more American households have televisions than have indoor plumbing. Television enables us all to be entertained in our homes by people

we would never invite into our homes doing deeds we would
never tolerate in our homes. It is thus what Dan liked to call a
kind of social and cultural Trojan horse.

Amazingly, American children watch an average of nearly
sixty hours of cable and network programming a week. Teens
see an average of almost seventy full-length feature films per
year either in theaters or on video—more than one each week.
They own an average of just over forty musical compact discs,
fifteen game cartridges, and half a dozen computer games.
More than a third of American teens have their own televisions; more than three-fourths own radios and cassette or
compact disc players. And access to the Internet is nearly universal. There can be little doubt that electronic mass media
have become the dominating means of conveying and purvey-
ing modern culture in America.

As Dan and Bea stared at the cacophony of lights and
sounds, they both had to wonder, "Is this a good thing? Are
we satisfied with the way this revolution in culture has tran-
spired in our lifetimes?" The pioneering media analyst Marshall McLuhan may not have been very far off the mark when
he quipped, "Satan is a great electrical engineer."

Standing in Times Square with all the evidence of an
American cultural "mediamorphosis" all around them, Dan
and Bea became engaged and engrossed in a provocative conversation of ideas—alas, a rare activity in these hustle-bustle
days trumped by the tyranny of the urgent.

"It seems to me there are only a couple of ways by which
the spirit of a great culture may be undermined," Bea
observed. "One is portrayed in George Orwell's horrifying
novel of oppression, *1984*. It is a vision of totalitarianism."

"Well the other would have to be Aldous Huxley's equally
horrifying novel of debauchery, *Brave New World*," Dan replied.
"It is a corresponding vision of concupiscence."

"Hmm. That's an interesting parallel."

"It is. But the more I think about it, the more it seems to make sense. In the Orwellian vision, culture becomes something all too akin to a prison. In the Huxleian vision, culture becomes something more like a burlesque."

"I wonder why moviemakers, science fiction writers, and civil libertarians have focused on Orwell most. Huxley seems to have been a lot closer to the truth."

"Good question. Maybe it's the old 'frog in the kettle' syndrome."

As they talked, Dan and Bea were arriving at the conclusion that, in America, Orwell's prophecies had practically passed out of relevance, but Huxley's had gone a long, long way toward being realized. As they watched the horde of teens bouncing about the arcade like so many pinballs, they could hardly escape the conclusion that America had engaged itself in the world's most ambitious experiment to accommodate itself to the technological distractions made possible by the electric plug. Electricity was an experiment that began slowly and modestly in the mid-nineteenth century but has now, at the beginning of the twenty-first, reached a perverse maturity in America's all-consuming love affair with mass media. As nowhere else in the world, Americans have moved with amazing alacrity in bringing to a close the age of the contemplative, slow-moving, and objective printed word, granting the electronic media sovereignty over virtually all their institutions.

"By ushering in the age of television and all of its ancillaries, like cable, satellite, video, and the World Wide Web," Dan said, "America has given us all perhaps the clearest and most literal interpretation of the Huxleian future."

"I suppose what Orwell feared were those who would ban books."

"Yes. But what Huxley feared was something even more frightening—that there would be no reason to ban books, because there probably would not be anyone who would actually want to read them."

"That's a horrifying thought."

Dan nodded as he looked into the arcade. "Orwell was afraid of powerful elites who would somehow contrive to deprive the public of information. But I think Huxley was afraid of powerful elites who would somehow give people so much trivial and disconnected information that they would be reduced to passivity, egoism, and ignorance."

"This is hitting a little too close to home," Bea said as she sidled up to him on the crowded sidewalk.

"Orwell thought that the truth might be concealed from us in one way, shape, form, or another. Huxley, on the other hand, thought that the truth would be drowned in a sea of irrelevance."

Bea just sighed.

"Orwell feared that we might one day become a captive culture. Huxley feared that we would become a trivial culture, preoccupied with some equivalent of what he so picturesquely called 'the feelies,' 'the orgy porgy,' and 'the centrifugal bumblepuppy.'"

"Welcome to the hellish mess that we've made of America."

"It is no doubt appalling to consider that in 1984, people are controlled by inflicting pain. But in Brave New World, the situation is far worse—they are controlled by inflicting pleasure."

"Land of the free. Home of the brave, eh?"

"The bottom line is that Orwell thought that it might be what we hate that would ruin us. Conversely, Huxley thought that it might be what we love that would ruin us in the long run."

Looking back into the thronging arcade with the garish lights of Times Square as a backdrop, Dan and Bea were forced to face the possibility that Huxley, not Orwell, was right.

"It is not simply a clever slogan," Dan concluded. "Marshall McLuhan, William Bennett, Neil Postman, and the other critics of modern media culture are probably more prophetic than we may have realized. We have actually begun the process of amusing ourselves to death."

They stood there for a few moments, taking in everything. They were seeing New York with new eyes of depreciation.

"Gee, I'm encouraged," Bea quipped with no little sarcasm. "Let's go find another bookstore."

It is not necessary to imagine
The world ending in fire or ice.
There are two other possibilities:
One is paperwork,
And the other is nostalgia.

Frank Zappa

WASHINGTON DC
POPULATION 609,909

At the end of August 1814, the U.S. capital lay in ruins after a British army commanded by Maj. Gen. Robert Ross defeated the American militia at Bladensburg and put the public buildings of the city to the torch. Three weeks later, it would be Baltimore's turn to be bombarded by the British. It seemed the fledgling American republic was very nearly done for.

Incredibly, despite a grueling twenty-three-hour bombardment, from early daylight on September 13 until dawn on September 14, the city's primary defensive position, Fort McHenry, held out. A young American lawyer, Francis Scott Key, on board a truce ship to negotiate the release of a doctor who had been arrested by the British, was moved to write a poem, which he titled, "Defense of Fort McHenry." It was the first time that someone had put down in words their feelings about their country and its most visible symbol, the Star Spangled Banner.

Impressed by the poem, Key's brother-in-law, Judge Joseph H. Nicholson, himself a commander of militia artillery at the fort during the bombardment, rushed it into print. The

poem was subsequently put to the music of a British drinking
song, "To Anacreon in Heaven." A month later, in a playbill of
October 17, it was announced that after a play at the Baltimore
Theatre, "Mr. Harding will sing a much admired new song,
written by a gentleman of Maryland, in commemoration of the
gallant defense of Fort McHenry." Just over 116 years later, on
March 3, 1931, President Herbert Hoover signed an act into
law to make the song, since popularly renamed "The Star
Spangled Banner," the national anthem of the United States.

Although it is sung at virtually all sporting events, large
and small, as well as civic meetings, political rallies, and public
celebrations, most Americans are only vaguely familiar with
the first verse of the anthem—indeed, many are unaware that
there are actually four stanzas:

> O! say, can you see, by the dawn's early light,
> What so proudly we hailed at the twilight's last gleaming:
> Whose broad stripes and bright stars, through the
>   perilous fight,
> O'er the ramparts we watched were so gallantly
>   streaming,
> And the rocket's red glare, the bombs bursting in air,
> Gave proof through the night that our flag was still there:

> O! say, does that star-spangled banner yet wave
> O'er the land of the free and the home of the brave?

> On the shore, dimly seen through the mists of the deep,
> Where the foe's haughty host in dread silence reposes,
> What is that which the breeze, o'er the towering steep,
> As it fitfully blows, half conceals, half discloses?
> Now it catches the gleam of the morning's first beam—
> In full glory reflected, now shines on the stream:

> 'Tis the star-spangled banner, O! long may it wave
> O'er the land of the free and the home of the brave!

> And where is the band who so vauntingly swore
> That the havoc of war and the battle's confusion

A home and a country should leave us no more?
Their blood has washed out their foul footsteps'
    pollution.
No refuge could save the hireling and slave
From the terror of flight or the gloom of the grave!

And the star-spangled banner in triumph doth wave
O'er the land of the free and the home of the brave.

O! thus be it ever when freemen shall stand
Between their loved homes and the war's desolation;
Blest with vict'ry and peace, may the heav'n rescued land
Praise the Pow'r that hath made and preserved us a
    nation!
Then conquer we must, when our cause it is just—
And this be our motto—"In God is our trust!"

And the star-spangled banner in triumph shall wave
O'er the land of the free and the home of the brave.

Dan and Bea thought about the remarkable story and then gleefully sang all four verses as they passed by the Fort McHenry National Monument and Historic Shrine at the foot of Fort Avenue in Baltimore Harbor. Singing, particularly boisterous singing, is a bracing bromide for the soul, and they felt it.

They had been forced to cut their stay in New York short by a day. One of Bea's clients had encountered serious difficulties during an installation of a Y2K remediation software protocol. Bea had been unable to solve the problem off-site, so they were on their way to Washington.

The urgency of the project meant that Dan had to skip several restaurants he had slated for articles, particularly several Dutch, Polish, and German diners in the Philadelphia area. But it could not be helped.

Of course, they had to eat sometime, so Dan insisted that at the least they take the time to get some crab cakes on Maryland's Eastern Shore. Normally when he visited the Baltimore area, he tried to eat at Michael's in Timonium. As far as he was concerned it was almost the only place to go for delicious seafood. Michael's crab cakes were always out of this world and the service was invariably impeccable.

This time, however, Dan wanted to try something different. He had long heard about Gabler's Crab House in the outlying township of Perryman, which had been voted metropolitan Baltimore's best in six out of the last ten years running. It just so happened that on the day that Dan and Bea arrived, Bud and Irene Gabler's fifty-seven-year-old restaurant was officially reopening after the annual winter closing. So it was sure to be a special day there.

Dan slowly navigated the curvy, soft sand driveway up to the restaurant. The parking lot was already full, and there was a crowd of patrons waiting to enter. One elderly couple, still rubbing their elbows and knees because they were stiff from the two-hour drive from Hershey, in central Pennsylvania, were standing at the very front of the line. They had arrived more than an hour before opening time to ensure that they would get a table. The local hard-shell crabs, steamed to order, faultlessly fresh, big and plump and seasoned just right, are why they began making annual pilgrimages to Gabler's years ago.

The minute the doors were opened, patrons made a beeline toward the tables near the back windows, which afforded a spectacular view of the Bush River shoreline. There are few other amenities, however. The chairs are hard and straight-backed. Plain wood tables are set with brown paper, wooden mallets, and paring knives. The crabs come piled high on plastic beer trays. Background noises include the screeching of gulls and the booming of weapons being discharged at the U.S. Army's Aberdeen Proving Grounds nearby. For cleanup, customers go to two porcelain sinks in the middle of the room, which dispense cold water only.

The water is cold, the bread white, and the restrooms unglamorous and outdoors. But no matter. The reservations phone rings constantly. The minute a table is cleared, there is almost always a new group waiting to claim it. The food is worth the bother.

Bud Gabler's crabs are a big part of the secret of this place. The spry octogenarian buys crabs harvested from nearby waters, where he claims that just the right salinity helps the flavor. "They're a full size bigger than what most of the other places get," he argues. "We pay a lot more for a bushel of them than the standard crab house fare. But then, that's what keeps us in business." That and the chubby crab cakes served hot between two saltines. That and the good crab salad. That and the honest friendliness of the place.

Alas, authentic crab houses such as Gabler's grow scarcer every year as the crabs become more expensive and harder to find. The size that was a couple of dollars a bushel six decades ago costs nearly a hundred now. When the buyers are even able to find them, that is. For this year's opening day, Gabler was only able to scrape together enough to fill that single day's needs. At the end of the day there was nothing left—not a single claw to spare.

Fortunately, Dan and Bea were able to get their fill and then they rejoined Elvis in Virgil for the quick drive down to Washington—just a couple of hours to the south and west.

THE CAPITAL of the greatest democracy on earth is a gleaming city of stately monuments, classic-styled public buildings, broad boulevards, and verdant parks. Carefully designed by Pierre L'Enfant and meticulously laid out by Andrew Ellicott at the end of the eighteenth century, the city is arranged according to a gridiron of streets cut by diagonal avenues radiating from the mall that runs between the Capitol and the White House. Situated on the banks of the Potomac River, the city was, until the advent of the twentieth century, a rather remote and inaccessible outpost of urbanity amid distinctly rural surroundings.

Despite its lofty architecture and natural beauty, the city is inescapably linked to the rough-and-tumble world of politics—as most of its visitors have been only too quick to point out. Thus the resplendent sights and sites are often forced to take a back seat to the litigious cites and slights of partisanship. Indeed, Dan and Bea quickly discovered that Washington is one of the rudest cities on the face of the earth. The crass and inhospitable atmosphere is everywhere, evident from the demeanor of the shop clerks in the malls to the aggressiveness of the tailgaters on the roads.

The architecture is monumental, as befits a great city, the capital of a great land. The bustle about the streets is frenetic, as betokens its great energy and its great affairs. The aura of power is palpable, as expected in its great caldron and its great ire. Yet somehow it all disappoints as if America were actually elsewhere, as if America were absent from this seat of power.

The problem is simply that politics has somehow grown out of proportion to its relevance to ordinary life.

Dan lamented that every time a problem arises in society, the same litanies could be heard from the usual pundits: The government needs to do more . . . There ought to be a law . . . The president or Congress or the state legislature or the governor or the courts must act—and act immediately! The fact is, he liked to point out, it took us quite some time to get into the culture-wide mess we currently find ourselves in, and thus it may take us a good while to get out of it. The grave dilemmas of our time will not be solved through a bevy of new laws or by a slew of new programs or by a series of new institutions.

Like most Americans, Dan believed that what we really need are not new and more restrictive laws, stronger and more intrusive regulations, or larger and more comprehensive government agencies. What we need are grassroots renewals of those things that made America the greatest nation on the face of the earth in the first place. The crux of our current crisis is not economic, educational, institutional, scientific, or political. It is cultural. We have loosed upon our children a world of woe, and we have simultaneously stripped them of every moral and ethical apparatus necessary to adequately deal with that woe. Or, as Bea asserted, "Character is the issue."

Of course, most of us are prone to look for quick fixes. We want instant relief for that which ails us. But our long experience with politics ought to be enough to tell us that even if a magic bullet exists, it probably won't be found in the arena of politics and law.

As Dan's father often quipped, "Certainly, politics is important. But it is not all-important." He believed that those who lived and died by the electoral sword would probably be shocked to discover that most of the grand-glorious headline-making events in the political realm would probably go down in the annals of time as mere backdrops to the real drama of the everyday affairs of life. But it is so.

Throughout his career, Dan's father had tried to keep things in perspective. Even with as much emphasis as was placed on campaigns, primaries, caucuses, conventions, elections, statutes, laws, policy proposals, legislative initiatives, administrations, surveys, opinion polls, demographic trends, and bureaucratic programs, he knew that the importance of fellow workers, next-door neighbors, close friends, and family members was actually far greater. Political skullduggery—however much it may or may not upset us—in the end is rather remote from the things that really matter. Despite all the hype, hoopla, and hysteria of sensational turns-of-events, the affairs of ordinary people who tend their gardens and raise their children and perfect their trades and mind their businesses are ultimately more important. Just like they always have been. Just like they always will be. That, he believed, was the great lesson of history.

Through the ages the central message of all the most intriguing figures of all the most dominating movements of all the most compelling ideals has been that ultimately it is the simple things that matter most. It has been that ordinary people doing ordinary things are who and what determine the outcome of human events, not princes or populists issuing decrees. It has been that laborers and workmen, cousins and acquaintances can upend the expectations of the brilliant and the glamorous, the expert and the meticulous. It has been that peasants with pitchforks and babushkas with brooms can topple empires and kremlins while all the world looks on in awe. It has been that simple folks doing their mundane chores can literally change the course of history, because they are the stuff of which history is made. They are who and what make the world go round.

Dan's father had learned that lesson the hard way. As one of the founders of the nascent Christian Right in the sixties and seventies, he was constantly engaged in political efforts to get statesmen in office rather than mere politicians, to try to pass pro-family, pro-life, and pro-liberty legislation, to put together grassroots coalitions of concerned citizens, to restore and renew a vision for a moral order in American society and life. But after many years of writing, organizing, coordinating, giving, and sacrificing, he began to believe that his best efforts might be better used elsewhere. He began to realize that, even in Washington, sometimes the most important people, places, and things were away from Capitol Hill, not on it. By the end of his life, he had begun to invest himself, not so much in the powers that be, but in the powers that would be—in the next generation of leaders who were busy with the important work of everyday life.

It was a lesson he never forgot. Neither did Dan.

And now, it was a lesson Bea was about to learn, as well.

AFTER SHE got Dan and Elvis settled into a hotel not far from Capitol Hill, Bea drove to her appointment a few blocks away.

She pulled into the parking lot of the sleek low-rise complex. The buildings were rather nondescript. Smoky gray curtains of glass and steel sheathed each of the structures with the kind of anonymity only modern architecture can induce. They were featureless and efficient, like factories or machines or computers. Bureaucratic planners prefer such a mask for being less serious, less heroic, and less evocative than that to which architecture has always aspired before. Such a building might disguise anything—anything at all. Apparently, this one did.

Bea stepped out of the elevator and followed a colorless corridor into a windowless room two stories below ground level. She walked into a room that could easily have been a scene from the Cold War era. People were hunched in front of computers in cramped cubicles, speaking to one another in hushed tones—in Russian. But they were in Washington, not Moscow, less than twelve blocks from Capitol Hill. And they were engaged in an entirely different kind of global struggle: a Code War.

Lyudmila Voronyanskaya and about forty other immigrants from the former Soviet Union were in the sub-basement of the D.C. headquarters of the American Power Service Association, the nation's largest utility cooperative. They were there not because they understood Russian, but rather Cobol, a computer language that runs many of the mainframe computers in use throughout the United States. But this language is so antiquated that relatively few American programmers actually know it anymore, which explains why programmers from less advanced countries were now in such high demand.

Lyudmila, a twenty-something refugee from the economic chaos of post-communist Moscow, was one of tens of thousands of programmers throughout the world who had been tapped over the last couple of years to try to head off the havoc that experts thought might ensue because the computers that underpin today's wired society do not understand that a year can begin with a number other than nineteen. Lyudmila had been hired by the federal government to head up the Y2K computer remediation efforts of the public utilities consortium.

The fact that Lyudmila was in charge of the operation here practically made Bea's head swim. She was obviously quite bright and articulate, but she was very young. This was her first real job. She had only been in America for thirteen months and obviously not yet able to qualify for citizenship, much less the kind of security clearance necessary for such a sensitive post. But the federal utilities compliance oversight task force was desperate, and Lyudmila not only spoke perfect English, she was capable and, perhaps more important, she was also immediately available.

She and her colleagues had already spent the better part of a year painstakingly sifting through a program consisting of some seven million lines of code that, to the uninitiated, resembled gibberish. And that was just to fix one program. In all, American Power Service had nearly eight hundred programs with a total of some fifty million lines written in more than twenty programming languages. How well they were fixed or replaced determined whether the lights and heat would stay on around the country in the new millennium.

The Y2K problem, as it is known in computer jargon, had been draining hundreds of billions of dollars from companies and governments struggling to tame the so-called millennium bug, which was not technically a bug at all, but simply a seemingly insignificant programming shortcut turned time bomb.

Bea knew that the direst situations that had been predicted—financial chaos, societal strife, food shortages, and persistent, widespread blackouts—had already proved to be overwrought and exaggerated. But she was also only too well aware of the fact that it was not hard to find reputable alarmists, even at this late date; computer experts who asserted that they would not fly overseas any longer or economists who still insisted that the computer bug was sure to set off a domino effect of market stresses leading to a global recession.

The fact was the first wave of disruptions had already hit, long before the advent of the new millennium, with nearly half of the largest American and European companies experiencing at least minor breakdowns because some software already had to deal with dates in 2000 and beyond. Many retailers had difficulty processing credit cards that expired in 2000 or later, for example. At BankBoston, some ATM cards were seized because cash machines responded as if the cards had expired in 1900. Another spate of disruptions was experienced during each succeeding quarter, because a host of other computer programs—like those used to prepare budgets, schedule appointments, and pay unemployment benefits—dealt with dates up to a year or two into the future.

All the threats stemmed from the fact, by now well known, that computer programs frequently use two digits to represent years, like 98 for 1998. So when 1999 ended, many computers were baffled about what came next or responded as if 00 meant 1900 instead of 2000. Some of the afflicted machines crashed. Others, just as dangerously, spewed out erroneous data. With computers running everything from power grids to bank machines to air traffic control, the range of services that were affected was vast.

Bea's job was to get machines fully functional again by remediating the code, repairing the software applications, and coordinating the installation of the necessary communications upgrades. Her business had really taken off in 1997 when the June issue of *Newsweek* carried a cover story entitled, "The Day the World Shuts Down: Can We Fix the Year 2000 Computer Problem Before It's Too Late?" The story portrayed a rather dim vision of the next millennium:

Drink deep from your champagne glasses as the ball drops from Times Square to usher in the Year 2000. Whether you imbibe or not, the hangover may begin immediately. The

power may go out, or the credit card you pull out to pay for
your dinner may not be valid. Did you try an ATM to get
cash? That may not work either. Or the elevator that took
you up to the party ballroom may be stuck on the ground
floor. Or the parking garage you drove into earlier may
charge you more than your yearly salary. Or the car might
not start, or the traffic light may be on the blink. When you
get home the phones may not work. Your mail may come,
but magazine subscriptions will have stopped. Your government check may not arrive. Your insurance policies may
have expired. Or you may be out of a job. When you show
up for work after the holidays the factory or office building
might be locked up with a hand written sign on the wall:
Out of business due to computer error. Could it really
happen? Could the most anticipated New Year's Eve party
in our lifetimes really usher in a digital nightmare, when
our wired up the wahzoo civilization grinds to a halt?
Incredibly, according to computer experts, corporate information officers, congressional leaders, and basically anyone
who's even given the matter a fair hearing, the answer is yes,
yes, 2000 times yes. Unless, we successfully complete the
most ambitious and costly technology project in history.
One where the payoff comes not in amassing riches or
extending web access, but securing raw survival.

Y2K became the latest in a long line of fashionable wor-
ries. And that was extremely good for business. Companies
that assumed that they could procrastinate to the last minute
suddenly realized in a panic that the last minute had arrived.
And the suddenly incessant media carping would not let them
forget it, try as they might. Dire predictions were offered by
some of the most eminent and respected leaders in banking,
business, and government.

At last comprehending that the crisis was real, imminent,
and disastrous, minions of the press corps suddenly threw
themselves into the maelstrom with a vengeance. Their aching

questions poured forth in a torrent. And almost as fervently, the ready responses poured forth in a torrent as well. Even if those responses were not exactly clear-cut answers, they were confident and emphatic guesses. Indeed, a myriad of experts and authorities weighed in on the network broadcasts, the twenty-four-hour cable newscasts, the talk shows, the morning variety programs, the newspapers, the tabloids, and the news magazines. Already reeling under the tremendous pressure of meeting compliance deadlines, testing schedules, and shareholder expectations, the harried global technopoly was suddenly buried beneath an avalanche of analysis and apocalyptic hype.

Although most of the instant wits, wags, pundits, prognosticators, essayists, editorialists, commentators, and curmudgeons knew little or nothing about the Y2K problem, had never explored the technological issues involved, and had never thought through the immediate implications of the social questions it raised, they were quick to offer their opinions, explanations, conjectures, and theories concerning the coming calamity. Invariably they resorted to the maxims and axioms of pseudoscience, pop psychology, and fad sociology. Most seemed more than happy to seize the opportunity to ride a political hobbyhorse or mount a social soapbox for one pet issue or another.

For several months the media's incessant handwringing commentary seemed to produce as many opinions as there were opinion-makers. Experts seemed to come out of the woodwork. And each was ready to offer his or her authoritative voice to the cacophony of prognostication. Each was quick to offer easy answers, quick retorts, and hasty analyses. And the media are set up for the rapid collection of emphatic guesses on the causes of disturbing news.

It was not long until the Y2K problem had become a cultural phenomenon dominating technology journalism, featured in apocalyptic novels, appearing in comic strips, and inspiring Hollywood screenplays. For those prone to believe that the end of the world was nigh at the start of the new millennium, the computer bug looked like the means to the end, a digital echo of Noah's flood.

Contract repairs for Y2K projects thus proved to be an incredible economic windfall for Bea's computer consulting business. It offered her an abundant supply of clients—more than she could handle—and companies were willing to pay a premium for the various compliance, remediation, rectification, refurbishment, and installation services they offered. After all, it was terribly tedious and painstaking work.

If writing programs were software's equivalent of carpentry, a Y2K repair job was more like asbestos removal. It was a task as wearisome as replacing all the light bulbs in Times Square but not as easy, because most of the massive mainframe software programs in use today were customized as proprietary applications and written years ago by programmers who have gone on to other jobs, retired, or died. Thus remediation work was about as perplexing, intricate, complicated, monotonous, and vexatious as any work could be.

THE REPAIR project undertaken here in Washington by Lyudmila Voronyanskaya for the American Power Service Association, was a case in point. Lyudmila and her colleagues were the final backstop in a search through every line of program code for places containing two-digit years. Sometimes such work can be straightforward because programmers refer to dates using abbreviations like YR or DT. But in other cases the designations might be quirky and subtle, like the names of movie characters or the programmer's acquaintances.

One day earlier this winter, Lyudmila had been inspecting a tiny five-hundred-line segment in the heart of the APSA operations code. A special diagnostic program had already quickly scanned the lines, picking out eighteen with numbers that might have been dates. One of those lines contained a twenty-digit serial number. Suspicious, Lyudmila focused on this segment and found a bug. Six of the digits in the serial number referred to a date: two for the month, two for the day, and two for the year.

Now the question was how to repair it. The automated utility program wanted to expand the serial number to twenty-two digits, adding two digits to represent the year. But such an expansion was not as easy as it sounded, because it would throw off the position of the other numbers. A number that was in position fifteen, which might have stood for a customer's geographic location, would now move to position seventeen, which the program might read as a meter reader's route number. So expanding the serial number could require changes to an untold number of other lines in the program and perhaps even to the very architecture of the application.

Before undertaking this task, however, Lyudmila found that another programmer had encountered the same serial number in another part of the program and had already expanded it. But that programmer apparently made an error, so now even more work was needed to get the code back online and fully operational.

And that was just one line of code in one side program at the heart of the operations system. The process would have to be repeated hundreds of thousands of times throughout the remediation process.

Of course, APSA never planned to fix all of its software. More than a hundred programs had been replaced by new software that was guaranteed to be free of Y2K problems. Several programs were to be scrapped because the company could not find the programmers who knew the proprietary language in which they were written. A handful of others were being retired because the consortium managers found that no one relied on them for critical tasks anymore.

To save time, the APSA compliance team had decided not to expand years to four digits in most programs, but settled on using a technique called windowing. Years were to be left as two digits but the computer was instructed to interpret 00 to 49 as being 2000 to 2049 and 50 to 99 as 1950 to 1999. Of course, if the program was still in use in 2050, it would have to be fixed again.

As for crucial software that helped balance the supply and demand for electricity, the utility consortium was saving millions of dollars by not fixing it at all, because the company planned to buy new software eventually. Until then, it was simply setting the clock back so that the program would function as if it were 1972 instead of 2000; the dates in 1972 fell on the same days of the week as 2000.

The bottom line, however, was that, despite these shortcuts, despite budgeting nearly a hundred million dollars for Y2K work, and despite starting its cleanup more than two years previously—earlier than most of their constituent utility companies—APSA was not going to finish this task on time. So like many other federally mandated compliance industries, the management team had resorted to triage—fixing the most important programs first and worrying about minor ones later.

But none of that was the reason Lyudmila had issued her urgent call for Bea to come to Washington. The problem was that a rogue—or a group of them—had been detected on the remediation team. They were pirating information from the system and had been utilizing it to enrich themselves. The situation was a matter of national security, because ultimately the integrity of the entire electrical and telecommunications grid depended upon it.

One of the things that Y2K repair programming required was access to all the information, transmission, and processing systems within a given computing environment. The technicians had to have access to every line of code, every piece of software, every scrap of data, every password, every encryption device, and every shielding sequence. In other words, the programmers who walked in off the street to fix the millennium bug had to be able to put their hands on every detail of a company's or an agency's vital information with full disclosure of all the firewalls and security measures.

In the information age, comprehensive access to so much sensitive data at any one time by any one person was unprecedented—and extremely dangerous. But then the Y2K crisis was itself unprecedented and dangerous, calling for drastic steps and extreme measures. And such a situation would not actually pose a problem if the contract programmers doing the remedial work could be trusted.

Apparently, some members of the hastily assembled team should not have been trusted. Whoever the pirates were, they had acted like kids in a candy store who simply could not bear to keep their hands off the goodies. For them, the Y2K crisis seemed to be a dream come true.

According to Lyudmila, the pirates had taken full advantage of the extraordinary access they were given to the sensitive files of the consortium's utilities and agencies. They had immediately recognized the unique opportunity for what it was.

"They made the insertion of remote backdoor entries a part of the standard operating procedure for every system they worked on," she told Bea.

"Thus, bypassing all security?"

"Right. And then they wrote blind access codes for all of the client administration, product inventory, shipping and receiving, vendor conduct, customer tracking, and production control programs."

"What about the accounting, billing, data transfer, fund supervision, and portfolio management programs?" Bea asked.

"Those too."

"Do you know what they were planning to do with the data?"

"They created a dense web of phantom accounts, clients, vendors, payables, and receivables."

"That's not good."

"Then they manufactured reams of illusory data, profiles, balances, histories, backgrounds, and inventories."

"So they were attempting to fabricate a fog designed to shield them from the auditors?"

"Yes. I think the disinformation was a foil so they might be able to go undetected when they began siphoning off funds from the now vulnerable and accessible accounts."

"So how were you able to discover the ruse?"

"If, for instance, a careful portfolio manager or fund administrator regularly changed the configuration of the security mechanism or installed new firewalls sometime after the remediation team had completed a particular project, the pirates would suddenly lose their ready access, become exposed, and make themselves easily detectable."

"So they were trapped by their own game?"

"Well, it took several hits before we realized what was happening. And by that time, the pirates had figured out we were on to them and they quickly ducked out. So we were unable to actually identify them."

"And they still had their encoded blind access?"

"Yes, but fortunately we were able to catch on to that pretty quickly too. So whatever back doors they might have created were blocked when we upgraded the buffer program. Once again, hacking into the system was still technically possible for them, but now it was much more detectable."

The problem wasn't so much that Lyudmila wanted to find a way to catch the pirates. She just wanted to find a way to lock them out of the system, restore the integrity of a year's worth of repairs, and then move on.

One of the things that Bea always recommended to her clients was that they alter all their information and transmission security measures shortly after Y2K repairs had been made. In this case, she advised strenuous new procedures that would protect the data and ensure the integrity of the system.

In the past, perhaps the greatest risk she had faced in her consulting business was her legal liability. The prospect of being sued for a failed repair operation, lost data, corrupted code, service disruption, or embezzlement was not a terribly welcome one. But it was an all too real possibility that she knew existed. Some legal experts had worried that the Y2K crisis might provide the biggest litigation opportunity of all time. In an already litigious environment—Americans file about fifteen million civil lawsuits and pay out more than a hundred billion dollars in legal fees every year—Y2K lawsuits could potentially paralyze the economy, perhaps even threaten the stability of the entire social infrastructure.

As a result, Bea was meticulously careful to protect herself against any and all liability. And the best way to do that was to ensure that her clients and their data were as safe as she could make them.

But of course, in this case, the stakes were much greater than merely protecting herself against this liability. The security of the APSA system was necessary to preserve the integrity of the country's entire power grid. And as a result the remediation of the consortium's operations loomed larger than all the political brouhahas of the capital put together.

AFTER SEVERAL hours of walking Lyudmila through detailed implementation simulations, Bea was able to retrace her steps through the drab building and head back to the hotel. Although she would have several more days of follow-up tasks to undertake, the crisis was past and the new security systems were in place.

As she drove through the capital's rush-hour traffic to rejoin Dan and Elvis, she recalled how much simpler life had been just a few years earlier, before computers had come to dominate life so completely. Indeed, back then computers were little more than the backdrops for bad science fiction movies. Windows were things people hated to clean. A ram was just the cousin of a goat. A gig was a job for musicians. An application was for employment. A program was a television show. A keyboard was a piano. Memory was just something that most folks lost with age. Compress was something people did to the garbage, not something they did to a file. Log on was adding wood to the fire. A hard drive was a long trip on the highway, and a virus was the flu.

Oh how things have changed, she thought as she wove through the clatter of the capital's rudeness.

Modern things are ugly
Because modern men are careless,
Not because they are artless.

Maurice Baring

ATLANTA
POPULATION 394,017

L~IKE MODERN ART OR~ an avant garde poem or the latest haute fashions, the cultural pluralism imagined by the enthusiastic minions of modernity had always been more than a little difficult for Dan to define. Although often stated with algebraic lucidity, its topsy-turvy logic was often as unintelligible to him as the dog-Latin of monkish hexameters. It was a kind of upsidonia that was, to his mind, as fully fantastic as Abbott's Flatland or Swift's Liliput.

In practice, he knew that it was a well-intentioned attempt to forge a cultural consensus on the fact that there can be no cultural consensus. It was the unspoken assumption that a happy and harmonious society could be maintained only so long as the only common belief was that there were no common beliefs. It was the reluctant affirmation that the only absolute was that there must not be any absolutes. He had difficulty resolving such modern paradoxes, although they seemed to be assumed by almost everyone else.

Dan believed that it was just as absurd to say that any idea was as valid as every idea as it was to say that bad ideas are as helpful as good ideas. He was convinced that it was equally ridiculous to say that there was no difference between right and wrong and to say that there is no difference between right and left. Everyone he knew had comprehended since childhood that too many chiefs and not enough Indians would inevitably result in chaos, and yet they somehow failed to grasp the fact that too many moralities and not enough morals would likewise result in chaos.

"Why can't we all just get along?" was the mantra of this kind of modernist multiculturalism. "Don't condemn anyone. Don't judge others. Respect diversity. Different strokes for different folks. *Que sera, sera.*"

Dan appreciated such notions. They were nice sentiments. They were noble sentiments. But they were rather elusive propositions that were invariably difficult to inculcate in a diverse society, much less to enforce in a standardless society. It seemed to be obvious to him that any culture that ceased to hold in common certain essential assumptions about life and morals could not long survive. A hazy and nebulous social conscience with lowered standards, diluted ethics, and compromised integrity was not only insufficient to hold a culture together, it actually militated against the very possibility of cohesion. Justice was necessarily tossed to and fro on waves of doubt. Truth changed from one day to the next. And anarchy or tyranny had actually become the best of a host of other undesirable options.

Case in point: It seemed to Dan that the sprawling city of Atlanta proved that notion all too clearly.

MANY FIRST-TIME visitors to Atlanta come looking for the stereotypes of the Deep South—white-columned mansions surrounded by magnolias owned by genteel folks with accents as thick as sorghum molasses. What they generally find instead is a good deal more cosmopolitan and as a consequence, a good deal less interesting.

These days, anyone looking around Atlanta for hoop skirts, plantations, simple agrarian pleasures, and the graces of Southern hospitality probably had best curl up with a copy of *Gone with the Wind*, because those things are nowhere to be found.

William Tecumseh Sherman burned the city to the ground as he began his brutal march to the sea during the calamitously uncivil war between the states. In the bitter days of Reconstruction that followed, Atlanta arose from the ashes, not as an indigenous Southern city, but as a recast vision of progressive American industrialism. And so it remains to this day. Although the palimpsests of glittering modernity may be scraped away here or there to reveal a few isolated islands of authenticity—places like the Virginia-Highland neighborhood, the old Fox Theater, the DeKalb Farmer's Market, and the Oakland Cemetery—for the most part the communities in and around the vast metroplex are the artificial constructs of an advanced Gernsbeckian social phantasmagoria.

The gleaming skyline of the city—home to multinational corporations like Coca-Cola, Delta Airlines, United Parcel Service, Holiday Inn, Georgia Pacific, Home Depot, and Turner Broadcasting—bears vivid testimony to this fact. Great abstract shapes of reflective glass and steel, the unmistakable hallmarks of our characterless contemporary architecture, pierce the sky with a startling profligacy and prolificacy. It is a marvel of the age of technopoly—just like Los Angeles or New York or Dallas or Kuala Lumpur or Delhi or Lagos or São Paulo or Toronto or Brussels or any of the other major metropolitan cityscapes cloaked in modernism's smothering techno-uniformity.

From a great distance, Atlanta appears as magnificent as the Emerald City of Oz. But as Tom Wolfe recorded in his blockbuster novel of modern manners, *A Man in Full*, Atlanta is all simply "a grand illusion." And as H. L. Mencken observed a generation ago, the city is actually little better than a kind of "cultural wasteland," one that is terribly "out of proportion to the unfortunate people who must inhabit it."

The result of modernism is a crisis of the human habitat: cities ruined by corporate gigantism and abstract renewal schemes, public spaces unworthy of human affection, vast sprawling suburbs that lack any sense of community, sterile and treeless spec developments, a slavish obeisance to the needs of automobiles and their dependent industries at the expense of human needs. Modernism divorced the practice of building from the history and traditional meanings of building. It promoted a species of urbanism that destroyed age-old social arrangements. It created a physical setting for man that failed to respect the standards of beauty, goodness, and truth. It produced an architecture of broken dreams.

And it produced a good deal of grousing on Dan's part.

WE MODERNS are enamored of progress. We live at a time when things shiny and new are prized far above things old and timeworn. For most of us, tradition is little more than a quirky and nostalgic sentimentalism. It is hardly more than the droning, monotonous succession of obsolete notions, anachronous ideals, and antiquarian habits. Sound and fury, signifying nothing," he lectured in pious tones.

Bea sighed with a kind of resignation, knowing what was to come.

"Of course, many of the wisest of men and women through the ages have recognized that tradition is a foundation upon which all true cultural advancement must be built. That it is, in fact, the prerequisite to all genuine progress. A contempt of the monuments and the wisdom of the past may be justly reckoned one of the reigning follies of these days to which pride and idleness have equally contributed."

Bea's strategy was to remain quiet until Dan exhausted his bluster.

"But Henry Ford and his industrial ilk claimed that an awareness of our traditions and an appreciation for the manners, erudition, and customs of the past were bunk. And in Atlanta, dominated by his instrument of the modernist Copernican social revolution—the automobile—Ford's kith and kin have apparently had the last say."

It seemed to Dan that the inhuman dimensions of humanistic modernism in Atlanta were evident in the sundered race relations, in the dramatic disparity between the haves and have-nots, in the soaring crime rates, and in the middle-class flight that has swollen Cobb, Fulton, Clayton, Cherokee, DeKalb, Forsythe, and Gwinnett Counties into an exurban sprawl.

He had begun complaining about the city's knack for impersonalism, its lust for gargantuanism, and its bent for megalomania before they had crossed into South Carolina, as they passed through Atlanta's kissing cousin, Charlotte, driving south along I-85.

"But I like it," Bea finally objected.

"What is there to like? It is the epitome of the geography of nowhere," Dan replied.

"Well, I like all the trees. The pine trees, the peach trees, the oak trees, and the magnolia trees. I like the azaleas. I bet they'll be wonderful in another couple of weeks. I like the rolling terrain. I like lots of things about Atlanta. It's clean and neat and new looking."

"It looks exactly like every other overbuilt, car-choked, mall-mad, ersatz-blinkered, and fantasy-veneered disaster of urban planning the world over. How could you possibly like it?"

"Well, I do. I just do. I think it is a pleasant combination of the old and the new. And besides everything else, I like the fact that one of my best friends lives here. So stop your philosophical grousing. I refuse to let you spoil my visit."

Dan drove on in a harrumphed protest.

WHEN THEY entered Gwinnett County at the outskirts of town, they began to notice a striking series of billboards. As they got closer in, they observed that the ad campaign also appeared on the sides of buses and the backs of taxicabs. And by the time they passed the 285 Perimeter Loop, they began to see them everywhere. "Let's meet at my house Sunday before the game.—God," said the first few. Then they noticed several more, all in the same crisp, clean, arresting, professional design:

C'mon over and bring the kids.—God.

What part of Thou Shalt Not . . . didn't you understand?—God.

We need to talk.—God.

Keep using my name in vain and I'll make rush hour longer.—God.

Loved the wedding, invite me to the marriage.—God.

That Love Your Neighbor thing . . . I meant it.—God.

I love you . . . I love you . . . I love you.—God.

Will the road you're on get you to my place?—God.

Follow me.—God.

Big Bang theory. Give me a break.—God.

My way is the HIGHway.—God.

Need directions?—God.

You think it's hot here?—God.

Tell the kids I love them.—God.

Need a marriage counselor? I'm available.—God.

Have you read my number one bestseller? There will
be a test.—God.

Do you have any idea where you're going?—God.

Don't make me come down there.—God.

The comfortable admixture of such evangelical sentiments
with the sleek urbane ethos seemed ominously paradoxical to
Dan. Bea thought it was wonderfully wholesome. In fact, it
was probably both. Regardless, it was an apt introduction to
the character of this remarkable city.

BEA'S LIFELONG friend Sarah MacAfee lived in the Intown community between Piedmont Park and downtown. It was an
older transitional neighborhood bustling with activity, redevelopment, and ethnic diversity. And it fit Sarah's high-octane,
never-say-die, on-the-go, twenty-four-seven lifestyle. She was
a privileged scion of the black professional class, originally
attracted to Atlanta by the wild spring-break sojourns of
Freaknik. But later she settled here to help establish the academic extension program of the Jimmy Carter Presidential
Library in nearby Little Five Points. Her flat was in a turn-of-
the-century building with a Starbucks coffee shop and a funky
retro boutique downstairs and six quirky apartments upstairs.
It was perfect for her plants, her cats, and her penchant for the
très chic oblige. Elvis was not the least bit impressed. And neither was Dan.

The Gylberds arrived just after noon on Saturday. Since
the girls said they had an awful lot of catching up to do, Dan
decided to go out for a while and kill a little time until dinner.

Besides, he would have felt like an awkward fifth wheel if he had hung around the apartment.

Actually, he didn't mind getting out at all. Although he was still a little road weary from the long drive from Washington, he had places to go and people to see himself. While he was clearly no fan of the city, there were a few attractions even he could not resist.

He made a beeline to The Varsity at the edge of the Georgia Tech campus. It was the world's largest drive-in restaurant, opened in 1928 by Frank Gordy. Still run by the Gordy family, it is an Atlanta landmark. It is also a fast-food mecca. Behind a stainless-steel counter half the length of a football field, red-shirted cooks rush out thousands of orders with astonishing speed. They serve up every meal garnished with plenty of hash-slinger sass. Thus, the spartan drive-in on steroids resonates with a bodacious chorus of "What'll ya have?"

Without hesitation, the regular customers, such as heavyweight champion Evander Holyfield, former mayor Andrew Young, and Sen. Phil Gramm, respond with esoteric aplomb. "Walk a dog sideways" means a hot dog with onions on the side. "Bag of rags" means a bag of potato chips. "Yankee steaks" means hamburgers with yellow mustard. "Strings" means an order of fries.

Dan had a chili dog accompanied by a cardboard boat of crusty onion rings and a tall mug of Coca-Cola—he knew not to ask for anything else. He then walked into the linoleum-dominated dining room with seating for nearly a thousand. He enjoyed his fete without even a hint of guilt; after all, founder Frank Gordy proclaimed that The Varsity served only health food, saying, "A couple of chili dogs a day keep you young, smart, beautiful, and oh, so happy."

That evening, Sarah took Dan and Bea to her favorite soul food restaurant, which was in the Sweet Auburn neighborhood, also known as the Martin Luther King Historical District. Bettye Mae's is a small café serving traditional Southern fare. It had all the ambiance of a grade-school cafeteria, but Sarah knew that it was exactly the kind of place Dan would love. He did.

Shortly after they were seated at a table near a bank of windows, the matronly proprietor burst out of the kitchen and came straight to their table. She was a large woman, obviously having made it a habit to sample the restaurant's rich wares over the years. Even so, she was robust and vivacious. Her round face radiated wit and intelligence.

"There you are, Miss Sarah. And these must be the special friends you told me about. Welcome to Atlanta. You must be Mr. Dan and you're Miss Bea. I'm Bettye Mae. It is so good to have you here." Her words poured out in a torrent, sweeter and thicker than dark Karo.

"Well, thanks—" Dan tried to reply.

"Y'all just settle back," she cut in. "Make yourselves at home. It's not often we get a famous writer and food critic in here."

Dan shot a withering look toward Sarah. "Famous? Food critic? No, you must have misunderstood—" But he could hardly get a word in edgewise.

"In fact, we never get writers or critics in here. Who am I kidding?" She laughed heartily. "In a little old soul food restaurant?"

"Actually, I just write a little column in a Chicago tabloid. And I've only been doing it for a couple of weeks—" he attempted to explain.

"Miss Sarah tells me you're traveling. All across the country. Stopping whenever a place strikes your fancy. Eating at the little out-of-the-way cafés, diners, and kitchens that are all but forgotten these days. Sounds wonderful. Absolutely wonderful."

"Yes, sort of. We're really just taking a kind of sabbatical—"

"So what do you think of our fair city? How are you liking Atlanta so far?"

"We've only been here a few hours, but—"

"Oh, what am I saying? What a ridiculous question. Of course you don't like it. If you were the type to really like Atlanta, you'd be having dinner tonight at the Buckhead Diner or at the Ritz-Carlton or maybe even Bones. You sure wouldn't be slumming with us here at Bettye Mae's." Her eyes twinkled with delight. "That Atlanta, the chamber of commerce version of Atlanta, is Hades all made over for the *turistas*."

Dan, Bea, and Sarah were all laughing now.

"So I'll tell you what. I'm going to give you a taste of a whole different Atlanta tonight. I'm going to give you a little taste of heaven, of the real deal, of Southern cooking at its very best."

With that, she bustled off into the kitchen to serve up some of the best food that any of them had ever put in their mouths: succulent fried chicken, crisp greens, savory chitlins, smooth sweet potatoes, and spicy okra. It was a festive feast of delight and discovery.

"Sarah, I ought to be furious with you," Dan kiddingly shook his finger across the table at her. "But after this meal I couldn't possibly be upset with anyone about anything whatsoever."

When Bea first met Dan, Sarah was wary and warned Bea to steer clear of him. He seemed just a little too wild, a little too reckless, and a little too brash. The girls had grown up together, were best friends through high school, and were roommates in college. They went to church together, discovered boys together, and plotted their life destinies together.

Sarah saw Dan as a threat. And to the extent that he was still reacting to his father's legacy, he was. Although he was remarkably well versed in the Bible, he resisted all attempts they made to get him to attend church with them. While he was quite astute in theological issues, he was loathe to discuss them. Despite the fact that he had grown up with incredible opportunities to travel the world, meet celebrities, and experience life as few had, he seemed to want to distance himself from the past.

Remarkably, he made loud protests that he actually loved and admired his father. He simply felt as if he could never live up to his expectations. So he went his own way. Sarah believed that he was a prodigal and that until he came to his senses, he could only inflict pain upon Bea.

Ultimately, as Bea's relationship with Dan became more serious, inevitable strains began to show in her friendship with Sarah. Eventually they drifted apart. It was only over the course of the last ten years or so that the friendship was renewed. And that happened mostly by long distance.

As a result, their reunion today, only the third time they had actually seen each other since Dan and Bea married, was rather bittersweet. Their lives had taken starkly different courses.

After dinner, the three of them retired to the Starbucks beneath Sarah's flat for a cappuccino nightcap. They talked and talked. About anything. About everything. They reminisced into the wee hours. It was wonderful.

The next morning, even though they were still groggy from their late-night carousing, they were up early. They wanted to make sure they were at Sarah's church in time for the first service, which was the least crowded of the four that were scheduled every Sunday morning. Although a bit reluctant as always, Dan did not have to be cajoled into going with them. He was somewhat inclined to go. The congregation was well known for its innovative approach to ministry and Dan was curious; either that, he thought, or he was a glutton for punishment.

ORIGINALLY, THE church was a fairly traditional Presbyterian congregation in an area of Atlanta undergoing dramatic demographic changes. Worried about declining membership, the young, articulate, and entrepreneurially minded pastor decided to do something about it.

To start things off, he commissioned a comprehensive market survey of the surrounding neighborhood. Among other things, the poll found that people were put off by the word *Presbyterian*. So he insisted that the church change its name. It became the *People's Community Fellowship*. Dan thought that sounded more like a Marxist banana republic than an evangelical church.

The survey also indicated that most of the upwardly mobile families in the community—those the pastor most wanted to attract—placed a high premium on accessibility. So he wheedled and coaxed the leadership until they sold the beautiful old church property with its sculpted sandstone spire and stately cruciform nave. Then the church hired a fundraising specialist, to manage a monumental capital campaign, and launched a massive building program.

The congregation built a new campus on a prime plot of real estate near the freeway and in the path of the city's most explosive growth. There was nothing about the buildings to indicate that they served any kind of ecclesiastical function. In fact, they could have easily been the corporate headquarters of a computer software firm or a certified public accountant or a savings and loan or a holding company for commodities marketers. The low-slung, beige brick exteriors, accented with bronze glass expanses, were surrounded by carefully manicured lawns. There was no evidence of crosses, towers, bells, domes, spires, stained-glass windows, or any other obviously religious architectural symbolism on the property. Even the signage and logos were subdued and corporate.

The congregation's sanctuary—or the media center, as the pastor preferred to call it—was a spare but cavernous auditorium with efficient acoustics, the latest high-tech audio-visual equipment, a wide stage, and comfortable theater seating for three thousand. It looked more like the set of a television variety show or a university recital hall than a church.

Dan wasn't surprised but rather sorely disappointed when Sarah told him that all these changes were wildly popular throughout the community. As a result, the church had experienced unprecedented growth over the last several years.

But it wasn't just the facilities that the innovative pastor overhauled. He also undertook extensive renovations on the public services the church offered. There would be no liturgy, no sermon, no hymn singing, no responsive reading, and no sacramental ritual. Instead, he wanted to make certain that the congregation was able to communicate the ancient truths of the faith in creative new ways. There would be professional-quality drama presentations, monologues, videos, and soliloquies. The pastor would "share" while sitting on a stool rather than preach from a pulpit. He encouraged people to dress casually. Thus it was more common to see young families in cutoffs and flip-flops than in suits and skirts. The music he introduced was crisply produced with an ear toward pop accessibility. The choruses were simple, hip, contemporary, and up-tempo.

The remake of the church was comprehensive right down to the language the people used. The pastor made certain that they threw out all theological terminology. As he explained, "If we use the words *redemption* and *conversion*, people think we are talking about bonds." So he banished all difficult or unpleasant terms from his sharing session, words like *sin* and *guilt*. He even produced a series of booklets containing easy-to-read Bible excerpts combined with eye-popping graphics. During his sharing session, he always referred to page numbers in the booklets rather than verses in the Bible. And he always made certain that he steered clear of all contentious issues. After all, church growth experts had long asserted that controversial or confrontational preaching actually does more to drive people away than to draw them in. They generally advised that sermons ought to appeal to the lowest common denominator, that services ought to be simple and accessible, and that programs ought to be consumer-oriented and user-friendly. Otherwise they offend rather than attract. They argued that substantive theology would at best confuse average churchgoers and at worst alienate them. And so the pastor did his best to accommodate himself to the demands of the day.

The church members were ecstatic. The church was a hit. People thronged its services. Its commodious facilities were soon overcrowded and one expansion after another was required. In every way it was the poster child for the chamber of commerce version of the new Atlanta. Not only that, it became a national model for the church growth movement, a darling of the new seeker-friendly evangelical world. It was studied in seminaries and Bible colleges. It became a legitimate tourist attraction in and of itself. It was, after all, McChurch for religious consumers.

It was also everything that Dan held suspect in the contemporary American church scene. He worried that Christians had so completely capitulated to worldly standards of success that the modern church was now awash in compromise. Its flippant commitment to the slick contemporaneity, razzle-dazzle modernity, and gee-whiz fashionability of the world had made it very nearly indistinguishable from any other social institution or philanthropic enterprise in America. Its mimicry of the world and the ways of the world had transformed virtually every aspect of ministry from pastoral care and foreign missions to church growth and Sunday worship. It was almost as though Christians had caught the spirit of the age like a virus. As a result, they were afflicted by a plague of terminal trendiness. It was no longer a joke to him; they had actually become the "church of what's happening now."

Although in some ways Dan viewed the mission of the church as a slightly interested outsider, he was afraid that the result of this modern metamorphosis was that the church had begun to lose its ability to maintain old-fashioned stick-to-itiveness. The difficult vocation of what his father had vividly dubbed "a long obedience in the same direction" was almost entirely missing from the lives and ministries of believers.

Even in evangelical congregations like this one, Dan felt that the gospel was now being squeezed into the mold of this world with amazing alacrity. Christians tried their best to tone down their denunciations of sin lest they be accused of being *judgmental*. They minimized doctrinal distinctives lest they be accused of being *divisive*. They blurred the boundaries between virtue and vice lest they be accused of being *legalistic*. They brushed off heresy and heterodoxy lest they be accused of being *intolerant*. And they veiled their concerns about societal disarray lest they be accused of being *political*.

Dan's father had always warned that the day was coming when it was possible that even the mildest assertion of Christian truth might sound like a thunderclap because the well-polished civility of religious talk had begun to keep Christians from hearing much of that kind of thing.

Indeed, it was evident to him that the well-polished civility of religious talk had all but eliminated true religion from the talk, to say nothing of the lives of Christians today. Thus, recovery seemed to have replaced repentance. Dysfunction replaced sin. Drama replaced dogma. Positive thinking replaced passionate preaching. Subjective experience replaced propositional truth. A practical regimen replaced a providential redemption. Psychotherapy replaced discipleship. Encounter groups replaced evangelistic teams. The don't-worry-be-happy jingle replaced the prepare-to-meet-thy-God refrain. The twelve steps replaced the One Way.

Dan thought it was far better today to be witty than to be weighty. Most folks wanted soft-sell. They wanted relevance. They wanted acceptance. They wanted an upbeat, low-key, clever, motivational, friendly, informal, yuppiefied, and abbreviated faith. No ranting. No raving. No Bible thumping. No heavy commitments. No strings attached. No muss. No fuss. They wanted the same salvation as the Old-Time Religion but with half the hassle and a third less guilt.

Thus public services had become little more than entertainment extravaganzas. Pragmatic methodology had all but displaced dogmatic theology. Christian publishing seemed to emphasize self-improvement or private diversion and only rarely concentrated on theological or biblical studies. Ministry had become a consumer-driven commodity determined by a demographic study, a niche group analysis, or a market focus survey all in an attempt to attract the baby boomer, the channel surfer, and the media-savvy unbeliever.

Dan was concerned that in their haste to present the gospel in this kind of fresh, innovative, and user-friendly fashion, contemporary Christians had come dangerously close to denying its essentials. They had made it so accessible that it was no longer biblical. Of late, he mused, evangelicals had outliberaled the liberals with self-help books, positive-thinking preaching, and success gospels. Like Atlanta, these Christians had settled for an artificial city, a substitute city: the city of man rather than the city of God.

Perhaps, Dan thought, that is why the moral practices of the average modern Christian are not discernibly different from the average modern non-Christian. It did not take a rocket scientist or a social ethicist to figure it out: It did not bode well for society when the voice of virtue was silenced by the practice of vice. What most believers do or don't do, how they act or don't act, what they want or don't want are all likely to be practically identical to what their unbelieving neighbors do, how they act, or what they want.

Instead of striving to be a peculiar people as the Bible commanded, it seemed that Christians had done their utmost to blend in. In the process of doing so, they had muted the distinctiveness of their message. Whether this was due to a seduction of

Christianity or a reduction of Christianity was of little importance to Dan. It boiled down to the fact that most people—even
those who frequented church services—appeared to be ashamed
of the gospel.

And most of them had never noticed what was going on.

The worldliness of the modern church was thus not really
a matter of hypocrisy. Instead it was something Dan thought
might be far more insidious. The great evangelical disaster, he
believed, was not so much due to the fact that people did bad
things. Hypocrisy was a perennial fact of life in this poor fallen
world. There was nothing new about the church not practicing what it preached. What was altogether new was a subtle
changing of the rules that make hypocrisy impossible.
Hypocrisy was merely a lack of virtue, but the modern church
was actually suffering from a lack of knowledge of virtue.
Christians, like other sinners, have always been susceptible to
vice, but today they no longer seemed to know what vice and
virtue were.

As THEY pulled off the freeway, Dan, Bea, and Sarah were met
with a traffic jam. There were three off-duty policemen direct-
ing traffic onto the massive campus. They were a little late, so
they had to park in the remote lot and take a shuttle bus to the
media center. The first service was just about to begin; they
could hear a drum roll and enthusiastic cheering from the
throng inside the auditorium. The three took an escalator up
to the second-level gallery and were shown to the few remaining seats by a paunchy, balding, middle-aged man sporting a
rather thin ponytail, a nose ring, hipper-than-thou duds, and a
broad, welcoming grin.

The lights had been dimmed and a slick video was under
way. It effectively and humorously appealed to the sentiments
of guilt and nostalgia in pressing home the necessity of good
communication in marriage. It was followed immediately by a

rollicking medley of choruses, carefully arranged for maximum emotional effect, and artistically rendered by the "praise
and worship team." The lyrics, which were the moral and
intellectual equivalent of nursery rhymes, were Power-Point
projected onto a network of massive flat-panel monitors sus-
pended from the acoustic baffles stretched across the ceiling
above them. A special musical presentation followed, featuring
a recording artist Dan had never heard of before, but he got
the impression that he certainly should have. Then the pastor
sat on his stool with an open-collared shirt and an easy air. He
shared "what was on his heart." It took about fifteen minutes
and was vaguely devotional. Afterward, there was more music
and then the one thing from a traditional worship service that
Dan actually recognized: the collection.

Dan was astonished. But he was as astonished at the fact
that he was astonished as he was at how shallow and silly the
service was.

Dan was certain that all the towering materialism of the
popular evangelicalism evident there that day rested on one
assumption, and it was the false assumption that substantive
spirituality can be had apart from disciplined maturity and
diligent labor. The fact was, he knew, the compromise of the
church was not so much rooted in a revolt against sexual
mores or financial scruples or gender roles or spiritual
integrity. It was instead rooted in the infantilization of the
faith. It was rooted in the dumbing-down and the easing-up of
the demands of the gospel. It was rooted in the oversimplifica-
tion and the underestimation of discipleship. It was rooted in
an aversion to work, perseverance, and holy patience. It was
rooted in a revolt against maturity.

But he was equally certain that his concern about such
things, which he could see was bordering on obsession, had
awakened in him a profound conviction. It was not so much a
conviction about churches or traditions or innovations or any

of the other external evidences of internal things. Rather it was a conviction about the gospel itself. And more, it was a conviction about Him whom the gospel heralded.

His sensibilities had been offended. But he realized that it was not so much the callousness of pop evangelicalism that had offended him; it was that he had begun to seriously consider the implications of grace for the first time in a very long time. In seeing so clearly the fallacy of this church's hollow faith, he had caught a glimpse of his own. He had been the pot calling the kettle black. He had tried to identify the moat in another's eye while suffering from a beam in his own.

He squirmed uncomfortably. He remembered that his father used to quote the renowned English preacher of the last generation, D. Martyn Lloyd Jones, remarking, "The great effect of our Lord's preaching was to make everybody feel condemned, and nobody likes that."

Certainly, Dan didn't. But for some reason, in the midst of the latitudinarianism of this church, he had come face to face with the latitudinarianism of his own hard heart. It was a terribly difficult reality for him to reckon with. But conviction always is.

Dan was reeling. He had felt so superior walking into this place. Now he was feeling the weight of glory press upon him. And every aspect of its providential pressure seemed to be an affront to all that he was and all that he did. And he was offended by that.

He considered the fact that on almost every page of the New Testament, Jesus was offending someone. When He wasn't confronting the scribes and the Pharisees, He was rebuking the promiscuous and the perverse. When He wasn't alienating the Sadducees and the Herodians, He was reproving the tax collectors and the prostitutes. He even had a knack for estranging His own disciples with His *hard sayings* and *dark parables*.

Jesus meek and mild was rarely meek or mild when it came to sin. He pulled no punches. At various times, and when the situation demanded, Jesus publicly denounced sinners as snakes, dogs, foxes, hypocrites, fouled tombs, and dirty dishes. He actually referred to one of His chief disciples as Satan. So that His hearers would not miss the point, He sometimes referred to the objects of His most intense ridicule both by name and by position and often face to face. Christ did not affirm sinners; He affirmed the repentant. Others He often addressed with the most withering invective. He did not avoid using words and tactics that His listeners found offensive. He well understood that sometimes it is wrong to be nice. He was an equal opportunity offender.

Dan was only too aware of the fact that Christ came into this world to call all humanity unto repentance. What he had never really come to grips with was the fact that as a consequence, His message stood out as an unflinching condemnation of the fallen estate of all humanity: the great and the small, the good and the bad, the weak and the strong, the rich and the poor, the wise and the foolish, the trite and the profound.

Such a message, he realized, was never intended to be popular; it was intended to be true. And that is simply not a prevailing notion. Not now. Not ever. By drenching the notion of popular modern morality in what C. S. Lewis called "a perpetual lukewarm shower bath of sentimentality," Dan had momentarily avoided its disastrous illogic—but only momentarily.

None of us want to hear that our hearts are "deceitful and wicked above all things and beyond cure." We don't want to hear that "we have all sinned and fallen short of the glory of God" or that "the wages of sin is death." We don't want to hear that our corrupt lives have resulted in a corrupt culture where the innocent are exploited, the helpless are despoiled, and the downtrodden are utterly forgotten. We don't want to hear that there are very real and tangible consequences to our sin that ultimately must be dealt with. We would much rather find a series of steps that would "enable" us, "empower" us, or help us to "recover" than hear the clear message of grace: "Repent therefore, and be converted, that your sins may be blotted out, when times of refreshing shall come from the presence of the Lord."

Dan knew only too well that everyone would have liked it if Christ had come and told the world that the way of salvation was to consider a great, noble, and wonderful teaching and then to set out and do it. Thoughts of imitating Christ always please us, because they flatter our innate pride. They tell us that if we would only use our wills we could do almost anything.

The world today in its state of trouble is very ready to listen to sharing sessions that tell it somehow or another about the application of Christian principles. No one is annoyed at them.

"What wonderful thoughts," we say. "What a wonderful conception." "How nice." "Isn't it inspiring?" But of course the message of the gospel is, "The world is as it is because you are as you are. You are in trouble and confusion because you are not honoring God. You are rebelling against Him because of your self-will, your arrogance, and your pride. You are reaping what you have sown."

We naturally dislike that, and yet it is always the message of Christ. He called upon men and women to repent, to acknowledge their sin with shame, and to turn back to God in Him. But the message of repentance always has been and still is a cause of offense.

And Dan realized that offense is easy enough to give. All we have to do is to say what the Bible says. All we have to teach is what the Bible teaches. We wouldn't need to launch a crusade or provoke a revolution. We need not lower ourselves to rudeness, crudeness, or a lack of sophistication. The Bible is enough—*sola scriptura*—to send the purveyors of politically correct bibblebabble and multicultural willywonkism into absolute conniptions.

As these thoughts trundled through his mind, he was sundered, heart and soul and strength. He was wrenched from his high-horse critique of the hellishness of American culture by a sudden recollection that hellishness is only recognizable because there actually is a hell.

Amazingly, it was the stridency of his negative critique of the People's Community Fellowship that forced Dan to apply the same fierce analysis to his own recalcitrance. He had been living as if a comprehension of such intellectual precepts were enough. And so he fell under the bar of his own calculating judgment.

Tears slowly welled up in Dan's eyes. Bea looked over in surprise. She had fully expected him to lambaste the service. Even she was taken aback by how awful it was. Instead, he was clearly stricken. She smiled and tenderly touched the back of his hand.

"It appears that Pogo was right," he whispered to her. "We have met the enemy and he is us."

Individualism at first, only saps the virtues
Of public life; but in the long run
It attacks and destroys all others
And is at length absorbed into selfishness.

Alexis de Tocqueville

BILOXI
POPULATION 46,319

THEY HAD HARDLY EXPECTED to find the little Gulf Coast town in Mississippi between Mobile and New Orleans in such an uproar. There were any number of reasons why they had settled on Biloxi as their last stop before they headed into Tennessee, but chief among them was the notion that it would be quiet and restful. They were wrong about that.

Dan and Bea had imagined Biloxi to be a bucolic setting of antebellum charm, elegant Victorian grace, and enchanting Southern hospitality. They thought it would be a sleepy, serene, and soothing parenthesis between the aggressive ambitions of Atlanta and the nascent narcissism of Nashville. It was anything but that.

They were immediately confronted with floats, costumes, beads, moon pies, wild revelers in the streets.

"What is this?" Bea asked.

"I'm not really sure."

"It looks like some kind of street party or something."

"I guess it could be Mardi Gras."

"Mardi Gras? I thought that was supposed to be in New Orleans. What is it doing here?"

"I don't know."

"You don't know?"

"No. I know that Mardi Gras is a day, so it isn't necessarily tied to a single place."

"Didn't they say anything about this when you made reservations at the bed-and-breakfast?"

"No. I guess they figured we knew about it."

"How could we possibly know about it? This is the kind of thing that belongs in the French Quarter, not here on the beach. Not on the Gulf Coast of Mississippi, for heaven's sake."

"I guess that's just your opinion. I would have to agree, of course. But unfortunately, it looks as if all these people would tend to disagree with us both. And rather vehemently at that."

"I should say so."

They steered their car through the crowds along the beachfront highway.

"This is déjà vu all over again," Dan muttered. "Just like that awful protest up in Vermont."

"Don't remind me."

"But surely this can't be as bad as that. After all, Mardi Gras is a party, not a protest."

"Well, that's the theory anyway."

THE HISTORICAL origins of Mardi Gras are much debated, but many of its traditions seem to have their roots in early Celtic Christian rituals in ancient Gaul, Ireland, and Scotland, which, in turn, seem to have even earlier Greek and Egyptian antecedents.

Mardi Gras, or Fat Tuesday, is a celebration of life's excesses before the austere self-sacrifices of the Christian season of Lent. It receives its name from the tradition of slaughtering and feasting upon a fattened calf on the last day of the Winter Carnival that follows the Twelfth Night, or Epiphany.

Lent begins on Ash Wednesday, forty days before Easter, and includes a much more proscribed lifestyle for faithful Christian families—traditionally a season of severe fasting and asceticism. The day prior to Ash Wednesday is thus the final hurrah, and excesses frowned upon at any other time of the year are actually embraced and exulted.

The ancient Mardi Gras tradition was first brought to the New World by the French, and it became a vital component of the culture established by the early settlers along the Gulf Coast. Although it is most often associated with the city of New Orleans, all throughout the region, festive carousers celebrate during the two weeks before the beginning of Lent with parades, balls, masquerades, street dances, concerts, amusements, jocularity, and merry banquets.

On April 9, 1682, French explorer Robert Cavelier, Sieur de la Salle, claimed the region from the mouth of the Mississippi to Pensacola Bay in the name of Louis XIV of France. Spanish explorers had already discovered the region, but they abandoned it when they failed to discover gold.

La Salle attempted to return to the region two years later, but ended up in Texas instead. He spent the next two years searching for his discovery—a search that ended when his men murdered him.

War prevented France from continuing its colonization efforts until 1697. Louis XIV then commissioned a Canadian, Pierre le Moyne, Sieur D'Iberville, to secure a colony and French interests in the region. Iberville's flotilla finally landed in February on Ship Island, twelve miles off the Mississippi Gulf Coast, and established a headquarters on the site of present-day Ocean Springs. The following spring, he built a fort near present-day Phoenix, Louisiana—the first permanent French colony on the Gulf Coast.

But ongoing wars and other concerns kept the attentions of Louis away from the New World. When he died in 1715, he was succeeded by his five-year-old great-grandson in name and in practice by Philippe, duke of Orleans, who served as regent for the young king. One of the regent's friends was John Law, who devised a get-rich-quick strategy of promoting Louisiana's riches. The scheme virtually bankrupted France, but not before the dramatic expansion of the colony and the foundings of New Orleans, Biloxi, Mobile, and Pensacola in the spring of 1718.

Progress in the new towns was slow, but Mardi Gras festivities are believed to have begun in their earliest days. It provided the colonists with a sense of cultural cohesion and identity. Indeed, it seemed that early on the Mardi Gras of the colonies took on a character and a flavor it had never had in France.

In 1760 France lost its Canadian colonies to Britain. Disheartened by their failures in the New World, for its lands in Louisiana had never shown a profit and had been plagued with troubles, Louis XV and his ministers decided to focus their attention on the French colonies in the West Indies. Even though thousands of French Canadians were exiled to the region by the British, in 1762 France signed the secret Treaty of Fountainbleau, granting New Orleans, Biloxi, Mobile, Pensacola, and much of the rest of Louisiana to Louis XV's cousin, Carlos III of Spain.

Spain's control had an immediate effect on the Mardi Gras festivities that were presumably as old as the colonies themselves. Although Spain, like France, was also rooted in a Celtic Christian tradition, the influence of the church was far stricter than that in much of the rest of Europe. Parties and street dancing were immediately banned. Even so, and despite nine months of open rebellion in 1768, under Spanish rule, many local traditions were allowed to remain, and New Orleans actually thrived rather than merely survived as it had under French control.

Napoleon Bonaparte's ascension to first consul of France marked the decline of Spanish influence in the region, now known as the Western Floridas. After consolidating his strength in Europe, Napoleon turned his eyes overseas and pressured Spain to return the Gulf Coast colonies along with the rest of Louisiana to France. New Orleans, Biloxi, Mobile, and the rest of the Florida parishes came under French colonial rule according to the Treaty of San Ildefonso in October 1800. But U.S. President Thomas Jefferson viewed French control as a threat to America's ability to conduct unhindered trade. Rather than marching to war, as some members of Congress suggested, he sent secretary of state James Madison to France to offer to buy the territories.

Napoleon had concluded even before Madison reached France that he could not hold the colonies and that it would be in his best interest to sell it to the United States. Negotiations took about two weeks, and the territories extending from New Orleans to the Canadian border were sold for $15 million in 1803.

Specifically exempt from the sale was the land east of the Mississippi. After only a year or so of French rule, it too became independent and autonomous. Eventually, the settlers formed an independent nation extending from the Mississippi in the west to Pensacola Bay in the east and stretching as far north as present-day Montgomery, Alabama. The founders of this Gulf Coast state called the fledgling nation the Republic of West Florida and established a capital at Baton Rouge. President Jefferson's near relative Fulwar Skipwith was elected president shortly afterward. Skipwith encouraged the adoption of the Bonnie Blue Flag, the old Celtic symbol of covenantal freedom, as the nation's official banner.

Independence brought prosperity, liberty, and a return to open Mardi Gras celebrations. Public dancing and celebrating were allowed to return. Although costumes were worn for both, Mardi Gras was never confused with Halloween, another Celtic Christian celebration. Gore and mayhem were perhaps tolerated for All Hallow's Eve, but during Mardi Gras, it was glamour that was de rigueur. Feathers, beads, glitter, spangles, formal attire, tuxedos, ball gowns, and boas became vital aspects of the jubilant tradition.

In 1810 the independence of West Florida was brought to an untimely and ignominious end when U.S. President James Madison ordered a detachment of cavalry under the command of Gen. William Claiborne to conquer the territory for the United States.

Legislators were marched out of the capitol building at bayonet point and forced to pledge allegiance to the federal United States and its governmental emissaries. The Bonnie Blue Flag was torn down and replaced by the Stars and Stripes. Despite the imposition of such blatant imperial tyranny, the region continued to prosper, and Mardi Gras remained a hallmark of the distinctive region.

Such history hangs upon Biloxi like the Spanish moss that drapes her live oaks. Over the course of the past three centuries, the town, which is named after an Indian word meaning "first people," has served under seven flags: the French Fleur de Lis, the Golden Spanish Imperium, the Bonnie Blue of the Republic of West Florida, the Great Mississippi Magnolia, the Stars and Bars of the Confederate States of America, the Star Spangled Banner of the United States, and briefly, during the War of 1812, the British Union Jack. But it is under the banner of Krewe Rex, regent of the Mardi Gras celebration, that it seems most at home.

But Dan and Bea certainly did not feel at home under it. If they were looking for peace and quiet, deserted beaches to walk along at night, and sparsely populated seafood restaurants to enjoy, they had come to the right place at the wrong time.

DAN HAD planned to visit Beauvoir, the last home of Jefferson Davis, president of the Confederacy. The beautiful old estate facing the Gulf had been transformed into a museum of the Confederacy. Next door was a well-equipped library dedicated to the study of Southern historical, cultural, and literary concerns. And in the neighborhood immediately adjacent, there were several interesting antiquarian shops specializing in the memorabilia and books of the Lost Cause. But the crowds made him doubt that the visit would be possible. He suggested that they make a quick escape as they had done in Montpelier.

"You know, I'm too tired to drive any more," Bea said. "Let's just check into the bed-and-breakfast, hole up in our room for a couple of days, and read, write, and relax. Surely this revelry will be over by tomorrow."

"It's going to be tough to find a restaurant we can get into tonight though."

"So what? So far on this trip, we've eaten enough to last us for a year. Why don't we just stop by a grocery store and pick up some fruits and cheeses, a couple of loaves of French bread, and maybe some sausage? Then we wouldn't even have to emerge from our room all night."

Dan, who was beginning to get a little road weary himself, agreed. "All right, it's a deal. Let's wait out this storm of partying." But that was easier said than done.

Apparently the centerpiece of this year's Mardi Gras celebration in Biloxi was a special presentation of the World Wrestling Federation's "Nitro Night." It was to be held that evening at one of the massive gambling casinos that now lined the beach on the east side of town.

DAN AND Bea were only vaguely familiar with the WWF phenomenon. It seemed to be an omnipresent fixture of cable television programming so it was difficult to avoid awareness of it altogether. But they were about to get a quick education. It seemed that most of the stars were staying in the same bed-and-breakfast they were.

The WWF began in 1982 when Vince McMahon bought his father's wrestling company, Capitol Promotions, and set out to realize the vision known today as the World Wrestling Federation. Like other professional wrestling operations of the time, Capitol was a regional enterprise in the Northeast. But McMahon's innovative combination of arena sports and rock-'n'-roll style entertainment helped to give the WWF a much broader audience than before.

By the early nineties, McMahon had successfully enlisted a number of outrageous performers to make his events as brash and as crass as anything ever staged for a live audience. The biggest female attraction was Sable, a scantily clad femme fatale who body-slammed opponents, trash-talked announcers, publicly seduced referees, and flaunted brazen sexuality in and out of the ring. The biggest male attraction was Stone Cold Steve Austin, a hulk of a man who specialized in obscene gestures, blasphemous taunts, and bloodcurdling violence. They were joined by such performers as The Undertaker, XTC, and Demon Dan Do-Wrong.

Over the past few years the WWF had become a recognized leader in what McMahon liked to call "whoop-ass" sports entertainment, attracting half a billion global viewers each week in addition to enormous live and pay-per-view event success. It had become a multimillion-dollar enterprise. At the time of their Biloxi Mardi Gras extravaganza, eight of the top twelve rated cable broadcasts in the nation belonged to the WWF.

BEA KNEW something was up when she went to fill an ice bucket from a machine down in the lobby and saw wildly dressed, tattoo-covered, multiply pierced, and overmuscled men and their silky, busty, and sultry molls checking in. She thought that they might be Mardi Gras revelers or perhaps circus performers. But then on her way back down the hall she noticed a poster advertising the show later that night on a community events bulletin board.

Back in the room, Dan was on the verge of falling asleep in a wing-back chair by the window. He had a book open on his lap and Elvis curled up at his feet. A scented candle set on the barley twist table beside him subtly sweetened the air with a hint of citrus. The place looked almost too cozy and comfortable.

"Dan, we've got to get out of here."

"What?" He started, eyes widening.

"I've decided I don't want to stay."

"Why? What's going on?"

"This place gives me the heebie-jeebies."

"What on earth are you talking about?"

"You know that feeling you had in New York? Well, I just have a funny feeling that our quiet little refuge from the raucous crowds of Mardi Gras is about to become as much of a zoo as the rest of Biloxi."

"Huh?"

She explained to him what she had seen. It was not so much that she thought that the wrestlers themselves would cause a ruckus as that their fans and groupies might if word were to get out that they were staying here.

Dan tried to allay her fears. Funny feeling or not, he did not relish the thought of loading everything back into Virgil and hitting the road. He was just beginning to relax.

But Bea would have none of it. She was clearly distressed at the thought of having their quiet repose invaded by the WWF, its Mardi Gras–mad fans, or anyone else. "*Masque of the Red Death!*" she said.

"What?"

"*Masque of the Red Death.* Don't you remember?"

"What are you talking about?"

"*Masque of the Red Death.* Don't you remember?"

"The short story by Edgar Allan Poe?"

"Yes. That's the one."

"Yes, I remember it. What about it? What does it have to do with Mardi Gras and the WWF and your current sense of panic?"

"I'm not panicked. I just don't want to get caught up in a furor tonight. And I especially don't want to get caught up in a furor with wrestlers."

"All right. And what does this have to do with *Masque of the Red Death*?"

"In the story, a rich and powerful prince, Prospero, gathers all of his friends inside his palace for a masquerade ball. Outside the palace, a terrible plague rages through the populace. Inside all is well."

"And your point is?"

"Don't you see? Everyone inside the elegant imperial suites felt safe and secure. Little did they know that the instrument of their demise was disguised and stalking each of them in the midst of the merrymaking."

"Come on! Aren't you being just a little melodramatic?"

"There were all kinds of ominous warnings. But they were heedless in their frolic. There was the solemn tolling of the great ebony clock. There was the progression of color within the palace itself, from blue cobalt to black velvet. And we've had warnings too: Cooperstown, Montpelier, and New York. Each progressively more intense. You're the one who's been sensing this *thing* following us."

"Bea, you're driving me nuts. What are you saying?"

"I'm saying, I'm scared. I don't want to be under siege all night here. Wouldn't it be better just to hop in the car and drive to Jackson or Memphis or someplace?"

"You went into all that Poe stuff just to say that?"

"Well, I've been rereading Poe and the imagery just came to mind."

"Sometimes you scare me," he stood up and hugged her.

"You're trying to change the subject. I don't want to change the subject. Come on, Dan, really. Let's just leave."

"I'll tell you what, why don't we walk down the street and check out the shops we saw when we came in? It looked like they might have some really interesting books and other Civil War memorabilia."

"Pray tell, how does going shopping help the situation in this hotel? In this town?"

"Well, it doesn't exactly. But it does give us a little time to assess the situation."

"I really think we ought to just leave."

"And then if we decide after a nice leisurely late afternoon out that we really do need to leave, at the very least we will have had the chance to do something we like to do here."

Bea was unconvinced, but she relented nonetheless.

They walked around the corner and down the block where there were several antique stores and a couple of bookshops. In the first one, Bea found a fascinating biography of the adopted son of Jefferson Davis. He was an orphaned slave who was taken into the first family of the Confederacy. Bea was absolutely fascinated by the story, so much so that she almost forgot her discomfiting tension concerning the wild and woolly wrestlers.

BOOKS WERE a soothing salve for her soul, as Dan knew only too well when he dragged her down here. They were a kind of balm for her frazzled sensibilities. They were a ground of sanity in an all-too-often-insane world. It was probably a therapy that most of the Mardi Gras revelers roaming the streets of Biloxi would have not comprehended.

Long before the bane of television and its raucous entertainment spinoffs had invaded every waking moment, it was clear that while most people in modern industrial cultures were at least marginally *able* to read, they chose not to read.

The majority, although they are sometimes frequent readers, do not place much emphasis or importance upon reading. They turn to it only as a desperate last resource when there is simply nothing better to do. Then they abandon it with alacrity as soon as an alternative turns up. Reading is reserved for long waits at the doctor's office, tedious journeys through airports, nonambulatory illnesses, odd moments of enforced solitude, or for the process barbarously called *reading oneself to sleep*. They sometimes combine it with desultory conversation; often while listening to music and sometimes while watching television.

But bibliophiles—inveterate book people like Bea—are always looking for leisure and silence in which to read, and to do so with their whole attention. When they are denied such attentive and undisturbed reading for even a few days, they are left with the feeling of impoverishment. It is as if they had been denied physical nourishment.

Of course, there is a profound puzzlement on the part of the mass of the citizenry over the tastes and habits of the literate. It is fairly obvious that most people, if they spoke objectively and articulately, would not accuse bookish people of liking the wrong books, but of making such a fuss about any book at all. They would find it odd that readers could treat as a main ingredient in their well-being something that to most is marginal at best.

A recognition of this truth was not to imply any hint of moral turpitude on the part of modern bohemianism, rather it was simply an affirmation of the reality of the gaping chasm that exists between those who don't read and those who do, between the popular "many" and the peculiar "few," between the bibliophobes and the bibliophiles, between the Mardi Gras revelers and Bea.

That is not to say that nonreaders aspire to be nonreaders. Indeed, most folks would probably like to be well-read. They may even romanticize about becoming readers in the coming year in the same way that they romanticize about the washboard abs they would acquire if only they could be more consistent with their workouts at the local health club.

And there's the rub. Most folks today want to *have* their cake and *eat* it too; a prospect as improbable as a plausible *X-Files* plot coming out of Hollywood or a good piece of legislation coming out of Washington.

The problem with serious reading is part and parcel with virtually all the other problems of modernity: serious reading is often laborious work requiring unflinching discipline. If there is anything that contemporary Americans have an aversion to, it is disciplined work. In this odd to-whom-it-may-concern, instant-everything day of microwavable meals, prefab buildings, drive-through windows, no-wait credit approvals, and predigested formula entertainment, people tend to want to reduce everything to the level of the least common denominator and the fastest turnaround, which seems to be getting lower and lower, faster and faster with every passing day. In a world where Federal Express is too slow, where even faxes and e-mail have given way to instant messaging, paging, and call interruption, it is hardly a wonder that some people are impatient with the inherent inefficiencies of books.

As Dan and Bea realized anew while they were in Atlanta, even the church has fallen prey to this "spirit of the times." If most people really had their druthers, they wouldn't want worship to be too terribly demanding. They wouldn't want doctrine that challenged their pet notions. They want music that they are comfortable with. They want preaching that reassures them, that reinforces their peculiar preferences, that affords them a sense of serenity. And they want these things in record time. They want *quick* change, *cheap* grace, inspirational platitudes, bumper-sticker theology, and *easy* faith. They want Christianity Lite. They want the Nice News not necessarily the Good News.

For the same reasons, when the vast majority of people read anything, they prefer literary junk food. The predigested factoids of *USA Today* are much easier to swallow than Augustine's *De Civitate Dei*. John Grisham, Danielle Steele, and Tom Clancy are easier to digest than William Shakespeare, John Milton, and Dante Alighieri. Reading is a sober discipline, and all discipline is difficult. It requires work, diligence, concentration, practice, and maturity.

But that is the way it is with anything worthwhile. The best things in life invariably cost something. People have to sacrifice to attain them, to achieve them, to keep them, and to enjoy them.

That is one of the most important lessons anyone can learn in life. It is the message that most parents realize that they ought to instill in their children: Patience, commitment, diligence, constancy, and discipline will ultimately pay off if their children are just willing to defer gratification long enough for the seeds they have sown to sprout and bear fruit.

A flippant, shallow, and imprecise approach to anything—sports, academics, the trades, business, or marriage—is ultimately self-defeating. Instant gratification is not likely to satisfy any appetite, at least not for long.

But even if discipline were not an impassable obstacle on the pathway toward the literary life, most people wouldn't know where to start reading. And even if they had the least inkling of where they would like to start, hurdles galore are thrown across their path.

Dan and Bea knew this only too well. One day the previous spring, Dan stumbled across a recent paperback edition of one of John Buchan's classic series of spy novels set in Scotland during the First World War. It was published by a company he had never heard of before. He quickly discovered that no one else had heard of it either, including the bookstore that sold him the book in the first place. And of course, it was not listed in *Books in Print*. It took him more than a month of intensive detective work on the Internet, through connections at work, and on the phone long-distance to track down a source for the other volumes in the series.

Yet again he was reminded that, like the search of Demosthenes for the ideal honest syllable or the search of Diogenes for the ideal honest man, good books are notoriously hard to find. Although tens of thousands of volumes are churned out every year by the vast publishing industry, only a handful of titles are actually worth reading. And more often than not, they seem to be hidden like needles in a haystack.

Bea knew that she had found a prize in the little biography she held in her hands. There was a special pleasure in that; a pleasure she might have had a difficult time explaining to a WWF aficionado, but one that was palpable nonetheless.

Dan too had found a prize: a volume analyzing the political repercussions of the *Emancipation Proclamation* by George Washington Carver, the great Southern educator, scientist, and inventor. Dan had always known that despite the fact that much of the conflict between the North and the South in the years leading up to the Civil War revolved around the slavery issue, the North never adopted an abolitionist stance during the lifetime of Abraham Lincoln. In his first inaugural speech the great president admitted that in his view, the freeing of the slaves was not only inexpedient and impolitic but perhaps even unconstitutional as well.

What Dan didn't know was that to reinforce Lincoln's position, he allowed several of the states that remained in the Union to maintain slavery throughout the ensuing war, including Missouri, Maryland, Delaware, West Virginia, East Tennessee, and Kentucky. When the administration finally aced on the issue of slavery on January 1, 1863, it did not free any slaves within the jurisdiction of its governmental authority. Thus, Carver's book argued, the *Emancipation* was essentially

symbolic, designed to placate certain elements within the abolitionist constituency of the Republican Party and to provide
certain strategic wartime advantages, but not to actually free
any slaves under the Union's jurisdiction or authority. Nevertheless, the decree did lay the groundwork for freeing the
slaves, which came with the ratification of the Thirteenth,
Fourteenth, and Fifteenth Amendments to the Constitution.

The whole notion appeared at first glance to be so, well,
so redneck. But as Dan read the *Proclamation* itself and a few
pages of Carver's commentary, the complexity of the time, of
the issue, and of the war came into high relief for him. It was
always amazing to Dan what could be discovered and what
popular myths could be exploded if only people availed themselves of books.

By the time the Gylberds had perused each of the little
bookshops and antique stores, the sun was setting over the
Gulf. Dan and Bea walked back toward their hotel hand in
hand, their tensions altogether soothed. A cool breeze rustled
the Spanish moss above their heads. And the cacophony of
Mardi Gras was little more than a distant murmur.

Even in the midst of a hellish milieu of distraction and
diversion, solace may well be had for the resourceful.

BOOK 3

HOME

Silent, apart, companionless we went,
One going before and one behind,
Like Friars Minor on a journey bent.

And Aesop's fable came into my mind
As I was pondering on the late affray:
I meant the frog-and-mouse one; for you'll find

That if with attentive mind you lay
Their heads and tails together, the two things
Are just as much alike as Yes and Yea.

And, as one fancy from another springs
Sometimes, this started a new train of thought
Which doubled my first fears and flutterings.

Dante Alighieri

Gradually he mustered force
To put the sin at a distance.
And at last his eyes seemed to open to some new
      ways.
He found that he could look back upon the blast and
      bombast
Of his earlier gospels and see them truly.
He was gleeful when he discovered that he now
      despised them.
With this conviction came a store of assurance.
He felt a quiet manhood,
Nonassertive but of sturdy and strong blood.

                       Stephen Crane

NASHVILLE
POPULATION 487,969

Nashville is known the world over as Music City. While the metropolitan area boasts a diverse business and fiscal profile ranging from high-tech companies to heavy industrial manufacturers, from health-care management firms to aerospace engineering corporations, the omnipresent music and entertainment industry is an inescapable aspect of the city's identity. And these days that means it both enjoys an economic boon and suffers a cultural blight.

The great Scottish literary historian, Thomas Carlyle, once said, "Sing me the songs of a generation and I'll tell you the soul of the times." But most Americans would have a hard time taking Carlyle up on his proposition.

As Bea was wont to point out, much of popular contemporary American music is simply not singable anymore. Not only is it often without recognizable tune, pitch, cadence, or tenor—and sometimes even without melody, harmony, or regular rhythm—it is often so profane as to be unrepeatable.

Popular music has almost always been sentimental, sappy, and insubstantial. In the forties it tended to be romantic. In the fifties it was silly. In the sixties it was psychedelic. In the seventies it was carnal. In the eighties it was sensual. But in the nineties it became downright nightmarishly dystopian.

Rock music was, of course, the worst. With the advent of grunge rock, neo-punk, industrial rock, hip hop, goth rock, death metal, gangsta rap, rage rock, metal frenzy, rave rock, and speed metal, a new wave of wildly angry music with minimal melody lines or hooks, harsh and distorted electronics, incessant syncopations, and vile lyrics had swept onto center stage. Many rap and rock songs had gone far beyond the mere bounds of profanity to vile brutality, scatological filth, sadistic nihilism, blasphemous irreverence, and provocative decadence.

Country music, the pride of Nashville, while avoiding many of the discordant excesses of rock, had begun to perpetuate the noisome vision of a valueless culture gone awry. Steeped in a rather hopeless world-view of self-absorption, self-gratification, and self-consumption, the music tended to be depressing, dark, and deleterious, even in its most boisterous party-hearty mode. Its gleeful promotion of an ambivalent and irreverent lifestyle, its acceptance of a morally neutral and devil-may-care world-view, and its slavish adherence to a slovenly hip fashion sense was nearly as dire as anything in the world of rock 'n' roll. Garth Brooks had simply reinvented Led Zeppelin with a Stetson and a healthy dose of twang.

Even contemporary Christian music, also anchored in the Nashville area, was at the crossroads of a cultural crisis. Dan recalled an old *Seinfeld* episode that drove home that truth only too clearly. As Elaine Benes pulled into traffic, she turned on her new boyfriend's car radio and began bouncing along to the music. But then the lyrics sank in: "Jesus is one, Jesus is all. Jesus pick me up when I fall." Her eyes widened in horror. Suddenly frantic, she started punching one button after another on the dashboard console. "Jesus," she cursed ironically, discovering they all were set to Christian stations. Following the trademark bass riff, the scene shifted to the sitcom's typical diner chat. "I like Christian rock," said the ultracynical George Costanza. "It's very positive. It's not like those real musicians who think they're so cool and hip."

Dan chuckled as he remembered how the sitcom lords of Must See TV stuck in the knife and gave it a cynical, sinister twist. Contemporary Christian music, or CCM as it was often called in the industry, was "positive," not "cool" or "hip." It was nice, meek, and safe. After all, it wasn't performed by "real" musicians.

The *New York Times* had commented sometime afterward that CCM was simply "mediocre stuff, diluted by hesitation and dogmatic formula, inferior to the mainstream popular music it emulates." Since the gospel was comprised of truths that were literally larger than life, even such luminaries as Charlie Peacock—a respected author, producer, and performer with two decades of experience in both the mainstream rock and the CCM markets—had to wonder aloud why Christian music was smaller than life.

CCM was diverse. Its practitioners performed everything from classical to jazz, from pop to edgy rock. It was successful, having become a multimillion-dollar-a-year business. But by most counts it remained rather insignificant either because it had compromised itself by mimicking the standards of mainstream music or because it remained sloppy, tawdry, and unprofessional within a market niche ghetto of its own making. Whatever the case, even with the best of intentions, CCM was unable or unwilling to ameliorate the awful effects of music's modern downgrade.

Across the board, the music industry had somehow reduced humanity's greatest achievement—a near universal language of pure transcendence—into a knuckle-dragging subpidgin of wails, snarls, whines, moans, mewls, snivels, and whimpers capable of fully expressing only the more carnal forms of rapaciousness, egotism, libido, and concupiscence as well as the more cathartic forms of individualism, materialism, lasciviousness, and cupidity. In essence what the industry had accomplished was to brainwash the children of America to depreciate their legacy, to subvert their culture, to undermine their mores, to contravene beauty, to abandon significance, to despise authority, to slight substance, and ultimately to abuse each other.

DAN'S BROTHER, Tristan, had moved to Nashville more than a decade earlier to work in the recording business. Although he was able to carve out success as a session musician and songwriter, in the last few years he had devoted himself less and less to his musical career and more and more to Rivendell Academy, a fledgling private high school he had helped to get started in the area.

With the utter failure of most modern educational methodologies finally evident to all but the most hardened bureaucrat, the serious academic rigor, tutorial discipling, and familial involvement of the past were once again in vogue. In a little suburban community just south of the city, Tristan had gathered together a group of homeschooling parents who wanted to try to recover for their children the full spiritual, academic, and cultural inheritance of long-lost Christendom—no easy feat, to be sure. Through a rather haphazard process of trial and error, they began adopting the traditional elements of both classical modalities and covenantal methodologies to their little community effort of identifying, raising up, encouraging, and equipping the next generation of leaders. In short order, they found themselves on the cutting edge of a remarkable new grassroots movement.

It quickly became apparent to everyone connected with it that this movement was hungry for a rediscovery of the legacy of truth that had given rise to the remarkable flowering of beauty, progress, and freedom in the West. Curriculums would be needed. New co-ops would have to be established. Networks of communication and support would need to be put into place. Training would have to be provided. Resources would need to be made available.

It was all a bit much for Tristan. Like Dan, he had long rebelled against the undue pressures and expectations of being his father's son. But unlike Dan, in the last few years of his father's life, Tristan had become reconciled with both his father and the inheritance of faith and vision he had left behind. Now Tristan found himself walking in his father's footsteps in ways he could never have imagined just a few years before.

Now classical education was the "next new thing." It was the latest rage at curriculum fairs, academic conferences, and professional conventions. In fact though, it was anything but "new," as Tristan was quick to point out. Indeed, he had learned its most essential principles from his father, but beyond that, classical education was the age-old foundation upon which the entire Western academic tradition had been built. The carelessly discarded traditional medieval trivium, emphasizing the basic classical scholastic categories of grammar, logic, and rhetoric, had equipped generations of students with the tools for a lifetime of learning: a working knowledge of the timetables of history, a background understanding of the great literary classics, a structural competency in Greek- and Latin-based grammars, a familiarity with the sweep of art, music, and ideas, a grasp of research and writing skills, a world-view comprehension for mathematical and scientific basics, a principle approach to current events, and an emphasis on a Christian life paradigm.

Recognizing that all true education was the undertaking of mental and spiritual discipleship, covenantal learning—centered in intimate interpersonal, tutorial, and familial relationships—reinforced both the authority and the responsibility of parents in the process of training their children. After all, true education never was not an object, a product, or an outcome. It was the fruit of diligence and faithfulness in rightly related individuals.

This revival of classical education was clearly an approach that involved a good deal of hard work, as did practically anything and everything worthwhile, but it was not a system of education for intellectuals only. Rather, Tristan claimed, classical education was a simple affirmation that all students need to be grounded in the good things, the great things, and the true things.

Dan didn't really understand it all. But like Tristan, the older he got, the more attractive he found his father's legacy of art, music, literature, ideas, faith, substance, and vision. So he wanted to visit. He wanted to see Tristan's work. He wanted to experience his father's world, albeit in a new incarnation and a new generation.

DRIVING NORTH through Mississippi, Dan and Bea passed through Memphis before heading to Nashville. They stopped for lunch at the famous Rendezvous restaurant in the heart of downtown for a taste of spicy dry-rubbed ribs. It was quickly evident that while the blues clubs along Beale Street and the trinket shops near the Elvis shrine at Graceland remained vital aspects of the Memphis social climate, barbecue is one of the city's greatest assets.

The Gylberds didn't want to stay long in town, but they couldn't pass up the opportunity to get a picture of Elvis the dog standing in front of the home of Elvis the king. They found that Graceland was surprisingly small and unpretentious and at the same time predictably ostentatious.

"It reminds me a little bit of a mobile home on steroids," Dan commented as they were driving away.

About an hour and a half outside Memphis, they stopped in Jackson. Bea wanted to visit Casey Jones Village, a restaurant, hotel, and entertainment complex built on the site of the famous railroad engineer's home. It was comfortingly kitschy and the country cooking buffet was a delightful feast.

Through the rolling hills of Middle Tennessee, they finally ascended the Cumberland Plateau and entered Nashville. They were rather astonished to discover that the city had become a boomtown. Its forward-thinking leadership had long attempted to shed the city's image as little more than the capital of country music and home of the Grand Ole Opry. The once decaying downtown was now bustling with renewal efforts. A new football stadium, a vast new art museum, a new downtown library, a sprawling new public park, and a new indoor hockey and basketball arena were all either already open for business or under construction. With new NFL and NHL franchises and an attractive convention venue, the city was becoming a destination of choice for more than just die-hard Willie Nelson and Dolly Parton fans. A vibrant restaurant and shopping district had revitalized the riverfront, once a tawdry example of urban blight. And high-tech businesses with flashy corporate headquarters were moving in at a record pace, attracted by tax incentives.

The music and media industries were investing huge sums in the city's infrastructure as many companies decided to leave Los Angeles for more hospitable cultures and climes. Several fine universities and colleges, a massive medical research-and-training complex, an easily accessed world-class airport, and stunning natural beauty all made Nashville an attractive site for relocation. It had become an entrepreneurial hub for a myriad of graphic design, printing, publishing, video production, digital information systems, and telecommunications businesses. As a result, the small-town hospitality of the Old South was married to the hip progressivism of the corporate, academic, artistic, and entertainment worlds, which made an invigorating and inviting combination.

TRISTAN HAD a little piece of land south of town where he had been slowly building a small country homestead. Tucked away in the rolling farmland, it was picture-post-card beautiful. Set snug into the hugging hills, he had taken an old grain silo and refurbished it as a four-story home. Framed in rough barn timbers on the inside, the stone structure afforded him a kind of Celtic poet's tower, much like that of his hero William Butler Yeats.

The first floor combined an open commercial kitchen with a sitting area that opened into a greenhouse and conservatory. The second floor contained Tristan's vast library, much of it inherited from his father, but greatly enhanced by his own additions. The third floor was divided into three bedrooms, and the fourth floor was a music gallery and studio. All together there were less than two thousand square feet of living space in the house, but its twelve-foot ceilings and open design made it seem much larger.

The silo was surrounded by several carefully situated outbuildings, barns, pens, and gardens. And the homestead was crisscrossed by a series of fences, walls, pathways, and hedgerows.

As DAN and Bea drove up, a thin wisp of wood smoke rose from the chimney. A kind of indescribable glow radiated from the scene with all the deep inglenooks of memory and of home.

Dan was almost immediately transported back to his childhood. He was overwhelmed by a sense of joy. And that surprised him. "I don't know quite what I was expecting," he told Bea. "But it sure wasn't this. Somehow, I thought that it would probably be—"

"Sadder?"

"Yes. I suppose. I thought that it would be sadder."

Tristan had lost his wife, Lois, to cancer a few years earlier, back when the two of them were fixtures in the Texas folk music scene. They had never been able to have children, so their music became a way of life for them. Although they kept a small garage apartment in the Montrose arts district of Houston, they were rarely there.

Instead, Lois made a home for them on the road. She had a knack for making Tristan feel settled and rooted wherever they were. Their rumbling little camper was always adorned with wildflowers: bluebonnets and Indian paintbrushes in the spring, black-eyed Susans and Queen Anne's lace in the summer, chrysanthemums and marigolds in the fall, and pots of African violets and orchids in the winter. Their little foldout table was always elegantly draped with a fresh lace tablecloth and romantically lit by candles. And their constant companionship was suffused with an indescribable tenderness and joy.

After a rich decade of marriage, Lois was struck down by a virulent tumor in her liver. One week after they had played a gig at the big Texas renaissance festival in October—they had always fancied themselves as jongleurs and troubadours, so they relished the opportunity to play there—she began complaining of constant fatigue and an ache in her abdomen. The doctors initiated immediate treatments, but as is so often the case, the malignancy proved to be inoperable. And there was little they could do to stop the rapid growth of the feral cells. By Christmas she was gone.

Tristan was utterly lost without her. Although Dan tried to find a way to comfort him, he seemed utterly inconsolable.

At first, he just holed up in the little apartment. For weeks he did little more than subsist, wracked by grief, wearied by loneliness, and worn by restlessness. He couldn't sleep, and he couldn't stand to be awake. Dan despaired of ever seeing him return to even a modicum of normalcy.

But then, just before Easter, he began to read searchingly and substantively. For several months he resolved to read through the classics of what traditional educators have called the Western Canon. He read and read and read. He read widely. He read seriously. He found that the books afforded not only solace for the heartache of his unimaginable loss but vision for his unfathomable future. In the process, his faith was restored, his hope was revitalized, and his love was rejuvenated.

He enrolled in a graduate program at the University of Houston. Although he found most of the classwork rather pedestrian, he loved the academic environment. He picked up a dual doctorate in literature and philosophy in record time.

Tristan came to Nashville shortly afterward as a studio player, orchestrator, and sideman. He had always been fascinated with traditional Celtic and Gaelic acoustic music, and his versatility on tin whistles, uilleann pipes, Irish harp, recorders, and bagpipes enabled him to make a very respectable living on Music Row.

Before long, he launched the Rivendell school, began building his tower home, and thoroughly established himself in the community. He clearly was not maudlin about life. Although he still grieved for Lois, there was nothing sad about him and there was nothing sad about his place.

Bea let Elvis out of the back seat of the Bug, and he bounded off toward the edge of the verdant woods. Tristan met them at the door, beaming.

"Come in. Come in. Welcome to my humble abode."

"Doesn't look too humble," Dan answered as the two brothers embraced. "You're looking much too young and healthy. Baby faced, like always, little brother."

"Yeah, well, you look as surly and as ornery as ever, big brother. Bea, how on earth do you ever put up with this guy?"

"That's a question we've all been trying to find an answer to—for what? Twenty years now?"

As they walked into the house, Bea was struck by the simple beauty and domestic comfort of the décor. This was definitely the home of an artist. There were sculptures and paintings everywhere. The floors were either polished parquet or covered with rich Persian carpets. Decorative thrown potteries and woven wall hangings warmed the rooms. And old quilts were thrown over comfortable leather chairs, and antique signs were propped against the walls.

Bea felt a sharp pang of longing. She was tired of traveling. She was tired of the sabbatical. She was tired of the rootlessness, the vagabond attitude she and Dan had nurtured since the earliest days of their marriage. She was tired of being tired. She yearned for a place like this; a place she could call home.

Reminiscing through the afternoon, Dan was surprised by how comfortable he was too. Originally he had only planned to spend a couple of hours here. Now he was actually beginning to ponder what it might be like if he and Bea were to settle down near here. What it might be like to be connected to his family. To set down roots. To have a home to come home to.

Truth be told, he and Tristan had never been close. After he left for college, Dan had never looked back, rarely visited, and only occasionally called. They generally got together at weddings and funerals, if then. But for some reason, this time, he felt more at home than ever before with his brother. He felt a connectedness that was profoundly satisfying, as if it were the missing piece of the puzzle of his life.

That night, Tristan prepared a few of his specialties, which were in fact some old family recipes. He served smoked brisket, grill-roasted potatoes, fried new corn, a big fresh-green salad with a homemade vinaigrette dressing, and thick German bread slices. For dessert, he served Scottish shortbread, still warm from the oven, and Blue Bell vanilla ice cream. It was a perfect meal. Afterward, they retired to the studio upstairs to gaze at the stars through Tristan's telescope, listen to his latest studio tape, and watch his most recent effort at Claymation.

The next morning, Dan followed Tristan through a typical day. First, Tristan conducted several classes at the school. Dan was taken aback by the way the students seemed to come to life when his brother entered the room. He was also surprised to hear them address him affectionately as Dr. Gylberd; it was a moniker that had always been reserved in his mind for his father. Then he was struck by how much Tristan's teaching style was like his father's—animated, well-informed, carefully researched, and quirkily interesting. It left him feeling rather eerie.

When they left Rivendell Academy, Tristan said he had to make a quick stop at a studio near Music Row in town. He had been working on a special project—a benefit for the local crisis pregnancy center. Again Dan was struck by how much Tristan had become like their father in his interests, concerns, lifestyle, world-view, and habits. The project was an orchestrated medley of several classic Scottish folk songs. Again, something entirely too reminiscent of their father.

Dan had the gnawing feeling that in the same way he had spent half of his life avoiding the legacy of their father, Tristan had consciously tried to become just like him. And that irked Dan. He wasn't sure if he was feeling guilty, jealous, or angry. All he knew was that the same strange conviction that had suddenly upset his equilibrium in Atlanta was roiling within him, playing fast and free with his emotions.

When they got back into Tristan's Jeep, Dan couldn't hold back any longer. "Do you ever get the feeling that all you're doing is slumming with Dad's ghost?"

"What? What are you talking about?"

"It just seems like you've gone out of your way to become everything that he was. All this education stuff, the fascination with Scottish and Celtic culture, the cooking, the gardens. What's this about? You're not just becoming like him, it is almost as if you're trying to be him."

"Well, well. It finally comes out, does it?"

"Comes out? What do you mean by that?"

"Dan, you've been running from Dad's legacy all your life. You've run so far and so fast for so long that you've lost yourself in the process. I'm not Dad's clone. He wasn't an artist. He wasn't a musician. He wasn't me. And all the gardening and cooking—that was Mom's legacy to us, not Dad's. I'm my father's son. That's all. What he was necessarily affected who I am. If I were to try to excise all that he was and believed and taught I wouldn't have rid myself of something extraneous, I would have rid myself of my very heart and soul."

"Your heart and soul? I don't think so."

"When are you going to admit it? You've always played the prodigal. You've reveled in the role. But you've never really considered the toll it has exacted over the years. Not in your own life, marriage, and children or in the lives of others."

"What are you talking about?"

"When you left home, Dad wept for days. Mom thought he was being melodramatic."

"He wept? Dad?"

"Yeah, he wept. For days. Because he knew you were gone for good."

"I wasn't gone for good."

"Of course you were. You never looked back. You hardly even acknowledged the family's existence after that. You barely even touched the ground when you flew in for Mom's funeral. That really hurt Dad. And then when he died, you weren't even in town for a full day."

"It's not like you've actually been an angel all your life, Tristan."

"No, you're right. But I'm ashamed of some of the foolish things I did, the time I wasted, and the legacy I squandered. I can't believe I tried to live without a real home. I can't believe I never gave any of this to Lois." He swept his hand across the horizon of misty hills. "I am ashamed. Very ashamed. Have you ever gotten to the place where you can feel shame over anything? Has it ever hit you that you've tried to live life as little more than a sojourner, unconnected to anyone or anything? Have you ever come to terms with what it is within you

that you're so afraid of? What it is that you've really been running from all these years?"

Dan was silent. He hated to admit it, but Tristan was right.
It wasn't so much his father that he had been running from all
his life, although that is what he liked to tell himself. It wasn't
his upbringing. It wasn't his faith. It was himself. He had been
running from himself. All that he was supposed to be and all
that he was supposed to do. It was simply that his father, his
upbringing, and his faith were the sternest reminders of that
fact, and so they bore the brunt of Dan's rebellion.

He felt utterly deflated. He recalled the quip of Belloc that
pedants inevitably lose all proportion in such circumstances.
They never can keep sane in a discussion. They will go wild
on matters they are wholly unable to judge. Never do they use
one of those three phrases that keep a man steady and balance
his mind. First, "After all, it is not my business." Second, "Tut!
Tut! You don't say!" And third, "*Credo in Unum Deum Patrem
Omnipotentem, Factorem omnium visibilium atque invisibilium,*"
in which last, there is a power of synthesis that can jam all
their analytical dust heap into such a fine, tight, and compact
body as would make them stare to see.

To his considerable consternation, he had become the
quintessential pedant.

But the gibberish of his pedantry dissolved like an
enchanted castle when the destined knight blows his horn
before it. Suddenly it was as if the years had rushed by him like
wind. He saw not whence the eddy came, nor whither it was
tending. He seemed himself to witness their flight without a
sense that he had been changed, and yet time was beguiling him
of his strength, as the winds robbed the woods of their foliage.

He had somehow allowed an indiscriminant destruction
of variety, loveliness, and ancient rights in his life, all in the
name of a devouring and philistine materialism. It was then
that he came to the awful realization that it takes only the hand

of a Lilliputian to light a fire, but it requires the mellifluous powers of a Gulliver to extinguish it.

For the second time in a little more than a week, he wept. As they trundled along the highway, the car's engine hummed and his tears flittered onto the vinyl seat cover. And it was sweet music to his soul.

After the war, says the papers, they'll no be content
at hame,
The lads hae feucht wi' death twae 'ear I' the mud
And the rain and the snaw; for aifter a sadger's life
The shop will be unco tame; they'll ettle at fortune
and freedom
In the new lands far awa.
No me. By God. No me.
Aince we hae lickit oor faes and aince I get oot o'
this hell,
For the rest o' my leevin' days I'll mak a pet o'
mysel.
I'll haste meback wi' an eident fit and settle again in
the same auld bit.
And oh, the comfort to snowkagain the reek o' my
mither's but-and-ben,
The wee box-bed and the ingle neuk, and the kail-
pat hung frae the chimley-hook.
I'll gang back to the shop like a laddie to play,
Tak doun the shutters at skreigh o' day,
And weigh oot floor wi' a carefu' pride, and hear the
clash o' the countraside.

John Buchan

ALIO
POPULATION 4530

LITERARY EXPERIMENTS ARE DANGEROUS. By their very nature, they entail great risk and only very rarely does that risk pay off. The fact is, popular literature follows fairly predictable patterns, tends toward standard genres, and relies on the tried and true.

To attempt a work that crosses over or even flaunts convention is to invite disaster. Writing an article, a column, an essay, or a book like that is inevitably a process of uncertainty, self-doubt, and insecurity. When a genre-breaker does succeed however, the rewards can be great. Such works are delightful, refreshing, and full of surprises. Their innovation is provocative and inspirational.

Dan gravitated to such works. As a result, most of the books he had taken on at the publishing house turned out to be either total flops or stunning successes. They either fell apart altogether or they were unstoppable winners. People either loved or hated them; there was no in-between.

Not surprisingly, his writing was the same story. His column for instance, which was only published by the little arts-and-entertainment tabloid in Chicago at first, had elicited an altogether-unexpected wildly successful response. Like Dan himself, each installment of the column tended to be cranky, sarcastic, wide ranging, and only peripherally about what it was supposed to be about. It was, after all, a food column. You would think that he would at least write about the food every once in a while. Often it was little more than a series of musings on things as esoterically divergent as domestic architecture, bureaucratic bumbling, the pretensions of high art, and the wonders of pet ownership. Clearly, his sense was more wonderful than his genius. Even so, a New York literary agency negotiated the rights for national syndication, several proposed book projects, and included the possibility of a series of television specials.

For Dan, writing had always been a good staff but a poor crutch. But now Dan realized that he could quit his part-time arrangement with the publishing house and, best of all, Bea could quit her consulting business.

Bea really hadn't wanted to go to work in the first place. She hadn't wanted to deal with all the hassles of Y2K compliance and remediation. She hadn't wanted to leave the relative tranquillity of her kitchen, her hearthside, and her gardens for the jangling hustle-bustle of the corporate world. Although she loved computers, she really only did the work to bring in a little extra income while the kids were in college.

If she had her druthers, Bea would simply make a home for her and Dan. She loved planning menus. She found profound pleasure in planting and tending vegetables, canning jams and jellies, exercising hospitality, and discovering new cuisines, dishes, and recipes. She loved to pore over old issues of *Victoria* magazine and plan the betterment of her own sense of domesticity.

Such sentiments were surely anathema to the kind of feminist orthodoxy first popularized by Betty Friedan's blockbuster from the early sixties, *The Feminine Mystique,* now accepted as gospel by the arbiters of taste and propriety in American culture. In that manifesto, which helped to define the feminist movement, Friedan warned that depression, addiction, frigidity, menstrual problems, and even suicide stalk women who spend too much time in their home harboring Victorian ideals. Perhaps feeling that she wasn't quite making herself clear on the issue, she went on to argue that none but the mentally retarded could find housework fulfilling, and that women who accept the role of housewife are in as much danger as the millions who walked to their own deaths in Nazi gas chambers. Not too subtle, but she got her point across.

Friedan's rhetoric contributed mightily to the editorial profile of virtually all the women's magazines during the succeeding years of the seventies and eighties: *Cosmopolitan, Mirabella, Vogue, Ms, Ladies Home Journal, Good Housekeeping, Family Circle,* and *Redbook.* Each gleefully trampled upon everything associated with domesticity with the pious assurance that such things were not merely beneath the dignity of women, they were downright menacing. Thus it came to be that women expressing the slightest delight in affairs of the hearth risked seeming oppressed, frivolous, stupid, or all three together.

In 1987 though, Nancy Lindemeyer, Cindy Sperling, and Susan Maher—all veterans of the traditional feminist publishing industry—decided to launch their own revolution. They decided to reinvent the women's magazine. And they created the mother of all genre-breakers. At first glance, the product of their labors, *Victoria,* did not look terribly serious, much less revolutionary. A serious women's magazine, according to the tenets of feminist orthodoxy, had to cover politics, economics, science, business, and other worldly affairs. Even *Vogue, Mademoiselle,* and *Harper's Bazaar* regularly flirted with public issues to change the pace of their unrelenting fascination with fashion, sexual technique, and makeover beauty tips. *Victoria* by contrast was always resolutely, determinedly, and self-consciously domestic.

The magazine was intended to be rather like a Laura Ashley catalog with recipes. It was packed with soft-focus images of candle-lit dining tables set for the holidays with heirloom crystal and traditional meals; libraries stuffed with well-worn classics, family portraits, and rich tapestries; children in sunny fields wearing vintage dresses and apple blossoms in their hair; and verdant gardens redolent with a harvest of fragrant herbs, fresh vegetables, and sprays of wildflowers.

Victoria's critics hardly ever gave it credit for anything beyond its obvious commercial success; its premier issue sold an astonishing 320,000 copies, making it the most profitable publication launch in history. Its ad pages grew over the next two years faster than in any other publication ever. The critics regularly dismissed it as a hollow marketing coup, a shameless appeal to nostalgia, or a triumph of fantasy fulfillment. It had been called "a menopausal comic book" and "*Playboy* for wistful and sentimental women."

But Bea thought that such logic actually missed the point. *Victoria* was not escapism. It was instead a genuine exercise in social criticism. It was an authentic reinvention. It was a genre-breaker. To be sure, the magazine rarely made explicit comments on American society's lack of grace, virtue, and meaning, but when every page represented a choice of tradition over trend, beauty over convenience, home and family over work and career, the truth inevitably registered with readers, writers, and critics alike. And it did so profoundly.

For instance, the magazine often sprinkled quotations from classical literature throughout each lushly illustrated article or pictorial. Readers would find Shakespeare commenting on manners, Charles Lamb on tableware, Samuel Johnson on polite speech, Jane Austen on tea, Marcel Proust on carving sets, Isaac Watts on singing carols, Thomas Carlyle on neigh-borliness, Charles Dickens on city gardens, Emily Dickinson on keeping a journal, and G. K. Chesterton on celebrating Christmas. The quotations were often gratuitous, epigram-matic, and aphoristic, but cumulatively they demonstrated beyond any doubt that greater minds than Betty Friedan's had found meaning as well as intellectual and imaginative stimula-tion in the milieu and rituals of domestic life.

The effect of this women's magazine reinvention was to powerfully reinvest modern homes with mind and character and to rehabilitate the lost arts of hearth and home. *Victoria* even managed to lend housework a heady dose of dignity.

But it was ultimately able to do all this, not simply because some savvy marketers saw an enticing market niche among the suburban minivan crowd, but because its genre-breaking effort was rooted first and foremost in a world-view shift. As publisher Cindy Sperling said, "We have attempted to profile a kind of post-feminist world-view not just a pre-femi-nist world-view." Either way, it was a nonfeminist world-view that defined the magazine; it was a domestic world-view.

And that was a dramatic departure. It was indeed a rather remarkable revolution, a reinvention among all the other lock-step women's magazines, and a transformation based upon a radical reversal of the orthodox world-view.

Bea embraced this radical reversal, not just with her whole heart, but with her whole mind. The foundations of a civilized moral order are contentment with domestic conciliation, rev-erence for our forebears, and compliance with our prescriptive duties. In other words, the crux of social cohesion is necessar-ily the happy home. Home was the answer to virtually all the ills of the world, both the wider world of mayhem and woe and the inner world of mishap and worry.

Home is, after all, the basic building block of society. When the home begins to break down, the rest of society begins to disintegrate. There is no replacement for the home. The government can't substitute services for it. Social workers can't substitute kindness and understanding for it. Educators can't substitute knowledge, skills, or understanding for it.

There are any number of reasons for this. The home provides men, women, and children with a proper sense of identity. In the midst of their home, people can know and be known as nowhere else. They can taste the joys and sorrows of genuine intimacy. They can gain a vision of life that is sober and sure. They can be bolstered by its love. They can be strengthened by its confidence. They can be emboldened by its legacy. And they can be stabilized by its objectivity. Everyone desperately needs that kind of perspective. They desperately need to be stabilized in the gentle environs of hearth and home.

In addition though, home life provides genuine social security. There is no place like home. In times of trouble our greatest resource will always be those who know us best and love us most. Because family members share a common sense of destiny with one another and a bond of intimacy to one another, they can—and will—rush to one another's side when needed. And well they should. The home is an incubator for sound values. It reinforces the principles of authority, structure, liability, obedience, and selflessness. The accountability and discipline of home bring out the best in us. Typical parents, without thinking twice about it, would willingly die to save one of their children. While in most circumstances this human act would be regarded as heroic, for parents it is only ordinary.

BY THE end of their second day in Tennessee, Bea was beginning to think seriously about wanting to settle here, to make a home here.

Every man and every woman, although they were born in the very belfry of the bow and spent their infancies climbing among the chimneys, have waiting for them somewhere a home that they have never seen, but that was built for them in the very shape of their souls. It stands patiently waiting to be found. And when they see it, they remember it, although they have never seen it before.

Bea remembered this place from the great and distant longings of her heart.

Likewise, Dan found himself tangled in the skittering threads of memory. On the third afternoon at Tristan's homestead, Dan asked him to go with him to the cemetery. "I think it is about time I visited Mom and Dad's gravesite."

Tristan cast a questioning glance toward Bea. She just shrugged.

"Sure. Let's go. I'll take you there right now—if you want."

The cemetery was a small overgrown plot in the little town of Alio, about thirty miles outside of Nashville. It was here that their father had come to establish a small private liberal arts college more than twenty years earlier. It was here that he invested the last years of his life. It was here that he wrote prolifically. It was here that he buried his wife, their mother. And it was here that he himself finally succumbed to grief and overwork.

Alio was a fairly typical Southern antebellum town. The neat town square, dominated by its war memorial, was surrounded by little antique shops, a couple of cafés and restaurants, a small bookstore, and a bakery. Nicely restored, it had become a tourist attraction in recent days. The little college that their father had founded and their mother had run—in fact, virtually all of their father's big visionary efforts were actually brought into existence because of their mother's practicality, tenacity, and administrative acumen—still stood on the edge of town, just across Main Street from the cemetery.

The Gylberd graves were not difficult to spot. They were dominated by giant Celtic crosses of rough-cut stone. They both bore simple inscriptions: name, date of birth, date of death, and Latin inscriptions. Their father had chosen *Ex*

Aequo et Bono for their mother—"for mercy and goodness." For himself he had chosen *Alio Arx Axiom*—meaning, "somewhere a fortress of first principles."

Dan stood over the graves of his parents for a very long time. He contemplated his long wandering in the wilderness, all that had led him to this point in his life. He wished, as most people do at such times, for a restoration of the living years. A wave of regret swept over him, as well it ought. But with the regret also came a surprising new store of resolve.

Men ought to go somewhere. But modern man, in his sick reaction, is ready to go anywhere as long as it is the other end of nowhere. Dan loathed the impulse to modernity, and yet he had become the quintessential modern man.

He thought that he finally understood the truth of the truism: A person travels the world over in search of what he needs and returns home to find it—even if that home is a place he had never really seen before.

Every man, though he were born
In the very belfry of Bow
And spent his infancy climbing among the chimneys,
He has waiting for him somewhere a country house
Which he has never seen,
But which was built for him
In the shape of his soul.
It stands patiently waiting to be found;
And when the man sees it he remembers it,
Though he has never seen it before.

G. K. Chesterton

TOP MEADOW
POPULATION 2

During what a few unreconstructed Southerners sometimes call the "Late Lamentable Unpleasantness"—what nearly everyone else calls the Civil War—the Confederate government issued regulations listing the diseases that might afflict their troops and hinder them in battle. One of these was a peculiar problem for soldiers who hailed from Middle Tennessee. It seems that among the debilitating and sometimes life-threatening diseases on that list was an affliction that the field physicians aptly called Nostalgia, from the Greek word meaning "a yearning to return home."

As Dan and Bea stood upon the rocky top of a bluff overlooking a bend in the Harpeth River a few miles from Tristan's homestead, they suddenly succumbed. They were stricken with a longing for home. They realized almost simultaneously, it had been home. Home had been following them. No, not following them, they concluded. With them all along. Waiting. Waiting for them to recognize it. To welcome it. To embrace it. Why had it frightened them so? Home was what they had been searching for in their youth, in their child-rearing years, on this sabbatical. All their lives. And this was it.

The longing for home is woven into the fabric of the life of every man, every woman, and every child. It is profoundly affected by their inescapable connection to place, persons, and principles—the incremental parts of a covenant community. While the nomad spirit of modernity has dashed the integrity of community, it has done nothing to alter the need for it. Covenantal attachment has always been an inescapable aspect of the healthy psyche, and it always will be. Uprooted-ness has always been a kind of psychosis, and likewise, it always will be. Hearth and home are the cornerstones of help, hope, and happiness.

Virtually all of the Midsouth is marked by land resplendent with a variety of natural wonders. From the Smoky Mountains in the east to the rich Mississippi Delta in the south, from the lofty central highlands to the great valley of the eastern lowlands, it is a region blessed with both great beauty and generous resources. But Dan and Bea were particularly struck by the compelling attractions of Middle Tennessee with its voluptuous rolling hills all across the Cumberland Plateau.

Even so, it was not mere beauty that drew them to this place. It was something far deeper than that.

THE REAL estate agent was fidgeting back at the road. He had brought them out to see this isolated twenty-acre plot that had once been the back pasture and untamed woodlands of an old walking horse farm called Top Meadow. But Dan and Bea were heedless. Instead, they reveled in the moment.

Humanness cannot be found in escape, detachment, absence of commitment, or undefined freedom. Instead, its great promise may only be found in those rare places where people have established identity, defined vocation, and envisioned destiny. It comes from the sense of connection to land and people and heritage that occurs when people try to provide continuity and identity across generations. Such a commitment is inevitably costly, but that is precisely what makes home so infinitely priceless.

That kind of covenantal attachment to home simply cannot occur anywhere. It must be intentionally rooted somewhere specific, somewhere unique, somewhere preclusive, somewhere that is inherently good and right and true.

Although they had never actually seen this place before, Dan and Bea somehow remembered it anyway, as if it had always been an essential part of their lives. It was as familiar to them as the aspirations of their hearts. It was as comfortable to them as the contour of their hopes and dreams.

It seemed that Dan and Bea had been going somewhere all their lives. And now, at long last, they had arrived.

The End of the Beginning